Falling Deep

Also in the Nelson Island Series

Ever Always (novella)
Wanting Forever

Falling Deep

A Nelson Island Novella

DIANA GARDIN

New York Boston

This book is a work of fiction. Names, characters, places, and incidents are the product of the author's imagination or are used fictitiously. Any resemblance to actual events, locales, or persons, living or dead, is coincidental.

Forever Yours
Hachette Book Group
1290 Avenue of the Americas
New York, NY 10104
hachettebookgroup.com
twitter.com/foreverromance

First ebook edition: April 2015

Forever Yours is an imprint of Grand Central Publishing.
The Forever Yours name and logo are trademarks of Hachette Book Group, Inc.

ISBN 978-1-4555-6048-6

For My Mom

Acknowledgments

I'm so very blessed. I thank God every day for giving me the drive and the passion to be a writer.

To the very best agent in the whole entire universe, Stacey Donaghy. You are a complete rock star. Every time we talk, you build my confidence just a little bit more. I promise to leave you more voice messages in the future! Thanks for falling in love with Reed just as much as I did.

To Reed's very first readers, Skillet and Kate. Your opinions on my writing are always so important, and you really helped to mold my man Reed into something amazing. Thank you!

To my fabulous, super-smart editor, Leah Hultenschmidt, Nelson Island is coming into the light because you loved and believed in Sam and Aston! Thank you for helping Reed's story to be the very best version of itself.

To my other wonderful editor, Dana Hamilton. Thanks for coming on board for *Falling Deep*! Your insights were so valuable, and I couldn't have gotten it to its current polished state without your input.

To my publicists: Fareeda Bullert at Forever, you're a wonderfully refreshing woman to work with. You're fast and you're a fabulous communicator. Thank you, Fareeda, for your hard work on getting Nelson Island on the map! Autumn Hull, you are someone I wanted as a friend on my side. You're always in the know when it comes to New Adult, and you've done a phenomenal job of getting the word out on the last two books. Thank you, Autumn!

There are several bloggers and readers who have been there from the beginning, and I'm so lucky to have you on my side. Thank you so much for requesting advance review copies, and for loving what I do. You're just as invested in my books as I am, and that always feels so great. I still can't really believe anyone picks up one of my novels. Thank you for your love and your shares!

To my love, who has actually started reading my books, thank you for loving me enough to read romance novels. You're my hero.

Thank you to my amazing little family who lives with my crazy every single day. Our two little wild things are my entire world, and my husband is the sun in our galaxy. Without you all, I wouldn't have a purpose, or a reason to want to make our lives even better with this amazing career. Thank you for being perfect for me.

Prologue

How It All Ended…

She bit down hard on her bottom lip, the soft trickle of blood pooling in her mouth a welcome distraction from the terrible ache beginning to build in her chest.

She could see the darkness as it crept into his eyes. It was the shrouded darkness she had been so attracted to when she first laid eyes on him under the hot stage lights. The hard pallor that let her know, despite his glossy appearance and the obvious presence of prosperity in his life, he had clawed his way out of a long dark tunnel of pain similar to her own. She had been drawn to him because she hoped if he could get out, then maybe she could, too. Maybe he could pull her to the end of her very own darkness.

Then she'd made the mistake of getting to know him. She learned that he wasn't full of darkness, that he was full of the brightest light she'd ever dared to dream of. And when that light was directed at her, she'd completely fallen victim to his goodness and the shine that made him Reed.

But that hope was gone now, that flame had been extinguished, and in its place stood the bleak certainty that no matter how hard she wished, no matter how hard she wanted it, she was never going to be able to escape this life that karma had gifted her.

And Reed Hopewell wasn't going to be her savior, after all.

One

How It All Began…

He tried not to squint against the harsh lights aimed at the stage. He was beginning to get used to the feeling of all eyes on him, the palpable waiting that came with being the center of attention. His heartbeat soared with anticipation as he looked out over the crowd standing before him. He rubbed a hand over the scruff dusting his angled chin, and the audience emitted a collective sigh. He grinned, and the women in attendance screamed in response.

"Thank y'all for coming out tonight," he said, leaning into the microphone.

The crowd cheered, a swelling of sound that met his ears and pushed him to the limit of adrenaline that was currently pounding through his veins.

"I want to sing you one more before I go; would that be all right?"

Roars of approval consumed the club, and his grin grew. He

clutched his guitar a little closer to his chest and strummed out a chord.

"One day, I hope to be singing this for someone special," he continued over the crowd's growing noise level. "But for now, I'd like to throw it out to all the gorgeous ladies here in the crowd tonight. This one's called 'Endless Fall.'"

The biggest yell yet vibrated the rafters; Reed opened his mouth and the lyrics of a new song he had recently written came pouring out.

The crowd became hushed, swaying in rhythm to the rough beauty that was Reed's voice.

It was difficult for him to lay eyes on members of the crowd with the blinding lights in his eyes, but he scanned the faces to find his sister, Aston, and her fiancé, Sam. Her sparkling diamond glinted off of the light as she raised her arms above her head and swayed. One corner of Sam's mouth turned up at Reed as he wrapped his arms around Aston from behind and nuzzled her neck.

The vigor and nourishment he got from the stage coursed through his body as he finished the song, and the audience erupted into applause and cheers as he thanked them. Grinning and tugging on the strap of his guitar, he exited the stage.

"Well done, little bro," Aston said as he sat his burden in its case. "Amazing, as always."

He grinned. "Thanks, A. I'm not sure if Sam saw it, though; he was too busy sucking on your neck to notice anything I was doing up there."

Sam shrugged. "Have you seen this neck? No one would blame me."

Reed slapped Sam so hard on the back of the head that Sam almost inhaled the longneck bottle he was sipping. "That's my sister you're talking about. Lay the fuck off."

Aston waved her left hand in front of Reed's nose. "That's my fiancé you're slapping around there, Reed. I swear I'll pummel you senseless if you touch him again."

Sam smiled smugly. "That's my girl."

Reed rolled his eyes and turned his attention to Sam's other side. "What'd you think, Ash? You ready to leave your loser husband for me yet?"

Ashley smirked at Reed as the husband in question turned a full-wattage glare on him. "Nope. Still madly in love with Finn. Sorry, sweetie. But that redhead over there? She's another story."

Reed turned around, searching in the direction Ashley pointed. His sister's childhood best friend could always spot the groupies, and her radar was as deadly accurate as usual. At the adjacent table, a handful of young women eyed Reed hungrily.

It was how these shows went. Reed was announced as a guest performer for the club's entertainment, he sang, and panties dropped like leaves on a breezy fall day. It was a clockwork routine that Reed counted on.

He pulled out his chair and took a seat between Blaze and Tate. Looking his best friends over carefully, he frowned. "Where the fuck is the tequila?"

Tate Oliver slid a shot in Reed's direction and grinned. "Had one waiting on you, man. You did good up there."

Reed nodded, taking the small glass of golden liquid and tilting it up against his full lips. As he tipped it back and let the fire forge a trail down his throat, he hissed through his teeth and slammed the shot glass back down on the table. Glancing around him, he threw a dose of swagger at the table of gaping girls next door, letting them know that he'd be ready for business as soon as he oiled up his gears.

Blaze boomed out a laugh that seemed to ricochet through the rafters. "Take me as your wingman tonight! Please!" His gigantic body hunkered down over his own shot of tequila as he knocked it back.

Reed smiled and signaled the short-skirted girl with a revolving tray of drinks for another round. "Sam? You in?"

"Nope," he answered promptly. "I've got the princess on the bike tonight, Reed."

Reed grunted in response. He loved Sam like a brother, but he was shit for company on a night when all Reed wanted to do was find a warm body to celebrate with after a good night at the mic.

Tate scanned the room, clearly uncomfortable.

"Next weekend you'll be back at Sunny's, right?" he grumbled.

"Yeah," Reed answered, amused. "What, you don't like it when we're in Charleston, Tate?"

Tate and his twin sister, Tamara, had stayed behind in Nelson Island while the rest of them had attended the University of Charleston after high school. Tate never felt comfortable being off of the island, even when he was just right across the bridge in the Holy City.

"Don't worry, Tate," Reed said dryly. "Back in good ole N.I. next weekend. Sunny's as usual."

"Good." Tate nodded in relief. He sipped his beer and glanced over at the table of women, basking in the lustful glow that Reed cast over the female population of the club.

Reed glanced impatiently up at the bar in search of the drink runner. He scanned the crowd pressing against the current and stopped on a curvy figure with a short, sparkly dress and the longest hair he'd seen on a girl since middle school. He appraised her as she leaned into the bar, indicating to the bartender the drink that she wanted. Her back was facing Reed as he eyed her, and he took the time to drink in her shapely legs, the curve of her hips, and the glowing olive complexion. He whistled low under his breath, and glanced back at his present company.

"What?" Blaze rumbled, on high alert. "You spot another bad chick?"

Ashley exchanged an eye roll with Aston. "Ugh. Are you guys ready to get outta here?"

"Yeah, I'm pretty sure that was our cue," Aston agreed. She bent over Reed's head to kiss his cheek, rubbing off her lipstick as she pulled away. "Love you, Reed. Don't do anything Sam wouldn't do."

Tate choked on his Coors. "Yeah, right. *Everything* Reed does is something Sam wouldn't do. I think it's a rule."

Reed grinned. "Y'all be safe. Don't knock my sister up before the wedding, Waters."

"No promises," Sam answered, bumping Blaze's fist as they followed Finn and Ashley toward the exit.

When Reed moved his gaze once more toward the mystery girl at the bar, she was gone. He hadn't even gotten to see her face. Somehow, he knew that was probably for the better. Judging from the back of that woman, the front of her was likely to be a game changer.

Reed worked hard every day. He worked on his craft, and his music was what kept him moving through the motions of life. At night, after a show, he liked things to be easy. Nothing too complicated. Nothing he had to think too hard about.

Reed scanned the club again, and then shrugged. He rolled his shoulders once, loosening the muscles that tended to tighten while he performed.

With a half-grin, he refocused on the table full of very willing participants to a hell of a good night.

"Thanks, baby," he purred, grabbing the drink from her along with a handful of her curved backside as she eased around the edge of his chair. "You know just how I like it."

Hope somehow refrained from retching inside of her mouth and took her seat next to him. She crossed her legs and dug her nails into her thighs to prevent the crossing of her arms. Crossing her arms would be against the rules.

Slapping him across his smug, entitled face would also be against the rules. Hope itched to break those damn rules.

There had never been a date in her life where she appreciated the man she was with calling her "baby." She had never been anyone's baby, especially not the men she spent her time with. Trying hard not to curl her lip in disgust, she pulled them into a taut smile instead.

"You're welcome, *baby*."

He smiled indulgently and nodded. She looked away quickly.

It wasn't that he was an ogre to look at; in fact, most women would consider him handsome with his broad shoulders, thick, corded arms, and lush head of wavy blond hair. The success that rolled off of him with his expensive suit didn't hurt, either.

But to Hope? He may as well have been a monster.

She glanced back up toward the front of the club and stifled a groan. The performer for the night was making an idiot of himself. She frequented this club with a date, and the singer-songwriters the club owner hired were nearly always the same. Man-whores with guitars strapped to their chests, all of them.

This one was no different. He was attractive, like they all were. He could sing, like they all could. She ignored the fact that his singing style may have appealed to her more than most, and that rough-around-the-edges voice snuck up inside of her skin the way some of the others hadn't. As he sang, she had been lulled into a peace she hadn't felt in so long. But that didn't matter. He was still the same. Slobbering all over a table of classless bitches at the moment.

Just like the rest of them.

Said the girl with the minidress and mile-high heels. She tried to mentally shake herself for being so judgmental. The last thing she should be doing is placing the other women around her into a box and lashing out at them because of *class.* At least they were honest about what they were doing. They wanted a rock star. They wanted to see if the way he rocked the stage would be the same way he rocked *them* between the sheets. They made no game about it, implicating their desires like a neon sign blinking in a shop window.

"You ready to skedaddle?" Tyler asked suddenly, eyeing her over the top of his glass.

His eyes narrowed as he studied her face, and she realized he had followed her gaze and misread the reason for her focus on the singer. She tore her eyes away from the head of thick, dark hair and the stupid dimple appearing in the square chin and met the muddy eyes of her date.

"Uh, yeah. Sure. Do you have an early morning tomorrow?"

He smirked. "Something like that. Shall we?"

My, aren't we in a hurry tonight, she though wryly as they stood. For whatever reason, she threw one last glance at the front table again before allowing Tyler to place his hand on her lower back and guide her out of the club's front exit.

She nodded to the bouncer, whom she knew from school and from her frequent visits to the club, one of Charleston's hottest, and walked beside Tyler down the still-bustling street.

This part of downtown didn't settle down until well after 2:00 a.m., and as Hope glanced at her watch she noted that it was scarcely past midnight. She'd never been out with Tyler before, but she'd expected their date to last longer than this.

It was an uneventful evening. Dinner at a fancy restaurant with some of Tyler's colleagues and then out to the club to listen to some music and dance. Only Tyler seemed in a hurry to leave, before they'd even had a chance to make it to the dance floor.

Strange.

It was better for Hope, of course, to end the date as soon as possible. She was tired of pretending. Her whole life was a play, and she was always anxious for the curtain to close on another show.

She didn't need a jacket, as June nights in this southern, ocean-side city were nearly as balmy as the days. She was accustomed to the steaminess of the air; she'd spent her entire life here. Despite the cloying heat, Tyler slid a heavy arm around Hope's shoulders and yanked her closer to him. She was so tempted to tell him that the date was over, therefore so was the touching, the words just at the tips of her lips, but all she had to do was make it to the fancy limo they'd arrived in and she'd put some definite distance between them once inside.

But when Tyler turned her down an empty alley off of the populated street they had been traveling and pulled her closer still, she skidded to a halt and twisted her way out from under his arm.

"Wait, Tyler," she said. "I don't think this is where the limo is waiting. Let's head back onto the street."

She turned to go, her long hair flying out around her, and he grabbed her wrist hard enough to send a jolt of pain up her arm. She stared down at his hand and then scowled up at his face. Time suddenly slowed.

"Hands off." She'd meant the words as a warning, but they exited her mouth as a breath.

"Hands off? I don't think so, sweetheart. This is a date, right? Don't you know how dates end?"

The sneer plastered to his face was more frightening than she would have expected, than she liked to admit, because its ugly twist couldn't be blamed on alcohol. She knew Tyler wasn't drunk when they left the club. He was alert, bright-eyed, and walking a steady line.

"No, Tyler," she said, forcing an air of calm into her voice she didn't truly feel. "A date with me ends with maybe a kiss on the cheek and a sweet good night."

She turned once again to head back toward the busier street.

This time, Tyler wrapped an arm around her waist and wrenched Hope backward. His hot breath tickled her neck as he whispered loudly into her ear from behind.

"Oh, it'll be sweet, all right."

His voice had been kind of slimy all night. She'd noticed it and chalked it up to the fact that he was in the same category as all of the other older men she dated.

Sleazy.

A man who needed someone like her on his arm in order to make himself look more powerful, hotter, younger. It was a trait they all shared, and one Hope had learned to handle, manipulate to her advantage, as much as she detested herself for it daily.

But now, in the darkness of the alley, she realized she should have been paying more attention to the murky undertones in his voice, which would have indicated a much darker man beneath the glossy exterior.

With his free hand, he pushed Hope's head to one side and pulled her long hair away from her face. His fingers lingered at the nearly blond ends hanging past her waist. "I've been looking at this succulent neck all night, baby. Just waiting for a taste of it.

I couldn't wait 'til the limo. So we'll just have an appetizer here, and the main course later, when we're all alone."

To Hope's disgust, he licked the side of her neck. One long swipe of his tongue sent the vomit accumulating in her throat hurtling toward fresh air.

"Don't! Get off me right now, you sick bastard! This shit won't fly. You'll be spitting out your teeth for months if you don't get your dirty hands off of me."

In response to her words, he merely pulled Hope closer and slid a hand up her inner thigh. When it disappeared under her dress, she screamed. She couldn't help it; it was her natural response. She screamed because his greedy fingers had turned to claws, and they were raking desperately at her underwear. Hot, angry tears stung her naturally long lashes as she tried to blink them back and *fight*.

What had she learned in that class she had secretly been taking? He was behind her; she raised her high heel and used her foot to stomp hard into the instep of his foot. When he groaned as a result, she jabbed backward with her elbow with as much force as she could, catching him in the rib. Jerking with all of her might away from his stumbling form, she discovered it wasn't enough.

It's not enough. Her heart nearly stopped beating at the realization.

He kept a firm grip on the small of her back, and she was locked in an unwilling embrace.

She was pleading now, unintelligible words of fear leaving her lips, flying unnoticed into the heavy, still air around them.

Useless.

Until a new set of arms deftly reached in between them to wrench Hope free, pushing her behind a tall, muscular body and shoving Tyler away from her with amazing force.

The newcomer stood between them, and as much as she hated to do it, she gratefully cowered behind him as she peered around his tall frame at Tyler. Little gasps were leaving her throat as she stood there; her eyes were wild with fear and disbelief at what had almost just happened to her.

"Who the fuck do you think you are?" Tyler snapped at the intruder.

He shifted from side to side, clearly trying to figure out how to maneuver around Hope's human shield.

"That's funny," the tall man snarled—*snarled!*—back at him. "Who the *fuck* are you, and why didn't you listen when the lady asked you to let her go?"

The voice was simultaneously as smooth as satin and as rough as grainy sand, and it made Hope settle closer into his back. The voice was safety, and she held on as if it were a lifeline. Her heart was pounding much faster than it should; she could feel the blood pulsating in her temples as she sucked in harsh, ragged breaths. The humiliation of the attack was beginning to settle into her bones with a deep ache.

How could I have allowed this to happen? I'm smarter than this. I know better!

"Look, man. She's my date, okay? I wasn't roughing her up. She likes it like that, trust me." Tyler spread his arms wide and placed his most charming grin firmly in place.

The newcomer wasn't buying any of it. Tall and solid, he stood his ground, shaking his head. "She didn't like it. I heard her. You should have heard her, too."

Tyler took a step toward them, and the man standing in front of Hope reached behind him, grabbing hold of her and nudging her farther back. She swallowed her gasp when Tyler pulled out a pocketknife and flicked it open.

"Oh, are we doing this?" the man said in response to Tyler's forward progression. In the hush of the alley, his voice was flat and hollow. "Because if it's going down, I'm all about it."

He took a step to meet Tyler halfway. "You like to rough women up? I will handle your ass right here in this alley. You won't walk away from it, but I'll make sure and call an ambulance to pick up the pieces."

There was no mistaking his southern drawl, and although Hope couldn't yet see his face, she recognized his confident demeanor and unmistakable voice.

Tyler hesitated, clearly considering whether or not Hope was worth the risk of getting his ass beaten in a dark alley. She watched him shake his head angrily, and then throw his hands in the air.

"Find your own way home, bitch," he spat. As he turned to go, her saving grace rushed him from behind, whirling him around to face her and placing the blade of his knife firmly against the tender skin of Tyler's throat. Tyler probably soiled his pants at that moment; his face was a mask of terror and he actually whimpered when the cool metal bit harder against his neck.

And that was the moment Hope saw his face, under the glow of a bare bulb attached to the brick alley wall. The man who had leaped in between her and Tyler, had pulled a knife on a man for a woman he didn't know, and was now baring it against a monster's neck, all for *her*, was the rocker from the club.

She didn't even remember his name.

"Apologize," he growled into Tyler's ear. "Tell the lady you're sorry for calling her a bitch, and I'll let you go. Against my better judgment."

Tyler whimpered again, and the blade was pressed harder against his sweaty skin.

"Say. It."

"I-I'm sorry, Hope," spluttered Tyler. "There! Let me go, you psycho!"

The rocker turned Tyler loose and shoved him toward the end of the alley. They both watched him stumble his way out of the dark and disappear around the corner at the end of the street.

She studied the singer as he watched the end of the alley a moment longer. His broad chest was heaving, and his jaw, etched in scruff, clenched repeatedly, like a throbbing heartbeat. He wiped the blade of the knife on the thigh of his black jeans and snapped it closed, placing it back into his pocket.

When Hope realized she was still standing, the immediate danger gone but not forgotten, an animal-like noise escaped her throat, and her hand flew to her face in response.

He turned to face her, moving into the shimmer from the overhead light attached to the brick wall. She was met with eyes so darkly blue they glittered like jewels. Fascinated, she wondered stupidly what made them glimmer that way. Was it anger? Or were they always so iridescent?

Shaking her head, she took a step backward.

"Hey," he said, his voice unexpectedly soft. He reached out a hand toward her. "It's okay. You're safe. Did he hurt you? He didn't..." His voice trailed off into the night, as his eyes slid to her rumpled dress. Hope knew what he was asking.

His voice was so tender it nearly ripped a sob from her chest. The monster she'd chosen to be out with tonight had nearly *raped* her in a dark alley. She used the remainder of her strength to tamp the emotion down, and bit her bottom lip as she shook her head.

"Are you sure?" He stepped closer, holding both hands out in front of him as if to reassure her that he meant her no harm.

She just stared at him, full of doubt and uncertainty. She could count on one hand the number of men in the world she trusted, and now that she was alone with him she wasn't so sure he was one of them.

Except for the fact that he had just saved her from being violated in the worst way imaginable.

She allowed him to cross the divide between them until he was standing just in front of her. He put his arms down by his sides, but he stared into her face with those blue, blue eyes, and her own vision swam a little upon being at the receiving end of his stare.

"Hope, right? Do you need a ride home, Hope? I have a truck. I had a few shots in the club tonight, but I have a friend who's good to drive. Come with me, okay?"

She shook her head and found her voice. "That's okay. I'll..."

Suddenly, she had no idea what she would do. Tyler was her way home. And now he wasn't, and this man who'd saved her was offering her a ride and she was so overwhelmed she wasn't sure what to do.

Hope was never overwhelmed. She was never caught off guard. She made it a point to control her life, every single screwed-up detail, so that she never felt off-kilter or surprised.

And now, for the moment, all of that was shattered.

He reached out a cautious hand, brushing a strand of her hair from her flushed face. "Let me take you, please. And my name is Reed. So I'm not a stranger."

She studied him for a moment longer. She eyed the way his hair fell softly into his eyes when he spoke, and the way those long, dark lashes brushed his cheeks when he blinked. She took in his plain black T-shirt, and the thin leather jacket he wore over it. A metal wallet chain hung from his hip. She allowed her eyes to travel down his jeans to his black boots, and shuddered in response to the fact that from head to toe, he was probably prettier than she was.

"You must be hot," she blurted.

His eyes widened in surprise, and then his face broke into a huge grin, and he pulled his hand back down to his side. "I am. Thanks for noticing. Let's get to the truck so I can get this damn jacket off."

She finally nodded, agreeing to the ride, and accepted the outstretched hand he was offering. That unfamiliar feeling of safety cloaked her again at the touch of his hand.

He guided her back down the alley and out onto the busy street.

She saw two guys waiting just around the corner. They had obviously been looking for Reed; they started when they saw him appear with Hope from the alley.

"Seriously, dude? You needed to go down a dark alley to—" The one with copper-colored hair began to complain.

Reed shot his friend a stern look that shut him up. "Guys. This is Hope. She had a little, uh, problem. I helped her out, and now she needs a ride home. You still good to drive, Blaze?"

The huge guy with a dark complexion nodded his head and eyed her with appreciation. She stared back stonily.

Blaze and the Copper-Top took off for the parking lot across from the alley, and Reed angled his head toward Hope, indicating that she follow. After one more moment of hesitation, she did, placing her trust in Reed's hands for the second time that night.

Two

What were you doing with that guy, Hope?"

Hope had given Blaze her address and was settled into the backseat of a Chevy Silverado with Reed right next to her. Tate and Blaze were recounting the night's events in the front, but Reed was focused totally on her.

His intense attention made her feel like she was trapped in the frozen beam of his eyes. She tried not to return the gaze, but it was difficult not to notice his long and lithe body. She could see the hardness of his muscles beneath his snug-fitting jeans and under his tee, and all that dark hair caught the light shining in through the truck's windows. The thick, black lines of tattoos wound from his taut biceps, disappearing under the sleeves of his shirt.

The question was inevitable. Of course he'd want to know why she was dating someone like Tyler. How much of that question she could answer truthfully was minimal, and she hated to lie. She lied enough in her professional life; she didn't want to become a liar in her personal life, too.

Not that Reed was a part of her personal life.

But still, he was focusing on her so intently in the backseat of the truck it was beginning to make her skin itch. She now knew what the protozoa under the microscope in her high school biology class had felt like.

"You know what?" she said softly. "It's not important. I was on a bad date, let's leave it at that."

Reed's eyes narrowed. It was pitch-black outside the truck's windows; she lived out of the way, a fifteen-minute drive from downtown Charleston. She dreaded having the truck pull up to the gigantic home she shared with her mother, her sister, and her stepfather. But it couldn't be avoided.

"A bad date? You expect me to believe that someone like you *chose* to be out with that guy tonight?"

"What else would I be doing with him if I didn't choose to be there?"

She fired back a question for a question; that was the easiest way to avoid telling him the truth. Which she definitely wasn't about to do.

Reed sighed, aggravation vibrating through the deep sound, and threw his head back against the seat.

"It's fine," she answered. "You don't need to get wrapped up in my issues. You're dropping me off at my house, and I really appreciate what you did for me tonight. It's really rare that anyone would care enough to stop, let alone go to the extremes that you did, Reed. I have no doubt that if you hadn't been there..."

She shuddered at the memory of Tyler's hands all over her, and the overwhelming desire to rip off her dress and burn it washed over her. She tightened all of her muscles, attempting to ward off the breakdown she knew was coming. Reed reached over to cover her small hand with his large one. The contrast shocked her into silence, and she stared at their hands, trying to keep hers from trembling.

"Are you sure you're okay?" His voice had dropped lower; he hadn't told his friends what had happened, and she appreciated it. "He attacked you. Are you going to press charges? You're not going to see him again, are you?"

She pulled her hand out from under his and stared blankly ahead. "I'm a big girl, Reed. I can take care of Tyler if I need to. And yes, I'm okay."

She flashed back again to standing in the alley with Tyler, his hands crawling up her dress like scorpions intent on their prey. The shiver that wracked her couldn't be hidden, and this time Reed's arms went around her as the shakes threatened to consume her.

"Hey," he whispered into her ear. "It's okay. Guys who are like that…God, I really could have killed him, Hope. But you're safe now. And listen…I want to leave you my number, okay? You can call me anytime."

She looked up at him, resenting the weak portrayal of herself she was displaying.

"I'll be fine," she answered firmly, leaning upright. "You don't have to do that. Turn here, Blaze."

Blaze turned the steering wheel, and the truck was entering the long driveway of the large, plantation-style home that belonged to her stepfather.

Tate whistled. "This is where you live?"

"By association only," she muttered.

"What?" Tate glanced at her in the rearview mirror.

"Nothing," she said. "Yeah. This is where I live. For now."

Blaze pulled up to the three-car garage situated around the side of the house and stopped at Hope's direction.

Reed placed a hand on her arm before she moved to push the door open.

"Hope," he said, piercing her once again with those eyes she couldn't seem to stay away from.

"Yeah?"

He stared at her a moment, his eyes flashing, dark and brooding. "Be careful who you let take you out from now on, okay?"

She smiled, the first she'd bestowed upon him all night, and he reeled back in surprise. "Sure thing."

She thanked Blaze and exited the truck, slamming the door behind her. As she entered the access door beside the garage, she blinked the light once to let them know she was safe, and the big truck began easing its way back down the drive.

Once inside the cavernous garage, Hope leaned against the wall and closed her eyes. It was late; there was a chance that her mother and her stepfather weren't awake and waiting for her arrival. They grilled her after every date and she knew she'd be unable to sit through it tonight without either lashing out at them or disappearing forever under a deluge of tears. Neither would be helpful to her cause.

She opened her eyes when the mudroom entrance to the house opened at the top of the steps.

A sharp sliver of light bounced against the wall, growing as the door opened wider, and the fist in Hope's stomach unclenched as her thirteen-year-old sister's outline appeared in the doorway above Hope.

"Vi," she said, placing a hand over her chest. "You're up."

"Of course I'm up," Violet said, turning on the garage light and closing the door behind her. She descended the steps slowly, eyeing Hope with thought and purpose, the way she did everything. She stopped when she reached her, and they both slid down the wall until they were sitting on the floor beside each other.

"How did it go?" she asked softly.

Hope hesitated. Keeping her sister as sheltered as possible while she was young enough to avoid the cruelty of life was her mission, but having a sister as sharp as Violet made that difficult.

"It went," she answered vaguely.

Violet stared at Hope, her slate eyes telling her that she'd wait as long as it took for the truth to come tumbling out.

"Bullshit," she said calmly.

"Vi," Hope said, exasperated. "You sound like a trucker. For God's sake, teenage girls should *not* talk like that."

"And twenty-one-year-old girls should be out at a club having a blast with their friends. Life's full of twisted shit, ain't it?"

"Oh, my God." Hope groaned. "It's freaking impossible to keep you young and innocent, isn't it?"

"Not your fault." Violet shrugged. "It's the price we pay, having a mother who screws us over on a regular basis."

Hope reached over and clasped Violet's hand tightly in hers. She stared down at their intertwined fingers, noting the difference in their hands, one of the many dissimilarities in the sisters' appearance. If they were out together, no one ever guessed they were related at all.

Violet's hair was just as long as Hope's, but hers was so pale blond it was nearly white. This week there were streaks of teal running through it, but next week it could just as easily be the purple that matched her name.

Her long fingers were nimble enough to brush out on a canvas the emotions their owner tousled with, and Violet used them to create the most beautiful, ahead-of-her-time paintings Hope had ever seen. There was a clutter of her work in a corner of the garage where they sat, and Hope glanced over at it as a smile tugged her lips upward.

She reached out and pulled a piece of her sister's hair.

"Pretty color," she mused.

"Mmmm," Violet answered absently. She stared into the distance, and Hope tried to imagine as she watched those pale gray eyes, where her mind had wandered.

Had they been standing, Violet would have towered a few inches over her sister's head, making her look three years older than she really was. Violet's old soul made it impossible for Hope to keep her sister young.

"It went about as badly as any date could ever possibly go," Hope finally admitted quietly. "But I don't want you to worry about it, Vi. I'm home safe, and I promised I'd always come home to you."

Violet turned her striking gray eyes on her sister. "I don't think there's a God."

"What?" The comment was so casual, so off-kilter that it caught Hope totally by surprise. For the second time that night. She was beginning to feel an uncomfortable pattern forming.

"I don't. If there was, he'd never let someone as good as you deal with the perpetual shit storm you're constantly having to go through. And he'd never let me...you know."

Hope sighed. "It's a temporary shit storm, Vi. This won't be our life forever."

"Still." Violet used a thumb to gently rub the dark bruises beginning to form on Hope's wrist where Tyler had grabbed her. She stared down at her sister's arm, her expression so forlorn it caused Hope physical pain to see it, and to know the meaning behind it. Protecting Violet from the life she led was so much more difficult than she wanted it to be. Than Violet deserved.

Still staring at their hands, Hope marveled once again at the differences. She imagined it had a lot to do with the fact that they had different fathers. Hope remembered Violet's father clearly, although the younger girl couldn't recollect anything about him. He had been a genius of an artist, the only quality other than his appearance the girl had inherited from him.

Hope could remember being fascinated by the fury with which he painted, probably the same fascination that had drawn her mother to him. But she also remembered that in order to paint with that sort of crazed ferocity, he had to be sky-high on meth. And she remembered the monster he became when his artistic efforts were exhausted, thanks to the drug. She clearly recalled the nights she cowered under her bed while her mother screamed obscenities at the man in the next room as he stole everything they owned in order to buy more of the poison.

Hope recollected nothing of her own father. She only knew what her mother had told her, which was nearly nothing. She knew that his South American heritage was what gave her the thick hair, which started out dark at her roots and lightened to almost blond at the ends; it was the ombré effect most girls paid hundreds of dollars in a salon to achieve. Her hair matched her sharp hazel eyes perfectly, and the olive tone to her skin set the whole look on fire. Her cheekbones were high and pronounced, and it helped to balance out the fact that her forehead was a bit too wide and her face a little too full.

Men found her terribly attractive, which was why her dating life came so easily to her.

Much to her revulsion.

"Are they waiting up for me inside?" asked Hope.

Violet nodded. "Yeah. Do you want me to distract them for you while you sneak upstairs?"

"No," Hope answered, squeezing her sister's hand once before letting it go. "I want you to go to bed and dream of shopping and boys, like normal thirteen-year-olds."

Violet snorted. "I'll never be normal."

And a wave of sadness almost as large as the hatred she felt for her mother crashed over Hope, squeezing her lungs and leaving her gasping for breath as it subsided.

"Temporary," she promised again.

They stood, and Hope wrapped an arm around Violet before

they ascended the steps and entered the house. Violet flinched.

Stopping in her tracks, Hope turned to her sister. "Vi?"

Violet averted her eyes, staring down at the floor. Before she could pull away, Hope pulled the shoulder of Violet's shirt down to expose her sister's bare shoulder. A deep purple bruise stood out boldly against the milky skin.

"Oh, Violet." Hope's voice escaped in a tremulous whisper. "What'd she do?"

Blinking away furious tears, Violet began to mount the steps toward the house. "It's nothing, Hope. Forget about it."

"I never forget about it! How can I?"

When they arrived in the kitchen Violet whirled around. "You don't have to focus on me. I'm usually better at avoiding her, okay? Just worry about you. And how you're going to stop working this job."

With a sigh, Hope watched her sister disappear up the back set of stairs and squared her shoulders as she turned for the long hallway that led to the living room.

"Hope." Her stepfather Frank's heavy voice accosted her as she entered the room. There was a dark undertone of danger in his words. "An unhappy client makes a very unhappy business owner."

"Yeah, well a disgusting snake who puts his hands on me makes me a paying member of the unhappy club," Hope snapped.

Frank and Wendy were standing near the window, staring accusingly at her as she waited in the doorway with folded arms. She would have laughed at her mother's demeanor if it weren't so infuriating. Wendy had been married to Frank for, what, a year? And in that time, she'd managed to adopt her worst personality yet. One that made it seem like she'd been a millionaire her entire life, as if she hadn't been nearly evicted from a trailer right before she'd met Frank.

Wendy was a chameleon; she changed her color to match the surroundings she was placed in by whatever man she wrapped herself around at any given time.

"Well?" Wendy said, her voice sloppy with the effect of the liquor she'd surely consumed that night. "What do you have to say for yourself, Hope? If you did anything tonight to hurt Frank's business, I swear to God—"

"What?" Hope spat. "You swear to God what? You'll hurt my sister again?"

Wendy's eyes narrowed to slits. Frank placed a hand on her shoulder to silence her.

"Do you know who's on my client roster, Hope? Judges. Lawyers. Doctors. The mayor." Hope's heart plummeted down to her feet. "Who," he continued, "would believe your lies?" Frank's voice was steady, calm. Hope knew his placid demeanor was only a facade. Like the deep quiet before a tornado rolled over a town, leveling it to dust. "This is my business we're talking about, Hope. I have high stakes here. What happened tonight?"

Hope sighed, suddenly feeling so tired she could have crashed right there on the hardwood floor with those two hovering over her like vultures. "He attacked me. I had no choice. What was I supposed to do? Let him *rape* me?"

"That's not how Tyler tells it." Frank's deep voice slithered toward her like a python.

"Well, I'm your stepdaughter, and your highest-earning employee, so if I were you I'd listen to how I'm telling it. And that guy is a sleaze, not to mention dangerous. You should kick him out of the club."

Frank stared at her for a full minute before he answered. He pulled himself up to his full, terrifying height. His eyes were cold, hard, and unfeeling. Hope shuddered inwardly as she stared right back.

"You will never, I repeat, *never*, disrespect a client that way again. If you have a problem with someone, you take it up with me and I will handle it. Do you understand?"

"Oh, I understand perfectly," said Hope. "Basically, next time you want me to come crying to you *after* I'm violated, and you'll make it all better."

"You ungrateful little *bitch*." Wendy's words stuck her like needles from where she stood. "I've taken care of you your whole life, and now I've given you all of this"—she gestured around them—"and you want to ruin it for us. It's not going to happen. So you better get your shit together, young lady, if your little sister is as important to you as you say she is."

Hope turned and began to exit the room. Her body was numb; every time Frank and Wendy threatened her with Violet it was like awakening from a TKO just to be punched in the face all over again.

"Who was this other man Tyler told us about, the one who interfered where he wasn't welcome?" Wendy's cold voice dripped down Hope's neck as she walked away.

"No one, Wendy," she tossed back over her shoulder to her mother. "He was no one."

Three

There were a lot of aspects of Reed Hopewell's life he couldn't change, but living at the enormous ranch estate with his parents wasn't one of them.

Aston and Sam dwelled happily in the tack house on his father's property, but Reed couldn't do it. He endured a complicated relationship with his father, and he couldn't subject himself to the complexities of it now that he was an adult.

Reed stood out on the wide balcony of the condo he shared with Tate and gazed down at the waves crashing onto the sugary sand. He squeezed his mug of coffee tightly in both hands as he stared out over the ocean and thanked his stars that he hadn't left Nelson Island. He'd loved attending college in a vibrant, historical city like Charleston, but dreamed of moving to a place more musically saturated like Austin or Nashville when he graduated. In the end, N.I. was his home. And he was a hometown kind of guy. Even if he became a success in the music industry, he knew he'd always have a home here.

He had no intention, however, to begin a family here. Reed knew that having a wife and children and a white picket fence weren't in the cards for him. He loved it that his sister had found the right person for her and settled down, but he had no illusions about that ever happening for him.

He wouldn't allow it to.

He sipped his coffee again and took in one more lungful of salty air before turning and padding back inside on bare feet.

Tate was still snoring behind his closed bedroom door, but he didn't have to be up for hours yet. The job Reed reluctantly held at Hopewell Enterprises meant he was up and at 'em at sunrise. His daily mug of coffee came directly after his morning swim in the ocean just steps away from the condo's stilts, and if the mood struck, he sat down to write a few lines before hopping in his truck and heading to work.

Driving over the bridge from Nelson Island to Charleston was a daily ritual he treasured. When he looked out over the water from the highest arc of the overpass, he could see where blue horizon met the even bluer ocean. When he was a little boy, he wondered what it would be like to journey to that place where the two met, the place that he imagined heaven would be. Blue on top of blue, solitude with only the music of the waves for company.

He had been an escape artist as a boy, always finding new ways out of the gigantic home where tension between his parents and his sister always seemed to run high. Reed would sense his sister's distress and he would climb out a window, shimmy down a trellis, or walk right out the back door and disappear onto the acres of property behind the home.

Now, although he knew he couldn't disappear to that lonely spot, he still loved to stare off into that horizon while he drove from the town he loved into the city where he did his living.

"Good morning, Reed," Lena said brightly as he strolled past her desk with his hands in his pockets.

"Lena." Reed smiled at his assistant. "What does a hick like me have to do to get his assistant to call him Mr. Hopewell?"

Returning his wink, she shrugged from her place behind her desk located just outside his door. "A hick like you needs to start signing my paychecks."

Lena appraised Reed, shaking her head as her eyes ran up his body slowly. "When the real Mr. Hopewell sees you, he's going to inwardly cringe with disappointment, compare you to your perfect sister, and then offhandedly ask you about your show this weekend as he silently prays it was a disaster."

Reed nodded. "That's about right, Lena. But what the hell is wrong with my outfit?"

He evaluated his slim pin-striped pants and signature black boots. He had paired them with a tight, dark gray tee under a form-fitting black vest. His silver belt buckle peeked out from beneath. He thought he looked very put-together, while still being completely himself. And, at his father's demand, all his tats were hidden from view.

"Really, Reed?" Aston asked as she breezed past them and opened Reed's office door. She walked inside with sharp clicks of her heels, and Reed stuck his tongue out at Lena as he reluctantly followed his sister inside.

"*Really, Reed?*" he mimicked. "Aren't you sick of saying that to me? Shit, I'm here, ain't I?"

"Barely," Aston muttered. "This isn't Cali, Reed. We don't wear T-shirts to work in Charleston." She gestured down to her own impeccable pencil skirt and ruffled blouse and grinned.

"Daddy's gonna hate it," she said in a stage whisper. "But I think you look stellar, as usual."

He smiled and locked an arm around her neck, squeezing her close as she squealed. "Thanks, sis. Love you, too."

"So, Lena has the spreadsheet with the info on those calls you're supposed to make to London today. I'm so glad you're here to handle all those conference calls now. I kind of hate talking to people, and your 'life-of-the-party' outlook is finally coming in handy for a change."

"And you thought I'd never be useful," Reed teased as he sat at his desk and flicked on his computer.

"So, how'd the rest of the night go on Saturday?" Aston asked, perching on the corner of his desk and picking up the framed photo of the two of them.

"It was…eventful," Reed answered. "Drank some, talked to some chicks…you know the routine."

"Uh-huh," she answered. "I'm assuming Tate made it home in one piece, since Sam and I didn't receive a call from the ER."

"He did indeed," Reed said. "We're not as much of a train wreck as you'd like to think."

"Yes you are," she retorted. "Seriously, Reed…"

He groaned, and she giggled.

"Okay, fine. *Really*, Reed," she began again. "You're twenty-three years old. I know you love the music thing and you're really good at it. It's time to decide...are you going to make a life with us here at the company or are you going to get out there and do the singer-songwriter thing full-time? It's now or never, little bro."

He studied her hard, staring at her face until she finally shrieked at him.

"What?"

"Oh." He jumped, appearing startled. "I was just trying to figure out the exact moment you turned into our mother."

Those were fighting words to Aston. He watched her face turn from pink to red to purple, and she spluttered angrily as she tried to find the right combination of curses to send him spinning into oblivion.

Reed raised his hands in a sign of surrender. "I'm sorry. You were being such a damn boss, though, you kinda deserved it. You're not Mom, A. I swear, I take it back."

She spun on her heel and stalked toward the door.

"You know what else would help you with your whole growing-up process?" she threw back over her shoulder. "Quit sleeping with the female population of Charleston and get yourself a real woman in your life."

He jumped as she slammed the door, and then grinned as the company messenger icon popped up on his computer with a *ding.*

Lena: What crawled up her ass and died?

Reed: Hard to say. It's a different critter every day, is it not?

Lena: LOL

He laughed softly and began to read over the files Lena had e-mailed him this morning about his international call on the calendar for later that day. As he was studying the information, however, his brain began to wander. In his mind's eye, he saw curved, tan legs stretching out under a short dress. An endless net of hair, so long it must have brushed that tiny, cinched waist, and impossibly clear hazel eyes set in the most delicate, beautiful face he'd ever laid eyes on.

He shook his head to clear it, and sat back in his chair. He stared toward his office window and reluctantly allowed himself to wonder about her. *Has she seen that psycho again since Saturday night? Is she okay?*

And...farther down the list...was she thinking about Reed like he was thinking about her?

The entire situation just rattled him. He'd never been anyone's hero. That just wasn't part of who Reed was. He was a lot of things, to a lot of people, but savior wasn't one of them. Not once.

He was born and raised in the South, and he was innately a gentleman when it came to the general rules for treating a woman. He opened car doors, he pulled out chairs, and he let them walk through entries first. But he also loved them and left them, over and over again. The alternative, entering a relationship with someone and leaving himself vulnerable to the inevitable despair that came along with that, was something he just couldn't do. He'd never be able to open himself up to someone that way. He'd seen the destruction it caused.

Just look at his parents.

Aston would argue that their parents were still together, so his logic was twisted. But they had endured a lot to be able to stay together, and Reed knew he just didn't have the stomach for it.

Rescuing Hope the other night was out of character for Reed; he knew full well it was a circumstance that he wouldn't find himself in again.

But what if he saw her again, just out and about in the city, and she didn't need him to rescue her? What then? Would they speak to each other? Or would it be like they'd never met?

He didn't even know her last name, so it wasn't like he could look her up.

"Good grief, I was knocking for like two minutes!" Lena said from the doorway.

Reed looked up, startled, and focused on his assistant as she tucked her short blond bob behind one ear and tapped her foot.

"Well?" she asked.

"Well, what?" Reed asked sheepishly. "I didn't hear you."

"Oh, for the love of Jesus," Lena said, venturing farther into the room. "What was Reed Hopewell thinking about that kept his attention focused firmly in space like that?"

"Uh..."

Lena gasped. Reed's thirty-something assistant was a wife and a mother, and she tended to live vicariously through Reed's escapades when he came to work and told her about them.

"A girl?"

"Hell, no," Reed snapped. "Music. I was mentally writing."

Lena narrowed her big brown eyes. "Nope. That's a damn lie. I've seen you focused on writing before. But time will tell, won't it?"

"Did you need something, Lena?" Frustration crept into his tone.

"Yep, got a memo from your dad. He's out of the office today, lucky you, but he wants you at the ranch for dinner. Seven o'clock."

Reed nodded absently. "Yeah, okay."

Lena winked and backed out of the office, closing the door softly behind her.

Reed sighed and returned to his actual work. Hopewell Enterprises was a global energy corporation producing classic and futuristic types of fuel for industrial use. Reed was a marketing man, making sure the people on the other end of multi-million-dollar deals were comfortable and happy with the decision to go into business with H.E., and describing his family's company's plans for prospective partners.

As he pulled up his computer screen, he put all thoughts of a mysteriously gorgeous woman out of his head.

Hope turned her head and gulped a quick breath of air into her screaming lungs, then plunged her face back into the blue depths. She smoothly sliced her arms through the water in a fast, steady rhythm, blazing a trail from one side of the Olympic-size pool to the other.

If there was one benefit to living in Frank's house, it was the pool. The first thing she did when she woke was pull on her Speedo one-piece and head out to swim laps. And on a particularly stressful day, it was also the first thing she did when she arrived home after work.

She'd learned to swim in the pool of a Boy's and Girl's Club years ago, and no matter where she'd lived, she'd always found a way to keep swimming: dirty community pools, friends' backyards. Wherever she could find water, she dived in. It was an escape she'd learned early on would never betray her.

Work was spending the day at the Charleston Center for Girls and Boys, which she loved something fierce. That wasn't usually the source of the angst she felt churning inside her. But while at the center, she often had to douse little fires started by her *other* line of work.

She reached out to tap the side of the pool at the end of her last lap, and strong fingers grasped her tender wrist. She gasped, inhaling a mouthful of water in the process.

She sputtered, and heard laughing as she wiped the water from her eyes and cleared her lungs.

"Hey!" she said angrily. "Don't you know you're never supposed to startle a swimmer?"

Morrow Mathis squatted on the concrete directly next to the water, laughing his head off.

"No, is that a rule? I didn't know about that one."

She glared at him and pulled herself out of the water. She wrapped a towel around herself, took a seat next to him, and dangled her feet in the water.

"Who let you in?" asked Hope.

"The maid…what's her name again?"

"Maggie."

"Yeah, Maggie," Morrow said. "What's up with you? Your text had me worried. Bad day?"

"Bad life," she grumbled. "But yeah, today was no party, either."

"What happened?" Morrow stretched out his long legs next to the pool and kicked off his leather flip-flops. "I've known you, how long now? Nine years? You don't usually dwell on the negative. Why so glum all of a sudden?"

Hope's lips formed a thin line. "Yeah, well, the Hope Dawson of sixth grade and the Hope Dawson of the big, bad world are vastly different. A lot more mud under my nails."

Morrow shook his head. "Your life will change as soon as you allow it to, Hope." He frowned, staring into the softly lapping water. "You think I like seeing you shuffle through the shit show your life has become? I don't. I hate it, actually. But you aren't really willing to change anything."

"Row! I have my sister to think about! I don't exactly have the luxury of doing whatever I want, whenever I want to do it, do I?"

He sighed. "You're twenty-one years old. Shine a light on what's happening in your family. No judge would deny you custody of Vi."

She snorted. "I can't take that chance. Frank's so well connected. If I did that and lost, I'd never be able to protect Violet. I want to get her out of there, Morrow. But I have to wait until I have the leverage to be able to do that. If I ever have it."

She sighed, leaning back on her hands and staring at the picturesque chain of clouds chugging across the sky. "Right now, I need to suffer through working for Frank. When I have a chance, I'll make it all stop. But this is what I have to do right now."

She didn't want to tell him about the attack. But she desperately wanted to discuss Reed. She chewed the inside of her cheek, contemplating. Telling Morrow about Tyler would be stirring up a storm so violent she may not be able to rein it back in. Her friend protected her fiercely, when she let him.

While she mulled it over, Morrow shook his head and sighed. "Agree to disagree. New subject: your birthday. It's in two weeks. What do you want to do this year?"

Hope reached out a hand to brush a thick lock of hair out of his eyes. Women envied Morrow his dark brown curly tresses; they hung down just long enough to touch his collar, and a tendril or two always hung in his eyes. They envied him even more for his long lashes and flawless, light brown skin. She thought Morrow might argue that being a mixed-race individual in Charleston, South Carolina, had been more of a tribulation growing up than an asset, but he was beautiful all the same. His green eyes studied her, and she smiled back at herself in their reflection.

She and Morrow had been a pair ever since he threw himself in front of a rogue kickball for her in gym class back on the first day of sixth grade. Since then, he'd been her best friend, her confidant, and really the only person in her life other than Violet she truly let in.

"I want to get the hell out of this place, order a pizza, and watch a movie on the couch in your apartment. Oh, and beer. There needs to be lots and lots of beer."

"I thought you'd say that. That's why I made plans for us to go out. You're not staying in on your birthday this year."

She groaned and slapped the back of his head.

"Fuck was that for?"

"I'm not going to be able to get away on my birthday, Morrow. You know that." Her voice was quiet, and Morrow could read the serious expression on her face.

"You can. You will," he encouraged. "We're going to dinner at a fancy place, and then going to sing karaoke."

She brightened. "That actually sounds like fun."

"See? Leave it to your man Morrow."

She rolled her eyes. "Who else is invited?"

"Well...Violet's too young for this scene. But I'm going to talk to Beth and Xander from the Center. We'll make it a party. Okay?"

"Okay," she said happily. "Thanks, Morrow. I'd fall over and die without you."

More than one friend in their lives had wondered why she and Morrow were just friends. To tell the truth, they'd tried for more, just once. They'd kissed shortly after high school, and then both fallen over laughing when the smooch had revealed that they had absolutely no physical chemistry. Their relationship was based on pure, platonic, unconditional love. And she wouldn't trade it for the world.

He put an arm around her neck and pulled her into his side. He didn't care that she made a big wet spot on his thin Henley, or that she was dripping all over his khaki shorts. "Things have to go up from here, Hope. And maybe it will all start with your birthday."

She hoped so. She couldn't take much more of the downward spiral her life was currently on.

Four

Morrow whistled as she made the deposit.

"Having a paycheck that big would make me stupid," he said wistfully.

"Well, it always feels like blood money to me. But putting every penny of it into savings for the day I get to take my sister away from our mother is a hell of a lot of comfort."

Hope maneuvered her scrappy little car into the steady flow of traffic on the street in front of the bank and headed toward the Center. She and Morrow had been volunteering there since they were teenagers, but while Morrow had gone off to college to major in education, she had stayed behind in Charleston. College wasn't in the cards when she was trying to keep a close eye on Violet, and when her mother met Frank all of her spare time was filled with her second job. The volunteer time she spent at the Center turned into part-time work, and then she had earned a spot as assistant director in the last year and a half. It was a career for Hope, the only one she wanted to have. The fact that she had to balance her time there during the day with her time working for Frank's club at night was something she detested.

Now that Morrow was back home and teaching at a high school nearby, he volunteered at the Center on his summer break. They had just made a bank run for the fund-raising division, and Hope took advantage of the time to deposit the money she'd earned the night before. It was a percentage of what she'd really earned. Frank gave her a cut and kept the rest. For his stepdaughter, he kept a little more than he did from the other girls he had working for him. Just another special form of torture for Hope.

"Still," mused Morrow. "The fact that you're pulling cash for your trouble has to be kind of an upside."

She stared at him, her mouth hanging open and her hazel eyes flashing more green than brown at the moment. "Are you kidding me right now, Row? I'd give all of the money back if I could; I don't want to be anywhere near Frank's stupid club. But since I earned it, I'm glad I can put something away for when the time comes. I'm afraid that if I get another job, Wendy will be pissed. And when she's pissed…it's not good for anyone. Especially Violet. The only reason I stay in that house is for my sister. You know that."

He nodded, his face clouded with chagrin. "Yeah, I know, Hope. I'm sorry."

She sighed and pulled the car back into the parking lot of the Center. "It's forgotten. I only have to get through two more weeks until my birthday party, right? I shouldn't have to work any more nights for the club before then. I can do it."

They got out of the car and hurried to get out of the hot sun. Stepping inside the cool building, Hope took a deep breath in relief.

"Hell, yeah, you can." Morrow nodded his encouragement.

She still hadn't told him about Tyler, therefore not mentioning a word about meeting and being saved by Reed. There just didn't seem to be a right time to tell her very protective best friend that she'd almost been violated that way.

"Miss Dawson?"

Hope glanced down at the light tug on her jeans and smiled into the face of a little first grader named Jack.

She knelt down in front of him. "What's up, Jack?"

"I can't figure out how to make seven and three make ten. I know it's 'sposed to make ten, but it keeps comin' out only nine." The more the confused little furrow in his brow deepened, the more Hope melted inside.

Smothering a giggle, she let Jack pull her away from Morrow. When she looked back, he shot her a sunny smile and headed over to the basketball court where a group of high school boys were dribbling furiously.

Working full days at the Center over the next few weeks was exhausting, but in a fulfilling, endearing way. She adored the kids, and vice versa. Being one of the only adults in their lives who actually cared enough about them to make sure they were learning their numbers and letters gave Hope a strange sense of validation, like she was doing something important with her life no one could take away from her. But on the day before her birthday, coming home to find Wendy and Frank waiting for her in the living room was a whole different kind of draining.

"Now what?" Hope asked, not at all in the mood to deal with the two of them.

"You have to work tonight." Frank informed her of the news like he was commenting on the weather. His tone was so casual, she wished she could reach out and wipe the smug smile from his face.

"No," Hope argued. "I'm off this weekend, remember? Tomorrow is my birthday."

Wendy huffed out a breath and rolled her eyes skyward. Someone might have thought she was dealing with an irritating employee rather than her daughter. "Do you think adults actually get to take off work on their birthday, Hope?"

"How would you know, Wendy?" Hope said, her voice quietly bordering on rage. "When's the last time you worked?"

Wendy stood up, crossed the room to where Hope leaned wearily against the doorjamb, and slapped her hard across the face.

Hope raised her hand to her cheek, gaping at her mother. The stinging in her cheek began shortly after the burning in her chest. She quickly gathered her emotions and placed them in the deep, dark place in her heart where she kept them buried. Just another infraction of her mother's: the first of its kind, but no more catastrophic than what she'd already done.

"You've graduated to hitting *me* now?" Hope spoke with a

calm so forced it nearly broke her. "That's good to know. I'm actually okay with fighting back!"

"Hope." Her stepfather's voice commanded the room, and their attention. He stood; his height and girth best suited an NFL linebacker. In fact, he used to be an actual NFL linebacker, before he'd returned to Charleston following an injury and become the successful entrepreneur he was today. They were quite a pair when they were together; Wendy had all of her daughter's beauty but none of her warmth. Her long, dark hair didn't have the dark-to-light effect that Hope's had, remaining raven from root to end. She made a striking contrast to Violet's fair features, but it was obvious to anyone in the room that Hope was her daughter.

"I hit you because you're a disrespectful little wench," Wendy spat. "You deserved it. Frank said you're working, so you're working. It's not like we make you head out into the fray for free; you get paid, and your ass should be grateful."

Hope had heard it before. She should be grateful for what they made her do. She should be thanking them for allowing her sister and her to stay together. She should be kissing their feet for the home they provided her.

Sighing in defeat, she sagged slightly against the wall. "I need to get some ice on my face, *Wendy,* unless you want me to go to work with a welt. Is a limo picking me up?"

"As per usual," Frank said. "You're more trouble than you're worth, little girl. If you weren't my most requested employee, I would have canned your pretty little ass a long time ago. So fix your face, and then get happy. I picked out your dress; it's lying on your bed."

"Right," Hope muttered as she walked out of the living room and headed for the kitchen.

She needed to place an ice pack on her smarting cheek.

Another couple of weeks had flown by with plenty of sun, heat, and ocean. Reed had spent his days on international calls and coaxing deals out of conglomerates in faraway places. He'd spent his nights playing guitar and writing music, or downing beers with Tate on the beach at their favorite bar.

Among other things.

"Do you want coffee?" he asked the statuesque redhead as she stretched one long, bare leg out from beneath the covers on his bed. He didn't want to be rude, but his Saturdays were a precious commodity, and he wanted to get this one started, which meant the redhead from Sunny's last night needed to get out of his bed.

"Mmmm," she murmured as she stretched. "Coffee sounds good."

"Goddammit," he cursed under his breath. Aloud, he said, "Coming right up, uh…"

"Monica," she said, fully alert now. "My name is Monica. Did you seriously forget that?"

Reed cringed. "Coffee will be in the kitchen, Monica."

He ducked out of his room quickly and padded barefoot back toward the kitchen. He was certain Tate was in a similar situation behind his closed door, but he wouldn't be completing his send-off until later in the morning.

Reed listened to the percolating coffeepot as he sat on the arm of the sleek black leather couch. He placed his elbows on his knees and stared at his toes as he clasped his hands together pensively. Somehow, he found himself in this situation he hated on most weekend mornings, having to kick out a girl in the most unceremonious fashion possible. All the while trying not to come off like the asshole he really was.

"I didn't peg you for the deep-in-thought type," she muttered as she searched his cabinets for a mug.

He stood up and walked over, reaching around her to grab a travel mug and pulling it down for her.

Damn, he thought. *I lose more travel mugs this way…*

"Hard to tell what kind of person someone is when you go home with them after one night in a bar, huh?"

He couldn't help himself saying it. He might be the douche bag that drunkenly brought different girls home, but they were the ones who willingly flocked to his bed. Nelson Island was a small place; yes, most of the women in the summer were tourists, but they still had to realize what they were walking into.

She grimaced and grabbed her cup. Flouncing toward the door, she said, "Don't bother asking for my number."

"I'm heartbroken."

She slammed the door behind her.

Reed sighed, heading out the balcony door and down the wooden steps toward his morning swim.

When he returned, shaking water and sand from his hair, he found Tate in a lip-lock on the couch with his guest.

Reed sighed loudly as he slid open the door. Tate always had a more difficult time loving 'em and leaving 'em. He always let them stick around the morning after, and sometimes they made the mistake of feeling like a girlfriend.

"Yo," Reed greeted them. They ignored him completely, continuing their shameless devouring of each other in earnest like he hadn't even spoken.

Reed shook his head and headed to his bathroom to shower and dress for the day. The woman he spent the night with wore a perfume typical of all the women he brought home. They all smelled so similar, he could almost identify his type by their scent. He could never identify the scent, which let him know that she'd be a good one-nighter. It was always a cloying mixture of faux fruit and floral, and it stuck to his skin like sticky tape. The rigorous swim in the ocean hadn't been enough to remove it, and he scrubbed his skin raw in the shower trying to exfoliate the smell off of him. When he finally felt clean, he stepped out of the shower and stared at his face in the mirror.

He knew he was handsome—he'd had plenty of people tell him so all his life. His sister was exotically gorgeous, model material really, had she been interested. He was just as attractive, in a masculine way. Where she was dark, he was lighter. His eyes were a slightly lighter shade of blue, his hair a lighter shade of brown. Their skin was the same, pale in the winter and tan in the summer. He swam every day and played tennis all through high school, so staying physically fit wasn't an issue. His muscles stood out under his tight T-shirts and fitted clothing, and women liked to reach out and touch them.

But, staring at himself now, he wasn't happy with his appearance. His features were chiseled almost to a flaw, his lips were full, and the slight amount of dark scruff grazing his jawline drove women absolutely wild. But he was slowly learning that it had more to do with what was on his insides than what was visible on the outside.

Something was missing. *Or maybe it's just broken.*

As he was dressing, a loud knock resounded through the condo from the front door, and Reed wondered if Tate's guest had left yet.

He pulled on a dark blue plain tee over a pair of faded, worn jeans and walked out to the living room.

"Sam!" he greeted his friend. "What's up, man?"

"What's up is that we're headed out to lunch. You up for it?"

"What are we, chicks?"

Sam shrugged. "I'm hungry. You hungry?"

"Yeah."

"Then let's go eat. Tate, you in?"

Tate was slumped over the kitchen counter with a mug of coffee gripped in both hands. He muttered a response in the negative, and Reed waved him off.

"You know he doesn't actually wake up until two. Let me get my wallet and we'll head out. I assume I'm driving."

"Unless you wanna snuggle up to me on the back of the Harley."

"Ha! My sister might be in love with that thing, but I like to keep four wheels on the ground."

Reed and Sam both lounged in their seats in a seaside café that served sandwiches and kept the pitchers of sweet tea flowing freely. A light dusting of sand littered the sidewalk under their little round table.

"You and Aston going out tonight?" asked Reed, picking up his glass of tea to sip.

Sam rubbed the scruff on his square jawline and squinted into the sun. His huge, six-foot-four frame folded up into the medium-size wicker chair was comical, and Reed snickered as he watched him.

"I don't know, man. Wedding planning is keeping us pretty busy."

"I bet. I can't believe you two made it all the way through college, what was left of it, without getting hitched." Reed studied his future brother-in-law.

Sam and Aston had met a few years back when Sam had ventured onto the Hopewell ranch as a hired hand. He'd quickly worked his way up and into their father's heart, thus turning Aston from a potential enemy to the love of his life. They'd been through a lot since they'd met, including Sam's arrest for being wanted for murder back in Virginia a few months after arriving in Nelson Island. Sam had lost his girlfriend back home in the process, a girl he'd grown up protecting.

Sam was one of those guys who was just a born hero. He worked hard, lived on the right side of the line, and gave his entire heart to those he loved. And Reed loved him fully, like they were already brothers. Sam had been there for him many times over the past four years, always helping him out of tough situations and supporting his love of music completely.

If Reed was going to open up to anyone about what had happened a couple of weeks ago with Hope, and how it seemed to have changed something inside of him, it was going to be Sam.

Sam shrugged. "We like to do things right."

Nodding thoughtfully, Reed sipped his drink and stared out toward the water.

"I think Blaze, Tate, and Tam wanted to head over to C-town and hit a club or a bar. I'm not feeling it."

Sam stared. "You're not feeling it? That phrase isn't in your vocabulary, little bro. What's up with you lately? These past few weeks you've seemed...different. Too serious, maybe. Where's your head at?"

Reed heaved a sigh, propping a foot up on the chair beside him. "Man, I don't even know. I feel kind of different."

"How so?" Sam leaned forward and placed his forearms on the table, picking up his sandwich and taking a big bite.

Reed recounted the story of the night at the club when Reed had walked up on the alley to see Hope being roughed up by Tyler. He explained how he'd stashed her behind him and pulled a knife on her aggressor. Then he told Sam about giving her a ride home in the truck, and how he'd been thinking about her ever since.

"I feel really unsettled about the fact that I have no way to contact her now. Her whole demeanor that night screamed at me, man. She was tough and strong, but underneath that I could see this desperation. I think she needs help, but I don't know what the fuck to do about it."

Reed sat back, finishing his last words in a rush and gazing at Sam in earnest.

Sam nodded, smiling at Reed. "I'm proud of you, man. You did a good thing. When a woman needs help like that, you gotta step in and do the right thing."

"Well, hell, Sam, I was raised right. I wouldn't just leave a woman to get attacked in an alley."

"I know you wouldn't, Reed," Sam answered. "I think you're capable of a hell of a lot more than you give yourself credit for, though. Why didn't you get her number and call to check on her after?"

Reed shook his head and ran a hand along his jaw. "I don't know. That's the problem. I wish like hell I had. But when's the last time I asked a girl for her number? I don't usually want to call them afterward. So even though the thought crossed my mind…I didn't even know how to go about it, for God's sake. I felt like I was fourteen again, just trying to feel some tits for the first time or something. I offered her my number, but she turned it down."

He groaned, covering his face with both hands and dragging them downward.

"Yeah, but you didn't try to sleep with this one," Sam pointed out. "You rescued her. It's different."

"I know," Reed said. "But if I see her again…"

"If you see her again, you think you'll go man-whore Reed on her?"

Reed nodded. "Bingo. She's hot, man. Like…lingerie-model hot, only shorter. She's got this hair…never seen anything like it, it's so long and…and her skin is this bronze color that makes me crazy, wanting to touch it. And her eyes…her eyes are this brownish green that keeps glinting flecks of gold in the light. And she was so petite, I think I could fit my hands around her waist…"

Sam was rocking with laughter. "You got all that after one hour with her in the dark?"

Reed hung his hand, allowing his forehead to graze the table. He didn't look up as he mumbled, "Shit. Yeah."

"Well, if you see her again, and things go down with the two of you, I think you might just explode. I've never heard you talk about a girl like this, ever."

"Shit," Reed muttered again. "This is the last thing I need."

Sam laughed. "You're not singing tonight, right? The guys and Tamara want to go out."

Reed nodded, his head still scraping against wood. "I'm not going."

"No?"

"Nah. Dad has this business owners' banquet or something in Charleston. He wants me to attend."

Sam reached over and pounded Reed on the back. "Charleston is bigger than N.I. You probably won't run into her again, and then things will get back to normal."

Reed looked up hopefully. "You think so?"

Sam nodded with a quirk of his lips. "You better hope so. You can't let this girl get anywhere near your bed."

Five

Reed took a sip of fizzing champagne, trying his hardest not to look bored out of his damn mind.

It was difficult.

"Ah." Gregory Hopewell smiled and leaned in toward Reed. "There's Joseph Claremont. He owns Alpine Tech. You know, the software design company?"

Reed nodded, glancing at the ultratan face of the man his father was pointing out.

"We should speak to him about what his company can do for H.E."

Nodding again, Reed took a larger sip of champagne, downing the drink without tasting it.

"You're paying attention, right, Reed?" Gregory turned to face him, frowning slightly. "I usually bring Aston to these things. But now that you're more involved with the company, I think it's time you showed some more initiative."

It was a speech Reed had heard a hundred times before. And

he thought that showing up for work every day and completing his tasks there to the best of his ability *was* showing initiative. But he'd never be Aston. Working for Hopewell Enterprises had never been his dream like it was hers.

"Yeah, Dad," Reed answered. "I know. I'm here, aren't I?"

He was even wearing a plain black suit, against his better judgment. Gregory had insisted there be no "Reed fashion antics" tonight. Reed felt like he might suffocate.

His father led him around the room, introducing him to business contacts while everyone sipped drinks. There were hors d'oeuvres being served by waitstaff in crisp white shirts and black tailored pants.

While his father was deep in conversation with the mayor of Charleston, Reed stepped away to snag another glass of champagne and a crab puff from the tray of a passing waitress. The girl paused in her stride, staring at him with narrowed eyes.

He glanced at her curiously as she spoke. "Do I know you from somewhere?"

Sighing inwardly, he shook his head. The girl seemed about his age, maybe a year or two younger. When she wasn't waiting tables, it was likely she frequented the clubs and bars around the city.

"I doubt it," he answered shortly.

Normally, he would have jumped at the chance to tell her who he was, strike up a conversation that might end with her lying naked between his sheets. She was cute, her short dark hair streaked with blond, big gray eyes that seemed full of just the right kind of devilish merriment.

But tonight, his mind was elsewhere.

He watched her with an incredulous look on his face as she pretended to think hard, and then an imaginary lightbulb snapped on over her head and he nearly groaned in embarrassment for her.

"I know! You're that singer! I've heard you around town....you're ah-maze-ing!" She stretched out the word like it was something delicious on her tongue, and his stomach rolled. She looked him up and down, appreciatively, and then grinned at him. "You sure do look different tonight, honey. I almost didn't recognize you!"

This was normally the kind of attention he just sucked up through a straw. It was ridiculously easy for him to garner the attention of any pretty girl in the room, and turn that attention into a night of wild monkey sex in his bedroom at the condo. Then the next morning, he undoubtedly felt the heat of the mistake he'd made, and the horror of what an empty shell of a man he'd become hit him like a brick wall.

Tonight, he just couldn't do it. He was attempting to figure out how to separate himself from her when Sam strode up beside him. Aston was close on his heels, and she smiled widely at Reed.

"There you are," greeted Sam, grabbing a glass for Aston off the waitress's tray and turning his back toward her.

"Last-minute change in plans, little bro. I know how much you hate these things. Didn't want to leave you hanging, did we, Sam?" Aston took the glass from Sam and sipped.

The waitress scurried away, throwing Reed one last longing look as she went.

Reed sighed, relief flooding through his gut, and sent Sam a silent *thank you.* Sam nodded, his face full of concern.

Aston was glancing between the two of them, and Reed could see that she smelled something fishy. He just hoped she'd leave it alone, wait until a later date to grill him about his newfound aversion to meaningless sex.

She raised an eyebrow in his direction, with one of those superior looks that could only belong to a big sister. He returned her gaze with a blank stare, and she frowned slightly to let him know that she indeed knew something was up and certainly had no intention of dropping it. Then she flipped her long, thick raven hair over one shoulder and combed through it with her fingers. All the while, she kept one eye on Reed and the other on Sam. Sam wrapped an arm around her to draw her closer, and leaned down to kiss her cheek.

Reed stared at them, unable to help himself. He'd spent many an evening with Aston and Sam, always marveling at how perfect for one another they seemed to be. Before Sam, Aston had been dating her high school sweetheart, and she had never looked at him with half the amount of adoration she bestowed upon Sam. And Reed had witnessed Sam with his childhood love story, Ever, here in Nelson Island years ago. The connection he had with her was nothing in comparison to what he shared with Reed's sister. Their relationship was rock solid and full of a seething passion that drew them toward one another almost subconsciously. Even in a room full of strangers, they harbored an invisible connection that seemed to cloak them in a privacy all their own.

Reed thought it was a fluke. He didn't think relationships

like theirs existed for the rest of the poor folk bumbling around searching for their one true love. It was exactly why he wasn't searching. His parents were actually madly in love, even though his mother couldn't manage to keep her worldly gifts preserved for just his father. He'd witnessed it, and the havoc that was wreaked on their lives, as a small boy, and now he wanted nothing to do with any of it. Somehow Aston had managed to make it out of the muck their parents' tumultuous marriage had stuck them in. It wasn't going to happen twice.

Reed knew he was destined to lead a life that traveled one of two directions: never settling down and living fast and loose, or always miserably searching for the one person he was supposed to spend forever with.

He chose option one, a hundred percent.

"God, I would kill for that girl's hair," Aston mused. "I wonder how she gets it to be so shiny with all that *length*? Jesus, I think it's to her waist. And that color? I don't even think it's fake. I think she's a natural ombré: dark on top and blond at the ends."

Reed tuned back into his sister and Sam just as she was musing about some unknown girl across the grand ballroom. Her murmur was admiring and distant as she stared at the object of her admiration.

Reed was still thinking about his parents when Aston's words clicked in his brain. *Jesus, I think it's to her waist.* There was only one girl he could think of with that kind of hair. As his head was whipping around toward a table on the opposite end of the room for the first time all night, his eyes landed on the girl he'd been unable to pry from his thoughts since meeting her weeks ago. And the rest of the room seemed to fade away.

She was sitting at one of the large round tables set up for the sit-down dinner. Their own table was waiting for them nearby, and Reed shifted his eyes to see his father already sitting down, chatting with another man he didn't know.

She was sitting next to a man in a suit, and Reed's eyes narrowed as he inspected him. He expelled a breath when he realized it wasn't Tyler, the man who had attacked her the night they met.

Then who is she with?

The thought startled him as it appeared in his mind, but it didn't stop him from snapping to Sam and Aston, "Let's go sit with Dad. I think it's almost time for them to serve dinner."

As they arrived at their table and found seats, his eyes settled comfortably on Hope once more. She hadn't yet noticed his presence a mere two tables away, and he had the opportunity to drink her in unnoticed. Most of her body was hidden under the white tablecloth, but her torso was sheathed in a silver, sparkling dress with a very low neckline. Delicate sleeves fell off her shoulders, and her shining hair hung down her back. Her delicate neck was exposed, and he almost thought he could see the pulse beating softly underneath her flesh. His eyes widened, and a warm ache spread through his abdomen and up into his chest.

She was here. She was fucking beautiful.

And she was with another guy.

A waitress dropped off another glass of champagne at their table, and Hope grimaced at the sight of it. Frank was insisting she drink to stay loose and comfortable. Probably because he knew how pissed she was that she was here with him instead of out with Morrow for her birthday.

She'd had to text her friend earlier in the night to cancel after Frank dropped the bomb on her.

"You're coming with me tonight. I have a banquet I have to attend for business owners around the city, and you're a girl I want by my side to help schmooze some new clients."

Damn him. He could bring any girl he wanted with him to this event, and he knew it. Forcing her to cancel her plans was just another way to demonstrate he had full power over her and her life. And there wasn't a damn thing she could do about it.

"Frank," she whispered, leaning toward him. She didn't want the young millionaire on her other side to overhear her. Frank had sat them beside each other because he thought the young man would "enjoy" eating beside Hope. "I seriously don't think I can handle any more alcohol. Do you want me walking out of here, or do you want to have to carry me?"

"You need to relax. You'll drink one more," Frank said through gritted teeth, before turning back to the owner of the largest engineering firm in the area. Frank was here to win new clients, and her job was to look pretty and show them what they could have on their arms if they joined Frank's club.

She could hear the slur in her own voice, and her normal mile-high inhibitions had left the building hours ago. She knew perfectly well she was going to end up regretting her third glass of champagne the next morning.

"Fine," she said, standing on wobbly legs. "I'll just run to the little girls' room first."

Frank sent her a hard glance, which clearly said "hurry the hell up."

She headed for the exit doors of the ballroom and up a hallway that housed the ladies' room. She had a feeling she'd end up sprawled out on her ass in front of a lot of jeering people if she didn't walk slowly and carefully.

She made it safely to the restroom, and when she exited the stall and turned on the faucet, she stared at her reflection. She was missing Morrow something fierce. She felt awful about having to ruin the plans he'd made especially for her birthday. Today hardly felt like a special day. She never went out and just cut loose with her friends, and she felt suffocated. She was a prisoner of her circumstances, and there was no way out. She washed her hands and ran wet fingers though her hair to remove any knots. Then she inspected her face. Not much makeup; she hated caking on the stuff. Her cheeks were flushed from the alcohol and the heat. Her eyes began to blur with unshed tears, and she gulped. Quickly tamping down her emotions, she turned and headed for the bathroom door. As she walked unsteadily out into the dim hallway outside the restroom, she was caught in the strong and steady arms of Reed Hopewell.

What the…?

She was dreaming. She had to be. She'd fallen and hit her head in the restroom, and now this was a figment of her very active imagination.

She sucked in a breath that never made it back out again while she stared up at him. He didn't let go of her, and those bluer-than-ocean eyes bored into her as he held her still.

"Reed?" she asked in amazement. "What are you doing here?"

"You remember me," he observed. His tone was pleased, and she wondered why. She couldn't wonder long, though, because the sound of his voice was doing something strange to her insides, and she squirmed in his arms uncomfortably.

He continued to hold on to her as he chuckled. "You're tanked, aren't you?"

She shot him an indignant glare as she swayed on her feet. "No!"

"Right. It's nice to see you again, Hope. Very nice. But now, I'm wondering something."

She swallowed, gazing up into his beautiful eyes. "Wh-what?"

"From the last time we met, I kind of thought you were the kind of girl who maybe didn't have a smile. I kind of hoped that the next time I saw you, you'd be smiling. You know, so I'd know you actually knew how."

Tyler flashed through her head, his nasty leer and nastier words echoing through her muddled brain. She shuddered in response, and jerked out of Reed's arms.

"Yeah, well," she said sadly. "After a night like that, it's kind of hard to find your smile."

Reed followed her, not allowing the space to grow between them. "And tonight?"

She shook her head numbly, still not believing she was having this conversation with a guy she never expected to see again. "Haven't found a reason to smile tonight, either."

His expression clouded over, and she had the thought that a face as gorgeous as his should never look that troubled. "I'm sorry to hear that, Hope."

Her eyes were beginning to wander freely over his body; roving over the black tuxedo pants that fit him just right, his black-clad torso that contrasted perfectly with his tanned skin. She unwillingly envisioned what may be under those too-perfect clothes, and her unholy thoughts upchucked from her mouth.

"Do you have more tattoos under there?" she blurted.

He stared at her blankly for a moment, and then his whole face lit with a smile, and his mouth dropped open in shock. "Do you always just say whatever the hell it is you're thinking? Just blurt it out like word vomit? Or is that quality saved just for me?"

Her face had to be scarlet; she thought she'd never been so embarrassed in her entire life. She tried to remember the last time a man had affected her this way. Causing her thighs to clench with anticipation, her hands to become clammy, and the object in front of her—Reed—to become the only thing she could see.

"I—"

"Hope?"

A voice cut through the moment, saving her from saying anything else to further humiliate herself. It was the young millionaire; Hope couldn't even remember now what his business was. He moved toward them, eyeing Reed with suspicion and reaching out to pull her to his side. What the hell? The man hadn't even officially become one of Frank's clients, and he was already manhandling her. *Figures. He'll fit right in.*

"I wondered where you'd gotten to."

"I'm fine," she answered, not offering him any sort of explanation for Reed's presence.

Reed eyed Hope for a moment, his eyes sliding down to the

man's arm around her waist and then back to Hope's eyes. He nodded slightly to himself, seemingly coming to an inner decision. "See you around, Hope."

He headed off down the hall, and with his departure, Hope felt a little bit of herself seep away. She thought...well, she didn't know what she thought. That he'd ask for her number? That he'd ask her out on a real date? That he'd be remotely interested in her at all? It didn't matter, even if he'd done any of those things.

She was firmly planted in a not-available zone because of her mother and Frank. The last thing she needed was a man like Reed Hopewell invading her privacy and her life in general.

But somehow...she thought maybe she wanted him to.

Six

As hard as Reed tried to keep his eyes and attention on his own table, he was fighting a battle already lost. He was unable to tear his eyes away from Hope as she sat just a few tables over. More than anything, he just wanted to know what she was like. There had to be more to this mysterious beauty whose smile was noticeably absent from her exquisite face. This couldn't be the only facet to Hope. There had to be more.

Aston snapped her fingers in front of his face, and he jumped. "Reed? What the hell are you looking at? I asked you a question."

"What?" he hissed. He was more irritated with himself than with Aston, but she didn't need to know that.

"I asked you if you want to meet the CEO of Skinner Inc. You know, the company that does all the business with our natural gas division? But forget it if you're gonna be an asshole."

She gave him her haughtiest hair flip and turned back to Sam. Sam was eyeing him warily, and he nodded his head, not perceptibly, toward Hope. Reed nodded, and then leaned his head back far enough to look at the ceiling.

The frustration was bubbling up in his veins, replacing the blood that usually pulsed there with liquid anxiety. It was hotter than it should have been in the glitzy banquet hall, considering they were in an air-conditioned facility. Whenever Hope glanced at Reed, his chest constricted a little tighter into the knotted fist it had quickly become. And when she looked at the man who was apparently her date, he nearly lost his mind.

Mostly, he wanted to run over there, in front of the entire room, and ask why the hell she was out with yet another guy that wasn't Reed.

What was happening to him? The last time he had reacted this way over the mere sight of a girl...he couldn't actually remember it ever happening. He didn't know Hope. Not at all. Yet here she was, sharing the same space as him, and the fact that he wasn't touching her, talking to her, interacting with her at all was nearly killing him.

And when her date leaned over her, stretching one arm over the back of her chair, and whispered into her ear, all of the emotions he was battling pooled in his gut in the form of jealousy, and the growing rage in his body tightened to an uncomfortable level.

She slid back from the table, exposing her bare legs, and her heels were calling for him to lay her down somewhere and pull them off. Her smooth skin was begging him to run his hands all over it. The luscious rise of her breasts, visible above the neckline of her dress, screamed at him to take a swipe at it with his tongue. And her lips...those lips that would fit so perfectly around his own were puckering as she looked away from her date, and her hot pink tongue wet the surface.

"Hell," Reed muttered. He leaned over to Sam. "I gotta get outta here a minute."

Sam opened his mouth to respond, but Reed stood and nearly flew out of the too-crowded room.

"Oh, come on, man. You gotta get it together, Hopewell," he grunted as he paced the sidewalk outside. The street beyond the banquet hall wasn't the busiest in downtown Charleston, but it wasn't empty, either. He decided to stroll up the street and around the corner, where he didn't look like an idiot talking to himself in front of a crowded establishment.

He leaned against the brick, the heavy night air still cloaked with the day's humidity. The historic, charming streetlamp beside him on the sidewalk spilled a circle of yellow light onto the cement, and Reed stared at it blankly while his thoughts ran laps around his brain.

A couple strolled by him, stopping by the trunk of a statuesque palm tree to cuddle close and steal a kiss. The light from the lamp caught their faces, and when they pulled apart, Reed saw how adoringly they stared into one another's eyes.

He groaned and turned away, pressing his palms into the brick beside him. He closed his eyes, drawing breaths deeply into his lungs and releasing them slowly.

Why am I so damn affected? What does Hope have? Was it the fact that he had saved her from Tyler?

That had to be it. Some kind of special connection had formed between them that night. And now he felt responsible for her.

Although that didn't make much sense, because she clearly had someone inside the banquet who more than likely felt even more responsible for Hope than Reed did.

How was he going to get her out of his system? He couldn't take her home; she was here with someone. And anyway, he had a feeling that having Hope in his bed with him would have exactly the opposite effect of getting her out of his system. Just the thought of her long hair splayed out over his pillow, her naked curves laid out against his sheets caused him physical pain as his dick swelled in his nether region.

Reed shuddered visibly. No, the best thing to do would be to go on his merry way, never to see Hope again. He'd forget about her, and the way she affected his chest.

The chest that housed the heart that began to hammer wildly when he heard her soft voice behind him.

"Reed?"

He kept his forehead glued painfully to the unyielding brick in front of him, desiring simultaneously to turn around to make sure she was really there and disappear into the side of the building.

"Reed," Sam said sharply. "She wanted to know where you were, so we came to find you. Turn around. Don't be a dipshit."

Reed sighed, heavy with apprehension, and turned. Hope stood there looking every bit the vixen she had inside the bar, holding tightly to Sam's arm as they stood staring at him.

"Why?" asked Reed.

Sam looked down at her. "I'm going back in. It was nice meeting you, Hope."

She nodded, never taking her eyes off of Reed.

As Sam walked away, Reed stepped closer to Hope, like an invisible string pulled him.

"Why what?" she asked, her voice shaking slightly.

"Why are you out here? What does that guy in there think about the fact that you're outside with me right now?"

Her forehead wrinkled in confusion, which might have been the cutest thing he'd ever witnessed. He watched it in fascination as the wrinkles smoothed out and then appeared again as her thoughts whirred around her head.

"What guy? Why are you out here? You seemed upset when you left. Did I do something?"

Reed, still focused on the facets of her face, missed the question. "I'm sorry, what?"

"I mean...I know we didn't get a chance to talk the other week, but I wanted to tell you...I appreciate what you did for me. You didn't have to. You could have kept walking, and then...well, then Tyler probably would have hurt me." She shook visibly. "So, uh...thank you, Reed."

His name rolling off of her tongue like pure silk pulled him another involuntary step closer to her. Those hazel eyes held only a hint of green tonight, and they nearly sparkled in the lemony light of the streetlamp. Her lips pursed slightly as she watched him, and he could tell that although she was sincere, she hated the fact that she needed to be thanking him at all.

She was fierce, and he liked it. Oh, he liked that a hell of a lot.

And as he read all of that in her eyes, they suddenly softened, as if she knew what he saw there. And another step brought him closer still, until they were only inches apart.

She held her ground, not backing away from him like he thought she would. Reed pushed his hands deep into his pockets, ordering them to stay put.

"So, you're out here...with me. You wanted to thank me? I did what anyone would have done, Hope. No thanks necessary. I'm glad you're here, actually. I needed to know that you're doing well. And it seems you are. Very much so."

She nodded, and licked her lips the way she had inside. Reed's hands fisted inside his pockets as a fire began to burn so slowly inside of him. She shook her head, causing those deep waves of hair to ripple around her, and her scent reached his nose. She smelled freshly sweet, and also spicy, all at the same time. He inhaled deeply, closing his eyes.

He opened them quickly as he realized she didn't smell of cheap, fruity perfume.

"Well, yeah. I guess I'm okay. I don't actually want to be here tonight...I had to come. I'm actually supposed to be out with my friends, celebrating my birthday, but instead I'm here, and..." She trailed off, staring into his eyes.

Reed sucked in a breath. His voice came out low and strained. "It's your birthday? Well, hot damn. Happy birthday, Hope. I hope your date gives you everything you want."

There were those little confusion wrinkles again. "My date?"

Reed stared at her, the realization dawning on him. His hands slowly slid out of his pockets as he stared down at this girl who was every fantasy he never even knew he had.

"Hope," he said. His voice came out ragged and thick, emotion and unbridled desire clogging his throat.

"Reed?" She stared up at him, and the expression he read in her eyes this time was a sexy combination of longing and bewilderment.

"Are you saying that guy in there isn't your date tonight?"

Her eyes lightened and crinkled at the corners as she began to laugh. He waited, because although her laugh indicated so much, she hadn't actually answered his question.

Finally, she looked him straight in the eye and lowered her chin almost shyly. "No, Reed. I don't... I don't have a date tonight."

The mere inches between them disintegrated when he crashed into her, wrapping his arms around her waist and pulling her into his chest as his mouth melted into hers.

It felt like he'd been waiting years to kiss her, to feel her body molding against his, to feel her hands tangling in his hair as they now were. The little surprised gasp that vibrated against his lips as he grabbed her only fueled his need to get as much of her touching as much of him as he possibly could.

His mouth pressed against hers with no hesitation, no getting-to-know-you tenderness, only pure, raw want. Oh, *shit*, he wanted her like he'd never wanted anything in his entire existence. Right now, at this moment, he was living to touch Hope.

He lifted her effortlessly off her feet and turned her so her back was pressing against brick. His hands ran hungrily down the sides of her body. His tongue pressed insistently against her lips until she opened up to him with a little whimper and he plunged inside to massage her mouth. His erection strained against his pants as he pressed his body to hers. He wanted her to feel how much he wanted her, needed this.

Her mouth broke free and her eyes burned into his. "Reed."

There it was again, his name spoken from her mouth and the insane things hearing it did to his body. He grunted and trailed kisses down her jawline to her neck, and she tilted her head to the side when a hushed breath escaped her.

"Oh, God," she moaned, and her words merely reignited the fire burning inside him.

He couldn't possibly pull her closer, so he reached down to grab the back of her thigh, hitching her leg up around his hip as his knees bent to allow him more access to more skin.

She willingly pulled herself closer, and they were such a spectacle on the street that a whistle behind them made her freeze.

Oh, hell no, was Reed's thought as her hands stilled on his back, and he hauled her around the corner and into a doorway on the less-busy side street.

He hadn't received a clear thought firing to his brain since he'd touched her, and they weren't flowing freely now, either. He was acting purely on instinct, and every single instinct he owned was pointing him in Hope's direction. He'd never needed anything like this before. He'd wanted women plenty of times, and had no problem achieving his goal. But Hope? Right now, he *needed* her.

He planted his lips back firmly against hers but stilled when her hands found their way to his chest. She pushed slightly, and he pulled back, looking down into her eyes and panting slightly.

"What is it?" he asked in a breath.

"What are we doing?" she whispered, her eyes wide.

He stared at her, and the red haze of desire finally cleared a little. The beautiful woman in his arms was everything he'd ever wanted, and everything he'd spent his life trying to avoid.

He gently lowered her to the ground and leaned back to stare at the stars, muttering a curse into the sky.

"I feel like I should lie right now," he said. "And tell you I'm sorry. Do you like men who lie, Hope?"

"No," she said steadily. "I don't. But…I'm not available, Reed."

"But you said that—"

"No," she interrupted. "I don't mean I'm taken. I'm not. I'm just not available."

She pushed off the wall and began walking away from him.

It took all of two seconds of watching her walk down the road for his brain to catch up to the situation. He was relatively certain he wouldn't survive losing her like that. Not now that he'd touched her. As crazy as it was, he needed more of Hope. So much more.

"Hope, wait," he called, jogging to catch up to her.

She continued to walk briskly, and now she was angrily brushing at her eyes.

"Hey." He reached out to grab her hand. "Stop. Talk to me a minute."

She whirled to face him. "I'm not sure why you did that, Reed. I'm not sure why I let you."

"Shit," he answered with honesty. "I have no clue, either. But I'm glad you didn't stop me. And I damn sure ain't sorry I kissed you. There's something between us here. Don't run from it."

"I'm not running from you." She ran an agitated hand through her hair, and he momentarily lost his words.

"Then what are you running from?"

She stared at him fully, and he found himself wanting to reach out again and pull her into his arms. He wanted to do anything he could to rip that haunted look from her eyes, to twist the sad angle of her mouth. And it was another unfamiliar feeling he'd never encountered before.

"Trust me. You don't want to know."

Before she could turn away from him again, his big hands encased her face. His gentle touch contrasted with the way he kissed her: hard. He conveyed the strange emotions warring inside him with his lips, and when he pulled back, she blinked rapidly to compose herself once more.

"I want to know everything there is to know, Hope."

She shook her head. "I can't."

And this time, there was nothing he could do to stop her from walking away.

Seven

He kissed me, Morrow." Her tone was incredulous, her hazel eyes a perfect blend of green and brown today. She stared at Morrow in open bewilderment, as if she couldn't imagine why Reed Hopewell had done such a thing.

A few days before her birthday, the story about Tyler and Reed had finally spilled out. Hope had begged Morrow not to retaliate against Frank for not protecting her better, and he'd reluctantly listened. He'd been livid about Tyler, but more than curious about Reed. When she'd been unable to answer his questions, thus limiting the information he could gather about Reed, he ultimately dropped the subject.

Morrow whistled low. "And you liked it, apparently."

"Dammit! I knew he was going to, I could see it in his eyes. And in my head, I was going to stop him. I was! I don't know what the hell happened. It's those smoky eyes of his, all deepest-blue and expressive."

She hung her head in her hands while sitting in her office at the Center, the Monday immediately after her birthday night out at the Charleston business owners' banquet. Her desk was clear; she kept it impeccably neat and organized, and she had a nice clean space to lay her head.

"Um…maybe you were thinking that you like the dude? He's a good guy because he might have saved your life? Maybe you *wanted* to kiss him?"

And then she was sobbing. She cried like a blubbering baby, and embarrassed didn't even begin to cover how she felt about it.

Morrow wrapped his arms around her from behind and pressed his chin into the top of her head. Her body was wracked with heaves she was unable to control, and he held her steady.

She looked at her friend with wide, wet eyes. "What the hell am I going to do?"

Frank carried a strict no-boyfriend rule for all of the girls he employed in his club. The clients wouldn't like seeing the girls around town with an actual boyfriend. The club members paid a very high price to date *single* ladies. Not to mention the fact that an actual boyfriend would probably raise hell when he found out what exactly it was his significant other did to bring home the bacon after a night at work.

She had seriously considered what Reed had been offering the other night. What was wrong with her? She'd never entertained the idea of having a boyfriend before. With everything going on in her life, drama with a man was the very last thing she needed. She had a younger sister to take care of, a very demanding day job, and an even more demanding night gig. Her life was full to the brim in every respect, and Reed Hopewell didn't fit into any of it.

Not to mention the fact that that man was going places. The way he sang, it was just a matter of time until he was on to bigger and better things outside of Charleston. What would she do, hope to the stars every night that he would take her and Violet with him? She couldn't afford to be that kind of girl. She made her own way.

So, Reed and everything he had to offer her was out of the question. Thinking about a relationship with him was beyond premature, in any case. It was a pure, animal, chemical attraction that drew them together. She didn't know him. She certainly couldn't ever love him. She had no prospect of ever loving him, or anyone else for that matter.

So, that was that.

And she was going to forget all about him. Him and his sexy, muscular body, and those burning blue eyes with the curling lashes, and the plush mouth that had claimed hers so completely. If she was wondering what other parts of her those lips could completely envelop, she wasn't admitting it.

"I've got to get out of here today," she told Morrow suddenly. "My head isn't in it. I'm going to go tell Felicia I'm not feeling well and head out, okay?"

Morrow nodded, the sympathy in his green eyes unmistakable. "I got you. Go."

She shot him a grateful smile, which he returned, and left the building as quickly as her legs would carry her.

Sitting in her car with the day ahead of her, she suddenly found herself stumped. What to do with the time? The last thing she'd ever want to do with an unexpected day off was go home to Frank's mansion. Her best friend was currently working in the building she just vacated. Actually, everyone she knew was at work. She squinted into the late morning sunlight. Then she put the car in drive, and eased onto the road. She cruised past shops she had no desire to spend money in, and restaurants with southern delicacies she wasn't hungry for.

She drove around the downtown Charleston streets aimlessly for a while, and once she pulled around a horse and carriage trotting happily on the cobblestone, she zeroed in on an interstate sign up ahead.

A smirk finally found her lips, and she headed for the highway. Pulling into the relaxed-pace traffic, she sailed for the coast. She glanced in admiration at the signature South Carolina palms as she drove. She appreciated the fact that she lived in a state that was known not only for its year-round pleasant temperatures, but also for the beautiful palm fronds currently waving at her from the side of the interstate. If she and Violet ever lived anywhere else, palm trees and access to an ocean would be a requirement.

She smiled with satisfaction at the thought of her and Violet living anywhere else, because anywhere else meant anywhere away from Wendy and Frank. Her expression darkened again as she flashed back to the previous night.

She'd walked into the house through the garage as usual, noticing that Frank's car was missing.

"Where are they?" she asked Violet curiously when she'd stepped inside.

It'd been late, after midnight.

Violet, sitting alone at the kitchen table, shrugged. Her eyes dropped to the kitchen table.

"Vi?" she'd asked, rushing over to her sister with alarm. "Who's here with you?"

Violet shook her head, and then looked up and squared her shoulders. "No one."

Hope's mouth had dropped open in disbelief. "No one? Frank and Wendy left you here *alone?*"

Violet scoffed. "Yeah. And being here alone is five hundred times better than being here with those two psychos."

Fear had clutched at Hope's heart. Her little sister had been left alone, in a mansion, at night. When she thought about what could have happened…

An exit sign flashed in front of her vision: NELSON ISLAND, 4 MILES.

Nelson Island? She'd lived in Charleston her whole life and had never actually been to the picturesque town. Too fancy for the life she had lived thus far, and she'd had no reason previously to visit. She supposed she had no reason now either, except for the fact that she had a day to herself with absolutely nothing on the agenda.

She took the exit, grinning widely with pride at her spontaneity.

Driving along the bridge into the town, she experienced what life in a postcard would be like. The ocean seemed bluer here than it did on the waterways in the city, and the gentle arc of the bridge allowed the sails from fishing and leisure boats to reach for the sunlight glittering overhead. The pale pink sand on the coastline stretched for miles, and the beach's pristine beauty was one of the most breathtaking sights she'd ever laid eyes on.

She ought to get out of Charleston more often. This gorgeous place had been right under her nose, and she hadn't even known it existed.

She pulled into a beachside lot, grabbing a ticket from the machine at the front, and exited her car, stretching with a luxury she usually hadn't felt in the summer sunlight.

Her stomach rumbled as she strolled up to a sandwich shop with small tables scattered on the boardwalk, and she smiled at the charming wooden SEAT YOURSELF sign. She did so, tucking her legs under her in the wicker chair and staring out into the water.

"Hey there!" a waitress said brightly as she set down a napkin and glass of water. "Welcome to Blu. What can I get you?"

"Oh," said Hope. "I'm not sure. This is my first time here."

"Are you visiting the island?" the young, pixie-faced girl asked her.

"You could say that," Hope answered with a small smile. "I want a sandwich, though. What do you recommend?"

"Shrimp salad," the waitress answered promptly. "Best shrimp salad you'll taste on the coast. You wanna try it?"

"I definitely do want to try that," Hope answered. "Thank you."

The girl smiled at her and sashayed away. Hope leaned back in her chair and glued her eyes back onto the horizon. It was a Monday, but the summer season was in full swing, and the beach was dotted with colorful umbrellas and children playing in the sand.

The boardwalk around her buzzed with conversation as people in bathing suits and cover-ups strolled by. Couples, families, and young singles seemed to enjoy the beach with like-mindedness. Everyone acted like they hadn't ever had a care in the world, and Hope soaked up their positivity like a rose in the sunlight.

It wasn't nearly as steamy here sitting by the ocean as it was in the city, either. The breeze wafted over Hope's face like a fan, and she tilted her head up toward the sky and closed her eyes with the sheer pleasure of it. Her bare shoulders were absorbing their own dose of vitamin D as she sat at the table, and she was glad for her tank top selection this morning, not to mention her choice of white knee-length shorts instead of slacks. She kicked off her sandals and placed her feet in the chair next to her as she totally relaxed. It was so unlike her, but her current environment was so different from her normal one that she caved to the beach glow Nelson Island offered.

"I was pretty sure it was you, Hope, until I saw the bare feet and the utterly relaxed expression on your face. Now I think I've got the wrong girl."

Hope's eyes flew open, only to stare into the glare of the sunlight. She squinted, shading her eyes, and her vision clarified that she was indeed looking up at Reed Hopewell.

Against her will, she thirstily drank in the sight of him. The professional slacks and button-up shirt he was wearing fit him like a glove, and she admitted to herself that he wore every look well. His signature boots were present, peeking out from under his pants, and his button-up shirt was missing its top two buttons. An open vest flapped freely in the wind, and she smiled in spite of herself. She glimpsed a peek of his chest underneath, and a lump formed somewhere in her throat.

"Reed," she squeaked.

She cleared her throat and tried again. "Hey."

"Hey, yourself." The smirk alighting on his face was full of swagger and meaning.

He gestured to the chair beside her, where her feet were currently taking up residence. "Can I sit?"

She gathered herself up, nice and neat again, and rolled her eyes. "It's a free beach, so I guess you can. What are you doing in slacks and a button-up?"

His eyes flashed. "Oh, so you noticed I'm departing from my normal wardrobe? Does that mean I might have possibly affected the cool and collected Hope?"

She shrugged. "I'm observant."

"Okay. We'll play it that way, Miss Observant."

He leaned onto his elbows, and the icy blue pools bored into her.

"What?" she asked, mentally checking her face to see if there were crumbs strewn across it. She brushed a strand of hair out of her eyes. The breeze next to the ocean was steady, and strands of her hair were constantly being lifted and carried away.

His eyes followed the motion as if transfixed, and then refocused on her face.

"What are you doing here, Hope?" he asked softly.

She gestured toward him. "I could ask the same of you."

"I live here. And I work here sometimes, too. But I was asking about you."

"You live here? On Nelson Island? I just assumed you lived in Charleston like... the rest of them."

His face changed from bemused to amused, and a wide grin lit his face. "The rest of who?"

She gestured lamely. "I don't know. I guess I was just lumping you into the 'guys who play guitar and perform at clubs' category. They all have apartments in Charleston, and all they do with themselves is play and have sex."

His grin grew with each word she uttered. "That's very interesting, Hope. Well, I live here. I grew up on Nelson Island, and I have a condo here now. My parents live here, too, and I work for my father's company when I'm not playing guitar, singing, or having sex."

His smug smile made her heart quiver in her chest, and she silently cursed her body for betraying her that way.

"Your father's company, huh? What do you do there?"

"This and that. Mostly, I'm the guy they call when they want to close a big deal." He leaned in closer, lowering his voice to a confidential whisper. "I think they think I'm a good schmoozer."

"And are you?"

"Why don't I let you be the judge of that? Can I stay and have lunch with you?"

The waitress chose that moment to bring Hope's sandwich out, stopping in her tracks when she laid eyes on Reed. Her face, which was previously friendly with a side of bored indifference, now lit up like a firework on the Fourth of July. She smoothed her hair and bit her bottom lip, and Hope could practically read the girl's desire for her and Reed to not be "together."

"Oh, I see you've added your…boyfriend to your party?" The waitress's hopeful expression nearly caused Hope to regurgitate her soda all over the table.

"Nope," Hope answered promptly.

Reed's eyes sparkled. "But, babe, I told you I was sorry about the other night. You have to forgive me!"

Oh, he wants to play? Hope narrowed her eyes.

"Don't 'babe' me! I told you, one more time with that tramp and I was out. This is *so* over."

The waitress's eyes pinballed from Reed to Hope and back again, her jaw falling open.

Reed reached across the table and took both of Hope's hands in his. "Please, baby. Just let me have lunch with you? So I can explain?"

Despite the sparks shooting up her arms from the sheer touch of the man before her, she was fighting back a giggle. Successfully suppressing it, she blew out a heavy sigh.

"Fine. Lunch, and then we're through."

Reed smiled in relief and squeezed her hands gently. Her heart throbbed against her ribs furiously, and the intense blush she felt in Reed's presence flourished across her face.

"I'll have a number six," he informed the waitress without breaking his connection with Hope's hands or her eyes.

Hope couldn't look away from him in order to see the waitress's face, but she would have bet money that it was lower than sea level. She bit her lip against the smile threatening to spread across her mouth.

As the waitress scuttled away, Reed fought against a smile of his own. "That was fun."

"You are evil," Hope said accusingly. "You knew that girl was practically drooling over you."

"I'm just sorry she was the only one," Reed said cheerfully.

"Who said she was?" Hope shot back, shocking herself into silence.

Reed gave her hands another squeeze before he let go and leaned back against his seat. "So, are we going to talk about the other night?"

"No," Hope answered, shaking her head. "Not necessary. I already told you I'm not available. It was a nice kiss, but—"

"I'm sorry," interrupted Reed, his voice low. He leaned forward, a sexy smile on his lips. "Are you saying that kiss was 'nice'? That's the word you're using to describe it?"

"I meant, it was...I didn't mean..." Hope fumbled for a better word to use but failed epically. Instead, she stared at Reed across the table, cringing at the blazing fire burning in his eyes.

"Okay," he said evenly. "Then I get a repeat. No wonder you don't want it to happen again. You only thought it was nice. So I guess I'm going to have to rectify that."

"No! I didn't mean—"

He held up a hand to silence her, and her words fell short. "Doesn't matter. I've already made up my mind. I'm kissing you again. Sometime today. You won't know it's coming until it comes. And there's no goddamned way you're going to call this one *nice*."

She felt the now-familiar blush creeping across her cheeks. She tossed her hair over her shoulders to camouflage it, and nodded. "I accept this challenge. But if this kiss doesn't get me to change my adjective, are you going to forget about trying to make something happen between us?"

He gazed stonily at her. "I agree to nothing."

She groaned. "You're one stubborn man."

"I know." He grinned wildly, and her traitorous heart flipped upside down in her chest.

Eight

Hope's presence in Nelson Island—the place where he slept, ate, hung out, and sometimes worked—was doing something to Reed he was trying his damnedest to fight. It was tough, though, and he couldn't figure out what exactly it was about this woman that completely captivated him the way she did.

Sure, she was beautiful. But Reed had taken so many beautiful girls to bed he couldn't even keep count. Okay, she was feisty. But he grew up with a sister who wrote the book on that character quality. Hope was a complete mystery to him—maybe that was it. Throughout the day, he had learned tiny bits and pieces about her life that weren't quite clicking to make a whole picture. That was puzzling to him, because most girls their age were wide open and ready to share everything.

Not Hope.

So far today he had learned that she worked with kids (which he found endearing and weirdly sexy), she had a younger sister whom she clearly adored, and she lived with her mother and her stepfather. Although her day job was working at the Center with the kids, she spent most weekend nights working for her stepfather. This portion of her life was unclear to Reed, and digging further to uncover the details seemed like invading Hope's privacy. So he'd backed off, filing the information away for a later date.

He'd also learned that she had a smile that knocked the goddamn breath right out of him.

He'd taken her all along the boardwalk, showing her some of his favorite shops and restaurants. They'd gotten in her car, and he'd driven her around the island, showing her some of the quiet beauty the place possessed. At one point, they'd stopped in front of one of Reed's favorite ocean views, a jetty that overlooked a private beach not far from his parents' ranch.

"This is probably the most gorgeous view I've ever laid eyes on," Hope had murmured, her voice wistful and longing.

Reed heard so much more than the innocent observation she'd intended in that statement. He heard the desperation he thought he'd glimpsed in her the first night they met. He heard the voice of a woman who wanted to get away, and maybe never return to her previous life. And he wanted to scoop her up in his arms and take her there, wherever she wanted to go.

And that was just insane.

After a day of sightseeing around the small island, they ended up at Sunny's for a plate of chicken wings and a beer early in the evening.

"So, do you like my island?" asked Reed, lifting an eyebrow in question.

"Oh, it's your island? I'm sorry, I thought your name was Reed. This is *Nelson* Island, right?" Hope met his gaze with a rare twinkle in her own.

Reed laughed. "You got me. Did you like it?"

"I loved it," she said quietly, looking him directly in the eye and causing a bit of heat to rise low in his gut as a result. "Thank you for showing it to me like this, Reed. I could have driven around for a week by myself, but I never would have seen half of the beauty that you just captured for me in one day."

Reed sensed that this dose of raw vulnerability was rare, and he wished he could bottle it up so he could pull it back out again when he was alone.

"You're welcome," he said, pleased.

"So this is where you play most of the time?" she asked, gesturing around the bar. "I still can't believe it's literally a part of the pier."

That was Sunny's claim to fame; it was perched atop a pier over the ocean sound, and plenty of tourists feared it might one day fall into the water. Those who grew up in Nelson Island, however, knew better. Sunny's had been standing longer than any of them could remember, and they knew it would be there long after they were gone.

"Yep, I play here most weekends. I've only just gotten into playing on the Charleston club circuit. It's a brand-new environment for me, playing there. Here, I know everyone. Hopewell Enterprises' main office is in Charleston, so it's familiar territory, since I work most days out of that office. And I went to college in Charleston, too. So I know people, but it's just not quite the same as playing at home."

"I guess I can understand that," Hope mused. "You know...I go to a lot of different clubs when I'm working on the weekends, and I've heard a lot of people play. I would never have admitted it that night, but you're pretty special. I've never quite heard a voice like yours, and coupled with the way you handle a guitar...you have star potential."

Reed allowed his mouth to drop open in mock surprise. "Star potential? Hope Dawson, are you telling me you think I've got a chance at making it in the music business? Like...you think I'm *good*?"

"Don't make me say it again, Reed," she warned. "But I'm just saying...why are you wasting your talent in Charleston at all?"

His brow furrowed in thought. "I honestly love it here. I thought about moving on to Nashville or Austin or somewhere like that after school, but I just never got around to it. And honestly, as much as I love playing, singing, and writing music? I think I love Nelson Island more. Don't ever tell my parents that, though."

She nodded. "I can totally understand why you love it here so much. I can't believe this place was only a bridge away and I never visited. It's a gem."

Reed noted that it was rare for a newcomer to notice exactly how special his hometown was. He'd dealt with hordes of "summer people," and they never seemed to grasp what a diamond Nelson Island was. He could always tell they thought of it as just another beach. And it wasn't. It was more special than that.

But Hope seemed to understand right away, and that made her special in her own right.

"So," he said, clasping his hands together under the table. He wanted to reach out and touch one of the legs that had been calling out to him all day, or rub a lock of that silky hair between his fingers, but he wasn't getting a vibe from her that she wanted him to touch her. She was very closed off, turning her body away from his whenever they were close. He could read the signs.

He just wasn't sure *why*. He knew she had enjoyed their kiss the other night just as much as he had. Why was she pushing him away so forcefully now? Had he done something wrong that night? They were two single adults who had a mutual attraction for one another. *What's the problem?*

He wasn't going to push it. He'd just spent an entire day with her and enjoyed it more than he'd ever enjoyed a day with a woman. Actually, he couldn't remember the last time he'd spent a day like this with a woman. A night? Sure. A day? Never.

He watched in utter fascination as she tore a wing apart with her teeth, sucking the meat off the bone and then daintily licking her fingers free of orange-colored buffalo sauce. He swallowed thickly as she finished. The sight of Hope gently dabbing at her luscious lips with a napkin sent a throb of pleasurable pain sizzling down to places she seemed such an expert at awakening, and he wanted so badly to adjust himself in his seat so he wouldn't embarrass himself or her when he stood up.

"You know what?" he said, by way of a distraction.

"What?" she said, her curiosity lighting up her beautiful face.

"You haven't had any word-upchucks today," he said.

"I know." She beamed. "Guess I haven't felt awkward enough today to blurt out anything embarrassing."

"Hmm," he mused. "Awkward moments cause it, huh? I guess it's a good thing I haven't made you feel awkward, then."

She smiled at him. A genuine smile that creased the corners of her eyes and wrinkled her nose the slightest bit. "You've actually made me feel very comfortable today, Mr. Hopewell. Thanks for that."

He returned her grin. "You're welcome, Miss Dawson."

"You ready to get out of here?"

Reed looked around. It was a weekday evening, so Sunny's was slow and relaxed, but he still thought he might see a friend or two. No one had shown up, so he nodded.

"Yeah, you want to drive me back to my condo?"

She agreed, and they walked outside toward where her little car sat, looking lonely in the gravel parking lot.

"Wait," Reed said.

She turned, both her eyebrows shooting skyward.

"The sun is about to set. Do you want to watch it from the second-prettiest view on the island?"

She nodded without hesitation and allowed him to take her hand to lead her out and over the pier that Sunny's was perched upon.

They walked out to the very end, and stood stock-still while the sun sank lower and lower over the horizon. It finally disappeared in a brilliant burst of purple and crimson and gold, and Hope sucked in a sharp breath as she watched.

Reed glanced at her, and she was holding her bottom lip between her teeth as her hazel eyes focused on the place where the ocean met the sky.

"You liked it?" he asked, his voice soft.

She tore her eyes away from the sight and met his steady gaze. "Beautiful."

He hesitated, keeping his gaze locked on her face. He scanned her hazel eyes, her glowing bronze skin on her high cheekbones, her perfect, round little nose, and finally her succulent, plump lips. Then he ripped his eyes away and took her hand in his once more.

"Now we can go," he declared.

Hope had agreed to spend an entire day with Reed, and if she was completely honest with herself, it was on the hope that he would make good on his promise to kiss her again.

And he hadn't. There were so many opportunities she didn't have enough fingers to list them on. Nelson Island was truly a gorgeous, serene place, and they'd stopped in spots that were beyond fitting for a kiss. But he hadn't touched her. She'd gone rigid in almost all of those spots in anticipation, but he'd never once looked at her like he'd even wanted to kiss her again.

Maybe she'd been imagining the whole thing. Maybe he wasn't really attracted to her at all. Hell, there'd been alcohol present on her birthday. He could have been just as drunk as she was, and the kiss, so hot it was stupid, they'd shared could have been a result of drunken idiocy, not genuine attraction or passion.

So when she pulled up to Reed's immaculate condominium community and left her engine idling, she was shocked to her core when he turned to her and invited her to come in.

"It's getting late," she murmured. "Don't you have to get up early for work?"

"I'm the boss's son," he reminded her. "I can get there when I want. Plus, it's not that late. Come on up."

She hesitated a second before nodding her consent. "Okay."

He led her up the steps to the third floor and unlocked the steel door. It was a surprisingly contemporary design; she wasn't expecting to see it on the island. It didn't match the traditionally kitschy designed beach houses and condos nearby. But its modern lines seemed to suit Reed's personality completely.

As he led her into the condo, she stared around her in appreciation. The place was all clean lines and smooth stone, from the dark gray concrete floor to the lofty, white walls. The kitchen was to the left, right off the entrance, and the stainless steel and rich, dark wood caught her eye.

"Oh. My. God." Hope breathed each word like a solemn prayer.

"What? Do you like it?" Reed's voice was reserved in his question, almost as if he was really nervous as to what her answer would be.

"I freaking love it!" she squealed. "This kitchen is so badass. Can I come cook in here sometime?"

His eyes widened and hers did, too, as she realized what she'd just asked. It was too late to take the words back, no matter how badly she wanted to.

"You want to come and cook in my kitchen," Reed said evenly, raw emotion brimming behind his words. "The answer to that is Hell. Yes."

She smiled in relief. "Good. I'd really like to. It's beautiful in here, and I love to cook."

"I seriously don't think Tate or I have ever cooked anything in here other than frozen pizza. So yes, you can come and cook anytime."

She beamed at him, and he smiled down at her in return.

They continued to walk through the space, with Reed pointing out facts about the architecture or Hope commenting on something she found pretty or interesting. Circling back to the kitchen, Reed opened a cabinet and pulled out two tumbler glasses.

"I have to ask this," Hope said with wide eyes. "Who decorated this place? I mean you and Tate are two young, single guys. There's no way you two did this by yourselves."

Reed actually flushed crimson. The effect was so deliciously adorable she reached out and touched his cheek where it flamed scarlet. She left her hand there for a second, feeling the heat beneath his skin and relishing it.

"Uh." He worked his mouth a few times before he answered. "No, yeah, our moms helped us out. Tate's is an interior designer."

Hope nodded. "Now that makes sense. The place is amazing. I could stay here for hours, just looking around at everything you've done with it."

She'd done it again, inserted herself into his life as if she'd be a regular fixture there. *What the hell is wrong with me?* She cringed, peeking at Reed's expression through the curtain of her hair.

And was floored by what she saw. His face was *glowing*. Like he actually liked the idea of her invading his privacy and his personal space that way. Like he wouldn't mind if she actually *did* stay for hours at a time in his condo.

Now she was just confused. Her best friend was a young, single guy. She knew how they operated. There was no way in hell Morrow would want some girl he barely knew staying at his place for a night, much less hanging around for hours at a time.

The more she got to know Reed, the more twisted her opinion of him became. Her entire life, with the exception of Morrow, the wants and desires of the men in her life were made perfectly clear to her from the beginning. And Morrow had never wanted anything from her other than friendship.

But with Reed, she just didn't know what he expected from her.

"So? What are you having?" Reed was asking as she snapped out of her internal reverie.

"Sorry. What are my choices again?"

"Okay, space cadet. We have Coke. I can put rum in it if you'd like. Or we have beer. Or water. Or OJ."

"Well I have to drive all the way back to the city tonight, so I'll just have Coke, no rum."

Reed opened his mouth, as if to say something, but promptly closed it. He obviously had more control over his speech than she did.

"Yeah, okay," he replied, fixing her a glass of Coke. He handed it over, and then gestured over the bar toward the couch in the living room.

She sat, sinking into the soft black leather, and emitted a sigh of comfort and relaxation. She never felt this relaxed when she was sitting on the couch in Frank's home. She couldn't remember the last time she felt like she could let her head roll back and stop worrying about who'd come walking through the door.

Never. She'd never felt like that once in her entire life.

She looked over toward the kitchen and was surprised to see that Reed was still standing by the bar, watching her.

"What?" She patted the cushion next to her. "You don't want to sit down? Do I look like I bite?"

His eyes flashed a darker blue, and he took a step toward her. She liked how casual his office look came off on him. His pants weren't typical office slacks, but more of a slim-fitted Dickies that spoke to his musician side. They'd both kicked off their shoes at some point during the tour, and Reed with bare feet was giving her insides the squeezes as she sat there staring at him.

"That's just too damn bad," he answered her. His smile became predatory. "I was hoping you would."

Her sharp intake of breath gave her away, as cool and collected as she tried to remain. He hadn't kissed her today, and he'd had a million chances. Was that about to change?

As if reading her mind, he continued to close the gap between them with slow, deliberate steps. His eyes were melded to hers the entire way, and when he reached her, he dropped to his knees in front of her. Without breaking his stare, he slowly placed his hands on her thighs, just resting his palms on top of her legs as he gazed up at her.

"I have a promise to keep," he said. His voice barely registered as a whisper, and the blue of his eyes was so intense and deep that she thought she might be staring into the ocean's depths.

She nodded numbly. "You said you were going to make sure that I never called one of your kisses 'nice' again."

"That's right," he murmured, and he slid his hands up her legs until they were cupping her hips and sliding her forward on the leather seat. "I did say that. Did you think I forgot?"

Hope's mouth was steadily going dry as she continued to hold Reed's stare. "No. I just thought you didn't want to."

He laughed softly. "No, beautiful. That wasn't it. I was just trying to read the moment, and it never seemed like you wanted it bad enough."

Her eyes widened as she took him in. This gorgeous man, with the face of some kind of devious angel and what she was sure was a body to match, was kneeling before her like she was a goddess. Her vision blurred a bit as his fingers grazed the bare skin of her sides where her skin was exposed above her shorts.

He continued to hold her gaze; he tilted his head slightly, as if trying to read her expression. Then she realized he was waiting for a green light, just as he had the first night he kissed her.

"I want it," she whispered. *God help me.*

His hands pulled her even closer as he leaned up toward her face. He reached one hand up and placed it firmly behind her neck.

"You want what?"

His voice had dropped an octave and the gravelly satin was now causing Hope's mouth to literally water. She felt deliciously helpless in his hands, and she was horrified to find that she was willing to do whatever he may have wanted her to at that moment.

"I want you..." She wet her lips. "To kiss me."

His mouth was on hers in seconds. He kissed her softly, just a graze of lips against lips, again and again until she was left breathless and quivering in his arms. Then he eased his tongue out slowly, parting her lips with its moist tenderness and dipping inside her mouth to begin an exploration that would render her body completely useless. He delved in again and again, and she wasn't sure what animal in the room was making those sounds she could hear in the background. And then she realized that they were coming from her own mouth. That she was quietly moaning into the kiss that was just too delicious to stay quiet for.

She was putty, something malleable for him to play with, in his hands, and she was powerless to stop the hold Reed was creating over her. His hands slid up and down her back underneath her shirt as his mouth plundered hers, and on one trip down, the clasp of her bra was miraculously undone. Then she was lying back on the couch as he covered her body with his.

She was so much smaller than he was yet she seemed to fit so perfectly into all the nooks and crannies his body provided as it sank over the top of hers like a blanket. The heaviness of his presence was welcomed, and she sighed as the very obvious erection he harbored inside his slacks pressed insistently into her thigh.

His lips left hers only to rush downward toward her neck, leaving a trail of warmth on her jawbone as they journeyed. She opened her eyes to stare up at the ceiling as she tried to register every sensation her body was currently feeling in so many places. She closed her eyes again as another moan escaped her lips.

She realized Reed's lips were climbing again, and opened her mouth to him as he covered it once again with his own. He kissed her so tenderly she could have cried, but instead she kissed him back with all the fervor she felt and all the passion he was invoking deep inside her achiest, neediest places. And he pulled away slowly, taking her bottom lip with him as he reared backward, holding himself up with his hands while he hovered above her.

"Was that nice?"

She blew out a breath that caused the hair over his forehead to flutter. She really liked how he looked at this angle, holding himself above her with all of the control. His face was flushed and his lips were a tender, swollen pink that brought the sparkle out in those eyes. The shallow dimple in his chin was a place she wanted desperately to kiss.

"That…wasn't nice at all." She breathed.

He laughed loudly, bringing a smile of pure joy to her face. "It wasn't?"

"Nope. That was the most not-nice kiss I've ever had. Thanks for that."

His laughter echoed under the high, vaulted ceilings and echoed around the huge space, making her smile grow wider.

"Can I just show you another version of a not-nice kiss?" she asked, feeling bold.

His eyes narrowed, and he pushed himself all the way up, sitting back onto the couch and pulling her up to sit beside him.

"Sure," he said, his voice low and rough. "I'm all yours."

God, she really hated how much she relished that little sentiment. Suddenly, she really wanted Reed Hopewell to be all hers. She wanted it so badly she could feel the need echoing in her limbs.

Could he be hers?

Nine

Reed had had a lot of women in his condo.

A lot.

But never in his life had he had an experience like the one he was having tonight with Hope here in his space. It was exhilarating, it was mind-blowingly sexy, and it was confusing as hell.

"Is your bedroom this way?" she asked innocently, pointing down the dark hallway.

All he could do was shake his head because words had suddenly left him. She was asking him where his bedroom was? Did he dare to hope?

He had just spent the last few minutes making sure he had the upper hand in the situation, because he had been feeling like she was in the driver's seat in more ways than one. That she was leaving him twisted up and hanging out to dry with no grasp of his emotions or his massive attraction lighting a fire in his boxer-briefs.

Then, the memory of his conversation with Sam punched him

straight in the gut. He'd decided that he wasn't going to treat Hope like she was just another pretty girl in his bed. That being with her sexually would probably fuck him up for good, and that this current situation in which he currently found himself should be avoided like the plague.

But as she stood in front of him, waiting for him to point her in the direction of his bedroom, he couldn't prevent himself from gesturing toward the stairs.

"Up in the loft," he said, his voice raw with want.

She shot him a grin that was somehow alluring and shy at once and he groaned, shaking his head.

He was making a mistake.

He was making the best decision of his life.

He couldn't stop this from happening if it was what she wanted. He was only a man, for God's sake.

She took off for the stairs while he watched, helpless to stop her even if he wanted to.

God, he didn't want to.

She turned at the bottom step and beckoned him with the crook of a finger. He obeyed like a puppet on a string that she controlled.

"Hope," he choked out as he reached her. She leaned against the wall next to the staircase and gazed up at him with those eyes that always seemed to see so much more deeply inside of him than he wanted them to. "What exactly are we going to my bedroom for?"

She shrugged. "You left it out of the tour."

"I was trying to be respectful," he pointed out.

She narrowed her eyes. "Reed. Are you saying you've never taken a woman up to your room before me?"

"Hell no, that's not what I'm saying," he said in exasperation. "But I'm saying that you're not...one of those women."

He waited for her to change her mind, now that he had called her out. But she merely stared at him with her deep-set eyes, challenging him with the slight rise of her delicate chin.

"Well, I'd like to see it." She was full of confidence, and it was damn sexy.

He leaned forward, just because she was so damn close and he couldn't help it. He inhaled as he leaned in and her fresh, feminine scent engulfed him now that he was paying closer attention to it. It reminded him once again that she didn't embody the heavy, cheap-perfume aroma that the other women he'd been with owned. She smelled lighter, softer.

And now that his lips and his hands knew from experience that she felt the same way, he couldn't be this close to her without closing the distance between.

She met him halfway, molding her body to him in one fluid motion that had him scooping her up into his arms with his hands cupping her ass. He pressed himself into her so that she would be totally aware of what she was doing to him. Grunting as she writhed against his arousal, he devoured her mouth with his own. He took the steps as quickly as he could manage without dropping her, never prying his mouth away from hers as he sped the well-traveled route to his room.

He kicked the door closed behind them and leaned against the wood with her still held fast in his arms.

"You're blowing my mind today," he said breathlessly against her lips.

She sighed in response, and pulled back just enough so that she could look at him. Her face was so mesmerizing in the darkness of the room that he was momentarily transfixed in her gaze.

"I don't know what this is," she whispered. "I shouldn't be here, shouldn't be doing this. But I can't seem to help myself."

He smiled, pulling her body even closer to his own, which had become so attuned to her physically. "Good. I don't want you to hold back with me, Hope. I want to know the real you."

She pressed her forehead to his. "Shut up and kiss me, Reed."

He smirked and obliged, and she slid down his body until she was standing directly in front of him. She tugged at the buttons of his shirt impatiently until she had them all undone, and pushed it down his arms without much help from him. Her petite hands ran down the front of his chest and stomach, breathing life into his nerve endings as they went.

He sucked in a breath, tensing his muscles as he luxuriated in her grasp. He'd been touched so many times before, but Hope's hands held some kind of magical quality that made his body crazy and had his mind swollen with thoughts of her and what they could do together. He didn't want her hands to leave his skin, ever.

She knelt in front of him—*knelt, holy shit*—and immediately became his every fantasy come to life as she unbuttoned his slacks and slid them down his thighs with ease.

"God," he groaned. "Who *are* you?"

"I'm Hope," she said surely. "And you're Reed, and we're about to get to know each other a hell of a lot better."

She continued sliding his pants down his legs, and he allowed his fingers to tangle in her long, thick hair as she placed her lips against one of his thighs. He shuddered. He realized he was in severe danger of falling to his knees.

He'd never been so into this before. Sex was always awesome, it was *sex*. But his body was in overdrive at the moment, and the way he was reacting to her was almost primal. He couldn't control it, he couldn't turn it off. This was pure instinct, and tonight he was going to thank his lucky stars he'd been chosen to save Hope Dawson that night in a dark alley.

She rose again, standing in front of him and studying his body with a glint in her eye that let Reed know exactly what she was thinking before the words fell from her lips.

"You…you look even more amazing without your clothes on," she murmured. "I like the tattoos."

He glanced down at the swirling ink on his arms. They covered the area between his elbows and the tops of his shoulders. He'd gotten them after he'd opened himself up to the music inside of him, and the fact that she liked them now was just a bonus.

He stepped toward her. "Your turn, Miss Observant."

She gasped as he lifted her and threw her bodily onto his bed. It was too dark for her to be able to see his room clearly, and he was operating purely on instinct and memory. She landed smack in the middle of his king-size bed, and he smiled in anticipation.

He reached her seconds after she bounced and straddled her body as he gazed down at the woman beneath him. He stretched both hands out to graze the skin of her stomach, lifting her shirt slightly as he did so and raising it up to her neck. She shrugged out of it, and he couldn't help himself; he leaned down to kiss the soft skin under the lacy bra adorning her plump breasts.

"Holy hell," he murmured against her skin. "I've done this before. I swear I have...why is it all so much...*more* tonight?"

"Because it's us," she said simply. "And there's something about us, Reed. I feel it, and so do you."

Still looking down at her, he knew she was absolutely right. He did feel it, and it was an emotion he swore to himself he was never going to feel, because it only led to trouble. Unable to wait any longer to feel his lips against her skin again, he brushed his lips across the rise and fall of her chest. He pulled one of the cups of the delicate fabric covering those succulent mounds of flesh to the side so he could pull one perfectly round, pebbled peak into his mouth.

She sucked in a breath underneath him and grabbed at his hair. It stung, but it was the sweetest pain he'd ever experienced. *Jesus,* if he died tonight, he would just thank God he'd had the chance to touch this perfect specimen of a woman before his demise.

Tap, tap.

A knock at his bedroom door had them both frozen, Hope staring in alarm at the door and Reed cursing wildly under his breath.

"Yo, Reed! You in there?"

"Yes." Reed's response was strained. "I'm in here, Tate. What the fuck do you think?"

"My bad, man. Brought dinner. You want?"

A real, animal-like snarl left Reed then, and Tate took the hint, tiptoeing back down the stairs.

Hope breathed a deep sigh that lifted her whole body from the bed. "Fun's over."

Reed let loose another stream of curses and lowered his body so that he was lying next to her.

"Doesn't have to be," he said. "You can stay, Hope. I want you to."

She stared straight up at the ceiling. "Actually, I needed the wake-up call."

What? She was reverting back to the guarded, reserved shell he'd met the night in the alley. Damn Tate!

"Don't do that, Hope. What we had going on here was real, and you were into it. Don't deny it. We don't have to do anything if you stay. I just...want you here."

"I'm not denying anything, Reed, I swear. I was just caught in a haze of...of *you.* I wasn't thinking straight. We can't do this."

"We *can* do this, Hope," he insisted, his voice strained. He stared at her in the darkness, but she wasn't meeting his gaze. "We don't have to do...you know, *this.* But we can do...*us.* I want to. You want to. Why wouldn't we?"

She sighed again. "There're a million reasons we don't have time to get into tonight, Reed."

She stood, and the absence of her in his bed immediately felt cold and *wrong*. He sat up, scrubbing a hand across his jawline in frustration.

"Give me your phone, Hope."

She hesitated, straightening her shirt back in place over her torso. "Why?"

"Because I'm not letting you leave this damn condo without being able to get back in touch with you. It was a fucking miracle that I ran into you today. I want to see you again."

He vacated the bed and came to her, wrapping her up in his arms and breathing in her scent. "I want to see you again. Soon. No interruptions, no excuses."

He pulled back to inspect her face in the moonlight streaming in through his floor-to-ceiling windows overlooking the ocean. "Okay?"

"Okay." Her voice was tiny in the stillness, but the fact that she agreed let him know that he wasn't insane. This was really happening. *She* was happening, and he wasn't about to let her go without a fight.

And when he laid eyes on Tate, his roommate would likely be leaving the condo on a stretcher.

Sitting in her car, away from the hurricane of manly sexiness and intense emotion that was Reed, her good sense slowly began to ease back into her consciousness.

What had she been thinking? She hadn't been thinking with her brain, that's for sure. She'd been thinking with her body, her heart, maybe even her soul.

She wasn't sure which part of her being was most attracted to Reed.

Ten

Three days following her impromptu outing with Reed in Nelson Island, and after a long day at the Center running around at the level of a first grader for the most part, all Hope wanted to do was have a long, tension-releasing swim and a steaming hot shower.

She knew she'd be arriving home close to the same time as Violet, and she planned to help her sister with her algebra homework after she relaxed for a few minutes. Math had been a strong suit for her when she was in school, and while every subject was a strong suit for Violet, she enjoyed working through the problems with her older sister.

Shock permeated her features and her insides turned gelatinous when she pulled up the long driveway and found Reed and Violet perched on the tailgate of his Silverado, chatting like a couple of old friends. She sat in her car for a moment, just watching them as she faced off in front of them. Reed appeared totally calm and cool, and Violet eyed her with a smug "I-know-what-you've-been-doing" grin.

"Oh, brother," muttered Hope as she opened her car door and unfolded her diminutive frame from the car. But even as she uttered the words, a shiver of delight and something else altogether jumped along her spine.

Neither of the pair spoke as she strolled, a bit cautiously, toward them.

"What's going on?" she asked. "Reed? Everything okay?"

He hopped down and reached up to pull Violet from the tailgate.

"Everything's fine," he answered easily, approaching her. The velvety side of his voice was in full effect. "I needed to talk to you, and this one came along before you got here. I got out of the truck and introduced myself."

"Yeah," Violet added. "And he's pretty damn cool, Hope. Were you keeping him a secret, or what?"

Reed smirked at Hope, a triumphant gleam in his eyes.

"Okay, okay," said Hope. "Enough out of you. And don't say *damn*! Homework, Vi. Go. See you inside in a few."

"Oh, there's no rush," Violet said with a sly smile. "I got my algebra in the bag. And it looks like you need to bag something else."

Hope groaned. "Oh, my God. Go!"

Violet laughed and walked up to the huge house, tossing one last look at Reed and Hope as she went.

Hope turned to Reed, her eyes accusing. "You were trying to win over my sister?"

He shrugged. "Hadn't planned on it. But she was a lucky surprise." His face turned serious. "She's pretty freaking awesome, Hope."

Hope smiled in spite of herself. "I know she is. She's the best kid there ever was. She's the reason I work with kids in the first place."

The corners of his lips quirked upward. "I think that's amazing. And she's good inspiration."

"Yeah," Hope answered, her face clouding. "She needs me."

Violet needed her more than Reed would ever know. And if Wendy and Frank came home to discover Reed in their driveway, Hope would have a lot of explaining to do. She was seized with sudden panic at the thought, her muscles tensing in dread.

"I really should get in to help her," Hope hedged.

"Want some extra hands?" Reed asked. "I pretty much could have taught my algebra class in school."

Her heart softened at the sight of him. His dark hair was windswept, his cheeks were flushed, and his blue eyes glittered with hope. He wanted to be here, with her. And he wanted to help her, help Violet. God, what was wrong with him? Something had to be, right? His bottom lip was caught between his pearly teeth, and she experienced a flashback of what that plump lip felt like between her own teeth. She barely hid her shiver.

She wanted him here. Well, not here, in this house. But here, by her side. And he was so obviously a willing companion. At the moment, she cursed her life and her circumstances even more than usual. They were holding her back, once again. This time from something potentially life changing and wonderful.

"I'm sorry," she finally said, the reluctance pouring out of her voice. "I wish I could let you. My"—she nearly choked on the word—"mother and stepfather will be home soon. It wouldn't be a pleasant meeting. I'd like to avoid it."

She risked a glance at his face, hoping with everything in her that he'd understand. Or at least that he'd comply without too many questions.

He studied her for a few seconds. Then he reached out and pulled her into his arms. She allowed herself a moment of leaning into him, resting her cheek on his chest. He smelled more than good, like sea air and light, musky cologne all at once. She inhaled deeply, wishing his scent could envelop her again like it had three nights ago. She hadn't actually spoken to him since then. He'd texted her a few times, but she'd avoided speaking to him on the phone. The way she'd felt with him that night terrified her, only because she knew she couldn't keep it.

She'd never be able to keep him.

He rested his chin on the top of her head and she sighed at how easily her body tucked into the solid mass of his.

"Hope," he murmured. "Is everything okay?"

"What do you mean?" she asked, hesitant.

"I mean…here? With your parents and Violet and you? I get a feeling…" He trailed off.

She sighed again and shook her head, pushing off his chest so she could stand upright again. Facing him, she steeled herself with a silent breath.

"Everything is fine. I've got it under control."

His azure eyes were too expressive, too vibrant, too knowing. "I'm sure you do. But I want to be here for you. So you don't have to keep everything to yourself."

He had no idea what he was saying. And she wasn't going to delve into the special circle of hell that was her family dynamics. As if sensing her hesitation, he pulled her into his chest and squeezed. She settled her head there comfortably, marveling at how the hard planes of his center could feel so inviting. So safe.

He didn't say anything, but she felt him rest his chin on top of her head.

"I'm here, Hope. When you're ready."

Reed seemed to have the kind of personality that could push until he got what he wanted. Like he was used to doing just that. But with her, he only pushed as far as she was willing to go. He never took more than what she wanted to give.

"Thanks for the offer. I'm good, though. What did you come to say?"

He dropped his arms from around her waist and squinted down at her. Caught in his stare, she felt as though she were made of glass. Completely transparent in Reed's gaze.

"I'm here to ask you out. Like, on a date."

She sucked in a breath. "Reed..."

"What, Hope? You're not seeing anyone, right?"

It was her turn to chew on her bottom lip. Nerves shot through her body, beginning down at her toes and firing what could have been fireworks of anxiety off the top of her head. "No, I'm single. I just have a lot going on right now. I don't know if I should be dating."

She actually knew for a fact that Frank would expressly forbid it, but she wasn't going to mention that to Reed.

He eyed her as if he was seeing right through to her depths, where she hid all her secrets. He tilted his head to one side, the corners of his mouth pulling down. "You're too young to have that much going on, Hope. Let's go out. I promise you'll have a good time, and then I'll bring you back home in one piece. Do you trust me?"

She was lost, once again, in the depths of those eyes of his. They told a story, one that she desperately wanted to know the ending to. They held so many promises for her: safety, adventure, a sense of home that she had never before experienced. And all she had to do was reach out and grab it.

"One date?" she asked. "And we're not, like, a *thing*."

He chuckled. "We don't have to be a *thing*. Hell, I don't even know if I'd know how to be a thing with someone. But I do know that I want to get to know you better. I know that I love going to sleep smelling you all over my bed. I know that I haven't been able to get you out of my head. And I know for damn sure that's never happened to me before. So, yeah, I want to go out. With you, and only you."

She reached out to clasp his hand, for no reason other than to steady herself. Her heart was rocketing away in a sporadic rhythm, and she was in real danger of falling over from the heat that was coursing through her body and into her heart. Not to mention the dampness in her underwear. No one had ever spoken to her like that. No guy, with the exception of Morrow, had wanted to get to know her.

Maybe it was because every guy she dated was there because he had paid to be.

"When?" she whispered. Her voice was no longer working the way it should, and a whisper was all she could manage.

"How about this Saturday night?"

Her heart plummeted from the height Reed had caused it to soar to. "I can't. I spend my weekends working for my stepfather."

"Your weekend nights?" Reed's forehead wrinkled when his brows rose.

She nodded grimly.

"Okay, then. You free Sunday night?"

She nodded again, this time with a faint smile.

"Then we have a date this Sunday night. I'll pick you up at seven."

Panic engulfed her. "Here?"

Reed nodded slowly, squeezing her hand in his warm fingers. "Here is where you live, Hope. So yeah, I was planning on picking you up here. Is that a problem?"

She shook her head. "No. I'll see you Sunday at seven."

He bent slowly, causing her heart to start out of the blocks once again. He pressed warm lips to her cool forehead, and stood looking down at her.

"I can't wait," he whispered, his eyes boring into hers. "Sharon and I will be here on time."

"Sharon?"

He reached out to pat the truck affectionately. "Shhh. You'll hurt her feelings."

"You named your truck?" She placed a hand over her mouth to cover a giggle.

"Of course. She's the most important woman in my life. Until someone comes along to change that, she's Sharon." His blue eyes twinkled merrily as he winked at her.

Hope managed to merely nod and smile.

She began walking toward the house, but yelped when he smacked her bottom. She turned back with narrowed eyes, and his were crinkling at the corner with mirth.

"Hey, Hope?"

She looked back over her shoulder.

"Sunday's not going to suck. And it won't be *nice*, either."

Violet was waiting for her at the kitchen window, and Hope groaned at the sight of her sister's huge grin.

"Seriously?" Violet shrieked. Well, as close to a shriek as Violet's ultracool demeanor would allow. She had none of the hotheaded tendencies of her mother and her sister. "He's so hot! Like, rock star hot! How have you never told me you have a boyfriend?"

"Violet!" Hope snapped. She immediately softened her tone; she never spoke to Violet in anger. "Sorry. But think about what you're saying. Reed is not my boyfriend. I cannot have one of those. You know that just as well as I do."

"Let's pretend for a minute that I know nothing. Why can't Reed be your boyfriend? He was here, sitting in his big-ass truck, waiting for you to come home. That's hot. He wants you. Why not?"

Hope stared at Violet. "Because he probably wouldn't appreciate the fact that I date other men every weekend. And I get paid for it. Not to mention what Frank would do if he found out."

Violet shrugged. It infuriated Hope sometimes, how simple

life was according to Violet. "So stop dating rich men for money. I hate it, anyway."

Hope sank into a chair at the vast glass-topped kitchen table, where Violet's homework was spread in a haphazard arc of loose-leaf paper. "If I could, Violet, I would. But my job at the Center pays, like, nothing. And if it were just me, I'd be so fine with that. But it's not just me. I'm working on putting away money for the two of us. So I can get you out of here."

Violet dropped her pale blond head and sighed. "Now that I know you have a guy like that out there, just waiting for you, how can I be okay with that, Hope? You need to stop working for Frank. Yesterday. It's not worth it. Plus, you could have all the money in the world. Mom's never going to let me go. And I don't want you to throw everything away to go on the run with me. I just don't want that."

Tears stung Hope's eyes as they threatened to spill out onto her cheeks. Violet was just so much wiser than any thirteen-year-old needed to be. "Don't worry about it, Vi. It's my deal. You just keep kicking ass in school and painting your little ass off. I promise I'll take care of the rest."

She wiped her eyes and quickly changed the subject to prevent any more argument out of Violet. "Let's get started on this."

Maybe Violet had forgotten what life had been like before Wendy had snagged Frank. Living in a shitty trailer or apartment. Barely any money for food. Thrift store clothing. Roaches. All of that on top of the pain. And it was only a matter of time before the three of them were out on their asses again. She would never leave Violet alone with Wendy. Never.

Violet leaned forward to reach for her textbook, and her shirt rode up on her back. Hope gasped.

"Oh, my God, Vi! What happened to your back? What'd she do?"

The bruise was healing, and Hope could tell it was a couple of days old. It wasn't violently black-and-blue the way a fresh bruise would have been.

"It doesn't hurt," whispered Violet.

Tears stung Hope's eyes as she pulled Violet in for a hug. "That's what you always say, sweetie. What happened?"

"I was getting ready for school. I guess I took too long in the shower. I don't know why it matters. It's not like we're all sharing one bathroom the way we used to. Anyway, when I came out, she shoved me. And I fell onto my ass. I think my tailbone got bruised."

Hope gritted her teeth. "Why didn't you tell me? You might have needed a doctor." Emotions were swirling around and around in her head, making her dizzy. She was pissed, but she was also heartbroken. Wendy had always treated Violet this way. Why? She sucked in a deep breath, letting the air out slowly as she focused on her sister.

"I don't want to go to the doctor every time this happens, Hope. I'm fine. Let's work."

Hope was reluctant to let it go, but she couldn't see another alternative. But the incident only made her more determined to find a way to get her sister out of this house. For good.

They worked for nearly two hours on Violet's mound of homework before Hope finally made it out to the pool for a night swim. She dived in and began pulling herself through the water, feeling the tension siphon off of her muscles as the laps ticked by. She swam until her limbs were heavy with exertion, and she pulled herself woodenly out of the pool and up to the shower. All the while, her mind kept shifting to a tall, too-sexy-for-his-own-good rocker.

A bead of sweat dripped down Reed's forehead as he leaned into the mic. He often sang his original stuff when he performed at Sunny's, because everyone there knew him and would support whatever he did. But when he had a gig in Charleston, he sang mostly covers, with a song or two of his own thrown in. He sang one now that he'd written not too long ago, entitled "You're Better Than Him." He crooned the lyrics with the softest edge of his voice, allowing just the slightest tip of roughness to slice through the audience during the most emotional peaks of the song. The crowd was settled comfortably into the palm of his hand, and he was loving every single minute of the performance. His friends occupied a table up front as usual, and after this song was finished, he'd be done for the night and able to join them for a drink.

Things were different now that Hope had agreed to go out with him on an official date. He'd thought she'd been heavy on his mind before, but now he pictured her face before falling asleep at night. His fingers itched to text her or call her as soon as he woke alone in his bed.

Because these days, he was always alone in his bed. Hope had said she didn't want to be a *thing*, but he couldn't bring himself to escort random girls home just to get laid. He wasn't sure, but those days just might be over. He didn't know whether to be excited or pissed that he wasn't getting sex on the regular, at the snap of his fingers. Tonight would be a long night. He could only take comfort in the fact that it was Friday, and in two nights he'd be wining and dining the woman he saw in his dreams at night. Hopefully, she'd be willing to budge on the "not a thing" criterion.

He walked offstage to the sound of whoops and loud applause, and he settled into a seat at the table. Tamara, Tate's twin sister, slid a longneck in his direction.

"I loved that song," she mused. "Your music always makes me think a little too much, Reed."

The melancholy tone she used wasn't something Reed was used to hearing from Tamara. She was usually bubbly and outgoing, and always ready to party. She was a little wilder than Aston and Ashley were, even before Ashley was married and Aston had met Sam. But lately she seemed different. Quieter, more stuck inside her own head.

"You okay?" he asked her, cocking his head to the side and studying her face. She and Tate shared a birthday and their coppery red hair, but not much else.

She sighed heavily, her chest rising and falling with the movement as she drummed her fingers on the table. "Just fine. It's nothing I can't handle. Just caught up in my own thoughts, that's all."

"That's not like you." Reed frowned while the noise level in the club continued to rise around them. "You're usually living in the moment. What's changed?"

Tamara glanced around the table. She shrugged, staring up at the bar. "I'm going to get a drink."

Deep in thought, Reed watched her go.

When Sam had first arrived in Nelson Island, Tamara had jumped at the chance to attract his attention. She was looking for love, all right, and usually in all the wrong places. She either didn't notice, or thought she could overcome, the way Aston and Sam looked at each other when they thought no one was paying any attention.

Reed jumped when Tate's elbow found his ribs. "What?"

Tate inclined his head toward the pair of blondes eyeing Reed from the bar. "Let's get down to business. Your wingman needs to get some ass tonight."

Reed rolled his eyes. How had he never noticed before how shallow and disgusting Tate sounded? And he used to sound the same way. He only just realized his heart had never been in the chase the way Tate's was.

"I'm good," he answered his friend. "That's all you, man."

Tate frowned. "But they're looking at you. I'm the wingman, you're the main man. Let's do it."

"Not tonight, Tate," said Reed, lazily propping his booted feet up on the table. "You're gonna have to suit up on your own, or take Blaze with you."

Blaze's eyes lit up from across the table. "I'm in, bro."

Tate frowned at Reed. "What's up with you?"

"Yeah," Aston butted in. "What *is* up with you? Not that I'm complaining, little brother, but this sure as shit doesn't sound like you. Are you sick?"

Sam shot Reed a knowing glance before settling an arm around Aston's chair. "Easy, Princess. Maybe Reed's just growing up a little."

Tate looked horrified. "Growing up? C'mon, Reed. Don't do this shit to me now!"

Reed chuckled. "Have fun, Tate."

Tate groaned and slammed his beer down on the table. "Come on, Blaze. The ladies await."

Reed watched them go with a small smile on his face, then he glanced back at his sister. "I'm fine. I'm just not into bringing randoms home right now, that's all."

Aston's mouth dropped open. "Why?"

Tamara plopped back down into her chair, a cocktail glass in hand. "Yeah, why?"

Reed sighed. The girls weren't going away quietly. So he decided to tell them the truth. Aston might actually have some advice for him that he could use with Hope.

"Remember that girl you saw that night at the business owners' banquet? The one with all the long hair?"

"No." Aston gasped. "I mean, yes! But…you aren't bringing random girls home because you're into one girl in particular? My little brother?"

"Maybe." He shrugged. "But I think she's gun-shy."

"Smart girl," said Tamara with a smirk.

Reed shot her a dirty look. She leaned into a hand, cupping her chin and grinning.

"I need to get her to trust me, so she'll open up to me. I don't think she's had the easiest life, even though her parents' house over in Charleston is almost as big as Mom and Dad's. I just get a feeling that she has a lot of heavy shit to deal with."

Aston was watching him in wonder. "You're not even my brother. I can't believe this stuff is coming out of your mouth right now."

Sam absently brushed a strand of hair out of Aston's eyes. "Take it slow with her, man. Remember what we talked about? Don't be *that* Reed."

Reed had the propriety to look chagrined as he fiddled with his bottle of beer.

"Aw, come on, man," Sam said, throwing his hands up. "Please tell me you didn't."

"I didn't!" Reed placed both hands in the air in surrender. Sam looked relieved, and then Reed continued. "Because Tate came home."

A real groan came from Sam then, and Aston was looking back and forth between them in irritation.

"You knew about this?" she asked Sam, poking a dark fingernail into his chest.

He kissed the top of her head. "Bro code, baby."

"We'll see if bro code keeps you warm tonight," she grumbled. He leaned down to whisper something in her ear, and her grumble turned into a breathy giggle.

Both Reed and Tamara rolled their eyes.

"Well," said Reed. "Maybe Tate saved me that time. I'll take it slow. I won't try to get physical with her. Maybe I can move a mountain with that tactic."

"You'd be surprised." Sam smiled down at Aston.

Now Reed had to figure out how exactly he was going to keep his hands off the hot little exotic package that was Hope.

A tap on his shoulder had him turning around in his seat to stare up at a man he'd never seen before.

"Reed, right?" said the man with a smile.

Reed eyed the man's artistic look. He wore black jeans tucked into open-laced combat boots, and a red graphic T-shirt with a picture of a conductor poised to direct a concerto. His wrists were covered with black leather cuffs, and the earlobes on both ears were adorned with button-size plugs. Reed glanced back up at the man's face, and he was grinning. He'd seen Reed's appraisal of him, and his dark eyebrow rose as if to say, "Approve?"

Reed grunted. "Who's asking?"

The man reached up to pat the random bleach-blond spikes poking out all over the top of his head, and then held out his hand for Reed to shake. "I'm Phillip Castille. I'm supposed to be on vacation with my wife, but I'm a music producer based out of Atlanta, and I'd really like to talk to you, Reed."

Reed's heartbeat was off to the races when the man announced his profession, and he stood, facing Phillip directly. "Yeah, okay. Um, you want to sit?"

Phillip shook his head. "I'm headed out. Let me get straight to the point. I saw what you did up there, and I fell in love. I want you, Reed. In my studio, making a demo. I'm handing you my card—you can think about it or talk to whoever you need to talk to. But give me a call in a few days so we can set something up for the next couple of weeks. Yeah?"

Stunned, Reed nodded. "Yeah! Thank you."

Phillip slapped him on the back and sauntered toward the door. He didn't even seem like he realized he had just thrown a grenade into Reed's life and walked away without watching the beautiful explosion.

Aston squealed as Reed sank back into his seat. "Oh my God! Did that really just happen? Reed! What do you think?"

He just shook his head numbly as he stared at his sister and his future brother-in-law.

Sam hurried to the bar and returned with a tray full of tequila shots, Tate, and Blaze. Everyone was slapping Reed on the back and congratulating him at once, but it was all traveling to him through the sound of the blood rushing in his own ears. He couldn't think straight; he couldn't answer their congratulatory remarks.

He'd done it. He'd caught the attention of a professional in the music business, and something real and concrete was going to happen to move his career forward. He knew it somewhere deep in his gut. And *excitement* wasn't even the word to describe his current state of being.

He allowed the shot of tequila to burn away his shock, and then a big grin spread across his face.

He'd done it.

Eleven

Most twenty-two-year-olds lived their lives looking forward to the weekend. Hope lived Sunday through Thursday dreading Friday like priests fear the apocalypse.

"You don't have to go, you know," said Morrow. It was a familiar discussion between the two. Every Friday at the Center, Hope looked like she was about to partake in her last supper. Morrow argued that she was under no obligation to go and work for Frank's club. And she explained exasperatedly that it was the only way she would make that kind of money, and that if she weren't working there Wendy and Frank would kick her out and she'd be too far away from Violet to be of any help to her sister.

And she refused to leave Violet.

Once, when Hope and Violet were younger, Wendy had been found by her two younger daughters bent over the coffee table snorting thin white lines of white powder into her nose. Hope had been appalled, but not surprised. Violet had been too little to understand how off balance their mother really was. She had gone running to her mother, arms outstretched, and Wendy had sat up quickly, too quickly. Her movement had sent little Violet spinning into the wall.

As unstable as Wendy and all of the men she paraded in and out of her and Violet's life were, Hope would never, ever, make Violet have to suffer through Wendy without her. Even now that Wendy was happily married to Frank, Hope didn't trust either one of them. She wouldn't let Violet continue to be hurt.

Hope locked the door behind them; they were the last people to leave the facility on a regular basis, and tonight was no exception.

Morrow gave up the argument, heaving a sigh so large that his broad chest swelled. He shook his head, causing his brown curls to shift around his face.

"So, then," he said. "What's the game plan for tonight? You know I always like to know where you are...just in case."

Hope nodded. Every weekend, Morrow made it clear that he didn't think that what she was doing for Frank's club was safe. Silk—the name of the club—wasn't a job where she would be looked after. Frank, no matter what he claimed, wouldn't take care of her. It drove Morrow a little off the deep end. And after what had happened with Tyler, Hope was beginning to take his concerns more seriously.

"We're going to Jet for drinks and dancing. His name is Giovanni, and he's picking me up at the house. Okay?"

Morrow nodded, his eyes cloudy with troubled anxiety. "Okay. Keep your phone close, and call me if you need anything. I think I know another guy who would appreciate a call, too."

Hope shook her head, almost frantically. "Reed doesn't know

about this, Morrow. He'd never understand. I don't even know what I'm doing with him, honestly. I agreed to a date on Sunday, but I know it will never work. I shouldn't have let him talk me into it."

"Then why did you?" Morrow shot back. "You're not the kind of woman who gets talked into things she doesn't want to do." His knowing smile irked Hope, and she frowned at him.

"His stupid eyes do something to me," she snapped. "Now shut the hell up."

Morrow laughed, and wrapped strong arms around her. "I love you, girl. Be careful. Call me tomorrow."

"Will do," she called, climbing into her beat-up little car.

In her rearview mirror, she watched Morrow watch her as she drove away, dreading the fact that in a little over an hour she'd be staring at another man she couldn't stand over a drink she never wanted him to buy her.

Two hours later, it was so much worse than that.

Her date, Giovanni, had paraded her around at a cocktail event with potential investors for his Internet start-up. He was a silver-spoon-fed, trust-fund kid from Mount Pleasant who was attempting to branch off on his own with no business training whatsoever. He thought he could totally make it on his family name alone, even though he claimed to want to get away from the blanket of an overtly rich ancestry.

Laughable.

And now his guests were gone, and Hope had to stand next to him at the bar while he ordered shot after shot of high-end vodka. She declined every drink he offered her, and she could tell that he was beginning to get annoyed.

"Come on, Hayley," he slurred. "One drink. We're supposed to be on a date, right? I paid a lot of money for you, and you won't even have a drink with me?"

She only just refrained from shoving his drunk ass crashing back into the barstool behind him. "You did pay a lot of money. *For my company*. And my name's not Hayley. It's Hope. I don't want a drink, thank you."

His face flushed an angry scarlet. "What if I said I'm not taking you home until you have a drink with me?"

Rage flared up inside of her. It never changed. These power-hungry men who joined Frank's club never differed one bit. They all looked different, and were different ages, but inside they were exactly alike. They all had far too much money to spend, and none of them had a trace of morality or spirituality to keep their egos in check. It was disgusting, and Hope felt like she had to take a long, cleansing shower after every date.

Giovanni downed another shot. "Well, I think you're a pretty boring date. How much would it cost to upgrade my package?"

The gleam in his eye was familiar as he turned around to face the rest of the bar, propping his elbows up on the counter behind him and grinning at Hope.

She took a cautious step back. "Upgrade? The package is a date. There are no upgrades."

"Really?" His stance was casual. "That's not what Frank said. And he's your boss, right?"

Now she was engulfed in white-hot flames of fury. "*What?*"

Her long, dark hair was piled up on top of her head tonight in an elegant style, and her short navy dress hugged her petite, curved figure perfectly. She shook her head so hard in her anger that a bobby pin flew out of her head and hit the bar beside her.

Giovanni grinned like a fat cat. "You heard me, baby. Your boss said that I could upgrade during the date if I so desired."

There it was; being called *baby* by this man sent her hurtling over the edge.

"Let me tell you something, you sick son of a bitch," Hope spat. "I don't know what Frank told you, but I'm a person. I decide what I do, not Frank. So I'm telling you right now. I'm. Not. Having. Sex. With. You. There will be no happy endings on this date. You got me, *baby*?"

He simply smiled harder, if that was possible. "You're a feisty one. I like that. Too bad I'll have to talk to Frank and tell him how dissatisfied I am with Silk's service. I'm sure he won't be too happy about that."

Hope was already stabbing the keys on her phone, sending a text to Morrow. "Tell him whatever the hell you want. This date is over."

She turned, digging her stiletto into the floor of the upscale bar, and exited through the front doors.

When Morrow pulled up fifteen minutes later in his Tahoe, she was shaking from head to foot with anger and humiliation.

Morrow reached over to push open her door, and she hopped in.

"Oh, my *God*," she fumed. "I can't believe Frank! He told that bastard I'd roll onto my back for this date."

"You did the right thing," he said quietly. "Glad you called,

Hope. You know I'll always come and get you when you need it. But I don't know why you're so surprised. If Frank is suddenly changing the rules on you...well, this won't be the last time. You know that, right?"

Hope's brow furrowed while she mulled over Morrow's words. She turned them over slowly in her mind, and a thick cloud of dread began to creep slowly into her stomach.

There were girls who worked for Silk that provided the service Giovanni was after. Although Hope didn't interact with the other girls working for Frank's high-end escort service very often, she knew them well enough to know that not all of them had the same moral standards and values Hope lived by. She knew that a lot of them were in the business in order to pay off student loans or to put themselves though school. They wanted the money, just like Hope did, but they didn't care as much how they got it. The more of themselves they provided on a date, the more paper went into their wallet at the end of the night. No matter what the other girls said at the mixers Frank sometimes threw for the Silk clients, Hope had decided long ago that she'd never cross that line.

No matter how much money it would add to her growing nest egg.

"Just take me home, Morrow," she said, her voice barely a whisper.

He sent her a sharp glance, then sighed and turned the big truck for the mansion on the outskirts of the city.

Reed, Aston, and Sam sat in tandem around the Hopewells' huge wooden table in the large, ornate dining room. Reed had sat at this table more times than he could count, but the room never seemed more stifling than it did that night. His mother was staring at him in astonishment, and his father's frown deepened the lines marring his handsome forehead.

"You're going to Atlanta?" asked Gregory Hopewell. "To work with a producer?"

"That's what I said, Dad," answered Reed, unable to hide his frustration. His teeth ground together as he fought to remain calm.

"But why?" asked Lillian. She kept darting furtive glances toward Gregory. "I thought you'd decided to fulfill your role at Hopewell Enterprises."

"I said I'd give it a chance," Reed said slowly. "And I am. But I never agreed to stop pursuing music. That wasn't part of the deal."

"All right, son," Gregory said, taking a bite of his tuna tartare and wiping his mouth with a cream-colored cloth napkin. "What am I supposed to do? Should I explain to our associates that you are out of town with your guitar until further notice?"

Reed opened his mouth to speak, but Aston spoke up. "You don't have to explain anything to anyone, Daddy. He's the boss's son, for God's sake. I'll take conference calls with clients until he returns. He's only going to be gone a few days."

"That's not the point, Aston," said Gregory, his face strained. He tore his eyes away from his beloved daughter to stare sternly at Reed. "He's got to get his life together. This nonsense with music has got to stop. I've built an entire legacy for you, Reed; all you have to do is reach out and take it. Music is a hobby. Hopewell Enterprises is an entire future. More than anything, I want you by my side. Just like Aston."

Sam cleared his throat. "Sir. I know how you feel about Hopewell Enterprises, but isn't it possible that Reed doesn't feel the same way about business as you and Aston do? He has a passion, a talent, and the drive to take it somewhere. It's the ambition that he inherited from you, with all due respect."

Gregory sighed. "Drive is important. You know I value that, Sam. But family businesses as successful as ours aren't built in a day. I've spent *decades* on this company with my children in mind. And I want all three of you at its helm one day."

Aston and Sam shared a special glance; Reed knew that when Sam had first come to Nelson Island, Gregory asking him to learn the business from the ground up had been a source of jealousy and devastation for Aston. She'd recovered from it, and she now truly loved working side by side with her fiancé.

Lillian Hopewell threw a pleading glance at her husband, and then cleared her throat. "We're ruining dinner with this conversation," she said firmly. "Reed, good luck in Atlanta. We'll leave it at that. Aston, tell me how the meeting with the caterers went?"

Reed wasn't going to be able to sit there for the rest of the meal listening to the women in his life gab about wedding plans. Aston and his mother's relationship had come a long way, and he was happy to see them planning this event together, but tonight wasn't the night for him to be a part of it.

He and his father obviously still had leaps and bounds ahead of them in order to mend their relationship. His father wanted a son who was a mini Gregory, and that simply wasn't, and never had been, Reed. When Sam had entered their lives a few years ago, Reed was hopeful that he was enough like Gregory that his father would lay off Reed, but that hadn't happened. Gregory was insistent upon Reed graduating from college, that he come and work for the company rather than moving away to pursue his dreams. Reed had relented because he loved his hometown, but he made it very clear that he was still playing and writing music, and if something happened to further his musical career, he was going to follow that path wherever it led.

Reed had lost respect for his father long ago. He only hoped that they could move forward without much more damage being done to their already fragile bond.

He pushed back from the table and stalked out of the room, heading for the front door. When he reached back to close it behind him, Gregory was there to stop the door from slamming shut.

"Dad," Reed warned. "I'm done for tonight. I'm all talked out. Or should I say lectured out?"

"Reed." Gregory's voice was tired. "Why can't you just accept that this is where you're meant to be? Nelson Island is your home, not some wild city where a music career may or may not be waiting. I've built something for you here. Look at your mother and me. Find a woman like her, settle down. Start a family. Live this legacy I've left for you, son."

Something inside of Reed snapped with his father's words; he felt like a tree toppling over in a forest after being struck by a violent bolt of lightning.

"Are you kidding me?" he asked, his anger evident in his tone. "Settle down with someone like Mom? Someone who will step out on me repeatedly so I can look like an ass and keep taking them back? No, Dad. That's not gonna happen. *I'm not you.*"

Gregory's head whipped back like he'd been slapped. An angry red colored his stunned face, and Reed turned away. He walked down the steps that led to where his truck was parked just beyond the porch.

He'd said enough for one night. It was time to get a drink.

As he drove, his mind wandered to a girl with long, dark hair and olive skin, beautifully tragic hazel eyes, and a body that made his own sing with desire whenever he laid eyes on it.

Where is she tonight? He wasn't sure which club her stepfather owned, but he imagined her pouring drinks for customers in something short and tight. The thought aroused him but also sent a bolt of jealousy rushing through his nerve endings. He didn't want other men looking at her while she was wearing something appropriate for tending bar.

Did that mean he wanted her all to himself? Now he wasn't sure. He'd just told his father that settling down was the last thing he wanted. He'd seen what his parents had been through over the years, saw what completely loving a woman could do to a man. He didn't want that to happen to him. It would *kill* him if he allowed that to happen. He couldn't fall for someone just to find out she'd been with other men during their time together. He would never survive it; he knew that in his soul.

But Sunday was just going to be a date. He was just getting to know Hope; that was all. She compelled him in a way he couldn't explain. He had to find out what put that despairing look in her eyes. Once again, the desire to be there for her hit him straight in the chest. He was powerless to resist it.

Twelve

Hope had told Frank and Wendy in no uncertain terms that none of her dates would, under any circumstances, be "upgraded." And that if the subject came up again, she'd quit. She didn't give a shit how popular she was among the clients. She couldn't understand why they loved her so much anyway; her attitude was atrocious and she knew it. She viewed her own reflection in the mirror every day; she knew men considered her attractive. But compelling enough for men to want to date her in spite of her unwillingness to give them any more than a peck on the cheek at the end of the night? It was unfathomable.

Frank had observed her tirade with moderate interest, but Wendy was livid, calling Hope every name in her arsenal and screaming about how ungrateful she was, yet again. Wendy's rants hardly affected her anymore, but Hope was terrified that her unstable mother would fly into a rage and really hurt Violet.

"Your aloofness only works well in my favor." Frank had finally spoken when Hope ran out of steam. "My clients think they can win you over. They're used to women falling all over themselves; you're a breath of fresh air to them. And the fact that you're beautiful and what they consider to be classy doesn't hurt, either."

Now, as Hope readied herself for her date with Reed, she glanced anxiously at her phone to check the time.

"Stop doing that," ordered Violet. "It's going to be fine. Mom and Frank are out, you're not going to get caught going out with Reed."

Violet was lounging on Hope's bed, watching her get ready. She lay on her stomach lengthwise, her long and slender hands framing her face while she watched her sister apply her makeup.

"I wish I had your skin," said Violet enviously. "You and your Latin hotness—it's like a work of freaking art. All I got from my dad was Irish skin that turns me into a damn tomato in the sun. All of this paleness probably hurts guys' eyes when they look at me."

"Stop it," ordered Hope. "You're gorgeous. One day you'll realize that you look like a model. And you have the brains to back it up. You're a gift, Vi."

"Sure," Violet answered. "I'll realize that just as soon as you do, Hope."

Hope knew she was right. They both suffered from their own self-confidence issues, thanks to their jewel of a mother.

"No guy has ever wanted to take me out," Violet continued.

"You're thirteen!" exclaimed Hope, turning around to stare at her sister. "No guy should be wanting to take you out yet!"

Violet shot her a you-don't-understand-at-all glare and changed the subject. "Where's the rock god taking you?"

Laughing, Hope applied lip gloss to her sensuously full lips. "The 'rock god' wouldn't say. He needs to learn that I hate surprises."

"You mean, he needs to learn that you're a control freak," corrected Violet. "Let go a little. I think he really likes you."

"You talked to him for what, ten minutes?" Hope squinted at her sister.

Violet's face turned serious. She blinked her big gray eyes at Hope. "That was long enough. I like him. You do, too, I can tell. So let go, Hope. Just a little."

Her little sister's words resonated with Hope. Could she let go with Reed? It was something she'd never allowed herself to do, much less with a man. Only time would tell.

The doorbell's chime echoed through the house, and Hope grabbed her clutch and ran for the door. Her wedges clicked on the hardwood as she descended the stairs, Violet quick on her heels.

When she opened the front double doors, Reed stood on the porch, looking for all the world like God's gift to musical, manly perfection. He was casual in army green Dickies and a tight black T-shirt. His black boots were the same muted leather as the cuff that adorned his wrist and the wide belt at his waist. A shiny platinum buckle gleamed at her exactly where she shouldn't be aiming her attention. His dark hair was a perfect mess, and his eyes sparkled at her when she finally dragged hers away from his taut body and up to meet them.

"Hi," he said softly as she stared. Then he slowly let his eyes rove her the way she'd just done him.

They scanned her face slowly, then dropped to the bare skin her strapless maxidress left exposed. A bit of bronzer allowed her collarbone to shimmer slightly, and his pupils dilated as he wet his lips. His eyes continued their journey down to the curves her navy blue dress didn't quite hide, and stopped at her cherry red toes, which peeked out from her nude corked wedges.

"You done?" she asked a little breathlessly when his eyes found hers once more. He looked so amazing just leaning against the doorjamb, she nearly jumped out of her heels when Violet cleared her throat.

"You kids have fun." She grinned.

Reed frowned. "You're staying here alone?"

Hope shook her head. "I'd never do that. I made sure that a member of the staff my stepfather employs here will be with her until I come home." She turned to Violet. "You text me if they come home earlier than I do, okay? I'll come right back." Violet nodded.

Reed held out a hand. "Well, let's get out of here, then." He winked at Violet. "See ya, kid."

Hope turned and grabbed Violet's chin. She gave her a quick kiss on the cheek before releasing her and taking Reed's proffered hand. "Love you. Be good. And call me if you need anything, Vi. Anything."

Violet waved and shut the door behind them. Then Reed was walking Hope to his truck, which sat waiting for them in front of the side-entry garage doors.

He opened the passenger-side door, and then stopped her with a hand on her wrist before she could climb up. She turned to face him and was startled when his body was only inches from hers. She braced her hands against his chest and looked up into his chiseled face. And thought to herself that she hoped she could get through the night without just staring at the perfection that was Reed's face.

"You look amazing," he said, his voice full of dark, sexy sin. "And I promised myself that I'd respect you, and that I wouldn't put too much pressure on you. But goddammit, Hope, you look good enough for me to eat right now, and I'm having a hard time remembering why I made that promise to myself."

A hot flush crept into her cheeks. Suddenly, she couldn't remember why she needed to keep her distance from him, either.

His eyes flicked down to her lips, and her knees weakened slightly. "Because we are a bad idea. And I've got too much going on in my life right now to be getting so…physical…with anyone right now."

He immediately took a small step back. "Yeah. I remember you saying something about that."

He let his eyes run the length of her once more. "But I don't promise it's going to be easy to keep my hands to myself. I'll do my best."

She smirked. Reed brought out a boldness in her she never knew existed where men were concerned. She'd never *wanted* to be bold before. "I didn't say you needed to act like a priest."

His eyes flashed, and she giggled and turned to climb into the truck. She felt his hands on her hips, lingering as he helped her up to her seat.

He closed the door behind her and she inhaled deep. His truck smelled like him, and she inhaled again as she watched him walk around the front of it to climb in next to her.

"Where are we going?" she asked casually.

"Nuh-uh," he answered. "You'll see when we get there."

She sighed. "Fine."

"How was work this weekend?" he asked as he drove with one hand on the wheel and one placed lightly on her knee. She liked it that he wanted to touch her. She *wanted* the contact when it came to Reed.

"Work?"

"Yeah." He glanced her way. "You worked at your stepdad's club the last two nights, right?"

He thought Frank owned an actual…oh, crap. *Is a lie of omission the same as a lie?*

"Oh, that," she said, dread coursing through her. "It was…eventful. I had to set down some ground rules for a creep who had the wrong idea, but other than that it was just a normal weekend."

Reed's hand tightened on her leg. "Someone touched you?"

How am I supposed to answer that?

"This guy thought I'd give him more of a good time than my rules would allow," she said carefully. "So I set him straight."

Reed's jaw tensed; she watched the vein in his temple throb and marveled at the sense of strength it gave him. "What did your stepfather say about it?"

She laughed out loud, and then covered her mouth with her hand. "Frank's not the protective type."

Reed's eyes slid toward her. "You work for him; he should take care of you. You have my number, Hope. Call me if that happens again while you're working. I'll be there."

"Now you sound like Morrow."

He slid her a sideways gaze. "Who's Morrow?"

She smiled. "He's my best friend. We've been friends since we were kids, and he's always trying to look out for me."

"Well, then this Morrow's a smart dude. I mean it. I want you to be safe. There's a lot of bad guys out there, especially when they're drinking at a club."

Hope rolled her eyes. *Tell me about it*, she thought. Aloud, she said, "I'll keep you in mind."

He nodded, and his hand relaxed on her leg. She looked out her window and noticed that they were driving on the bridge to Nelson Island. She sighed as happiness flooded through her. "I'm glad you're bringing me back here."

"Good. I hope you like what I have planned."

The sincerity in Reed's tone was disarming. When she glanced over at him, his eyes were fixed firmly to the road ahead, both hands were now gripping the steering wheel.

He's nervous. The thought brought a smile to her face. He was nervous about taking her on a date. This ridiculously sexy man, who wore a guitar like another limb and played it like he owned the room, this man who'd hinted at the scores of girls who'd been in his condo before she'd ever even heard of him.

She made him nervous. The thought eased the rest of the tension right out of her coiled muscles and softened her closed-up heart just a little bit more toward Reed. Because if he was nervous, that meant he was real.

And she could handle real.

Why the hell am I so nervous? He actually couldn't remember the last time he'd picked a woman up to take her on a date. Maybe high school. Prom? That was probably it. By the end of high school, he'd learned that it wasn't necessary, the whole courting ritual. Girls tended to end up in his lap at Sunny's, where'd he'd been using a fake ID since he was sixteen, whether he sold them promises of tomorrow or not. The ID was merely a formality; anyone who worked behind the bar at Sunny's knew exactly who Reed was and how old he was. They just needed the fake in order to look the other way.

And that had been before he'd been brave enough to strap on his guitar and bare his soul for a crowd mixed with strangers and friends.

He drove along the state highway that ran through the middle of Nelson Island and ended at the oceanfront. On the way, he passed the turnoff for the Hopewell ranch and pointed it out to Hope. She seemed interested in the ranch's business, and he spent the remainder of the drive explaining about the polo horses his parents bred and trained on the working ranch, and how his father had started Hopewell Enterprises as a young man not much older than Reed.

"Wow," she remarked, just as Reed was parking the truck in a sandy lot beside a little wooden bridge that crossed from asphalt over to sand. "Your father seems like kind of an amazing man."

"Yeah," muttered Reed "He's something, all right."

She glanced at him, but he didn't elaborate on his dry remark. She'd figure out sooner or later that his relationship with his father wasn't what it should be, and he'd rather it be later.

Behind closed doors and family walls, every impressive man had his secrets and downfalls. Gregory Hopewell was no different, especially in the eyes of his only son.

"Shall we?" He exited the truck and went around to open her door. He used the excuse of helping her out of the cab to get his hands around her slim waist. He let them rest there while he eased her to the ground, relishing the feeling of Hope in his arms. She fit so perfectly there. She was so tiny, and although Reed wasn't a huge guy, not nearly as big as Sam or Blaze, she made him feel like a giant. She was vulnerable as she trusted him to place his hands on her. He was beginning to realize how much it took for her to bestow that kind of trust, and he found himself wanting to prove himself worthy.

Another totally brand-new feeling this girl seemed to awaken in him.

He pulled a black bandanna out of his pocket and waved it in front of her. "I asked you if you trusted me a few days ago when I asked you on this date, and your answer was yes. Was that really true?"

She assessed him carefully, and he could see her mind working as she formulated an answer. Finally, she nodded, smiling almost shyly. "Yeah, Reed. I do."

He grinned. "Good. Because I'm going to blindfold you."

Her eyes widened. The golden flecks swirling in them glinted in the setting sunlight, and he caught his breath as he met her surprised gaze. She was just so damn beautiful he *ached*.

He pulled her close, taking the time to inhale her sweet, fresh scent, and turned her around so she was facing away from him. He tied the blindfold gently around her head, and waved a hand in front of her face. When she didn't react, he smiled.

"Okay, I'm going to lead you a little ways away, Hope. Just walk with me and hold my hand, okay?"

"You're not going to lead me into the ocean, are you?"

He placed his lips close to her ear when he answered. "No, gorgeous."

She shivered—he could feel her body quiver—and he was slightly awed that he had such an effect on her. He gently tugged her hand, and they slowly walked over the little wooden bridge. As soon as her feet touched sand, he asked her to sit so he could remove her shoes. He guided her to perch on the wood, and he ran his hands down one of her silky smooth legs to the strap of her sandal. He silently unbuckled the strap and slid off her shoe. Her cute little toes wiggled as they were freed, and he smiled in response. He couldn't help it; he bent down to place his open mouth to her calf. Her lips parted and the softest of moans escaped her. He was instantly hard; her sexy-as-hell noises were just as he remembered them from the night they'd rolled around in his sheets. He closed his eyes briefly without saying a word, just gathering his strength. He had promised to respect her, and that was what he was going to do.

He repeated the process with her other shoe, and placed one more chaste kiss on her ankle before clasping her hands in his and pulling her to her feet. He turned to face the ocean, and his little surprise was in full view.

As they began to walk, a trio of violinists began to play a quiet instrumental. Hope gasped beside him, and he was unable to keep the huge grin off his face as he led her toward a small table for two set just where the waves kissed the sand. He kicked off his shoes as they walked, and bent to pick them up as he continued to lead Hope toward a romantic dinner.

The chef he'd hired, a friend of his family, smiled at Reed as he pulled out Hope's chair. Reed guided her into it and pulled off her blindfold. Her wide eyes reflected the flickering candlelight from the table, and she glanced around her in shock. As the sun sank low over the horizon, Reed was almost as taken away by her perfection as she was by the scene before her.

"Reed." Her voice was the softest of whispers. "This is…I can't…" Words failed her as she trailed off. "This is too much. I don't deserve it."

"Hey, now," he protested, sitting across from her. He grabbed the bottle of wine, which was breathing in the center of the table. Picking up her glass, he poured the rich, crimson liquid. "Let me be the judge of that. Just enjoy it, Hope. I knew how much you liked it here the last time you were in N.I., and I wanted to bring you back and make it something special just for you. This is Chef Giovanni, by the way."

She stiffened at the name, and her eyes flew up to the chef's face. She seemed relieved when she laid eyes on the man, and then he smiled warmly at her.

"Hello, Miss Dawson," he greeted her. "I feel fortunate to have been able to prepare dinner for you this evening. My restaurant isn't too far down the beach, so the food hasn't traveled far from my kitchen. And anytime you want to stop by, you'll always be welcome."

Reed watched her while Giovanni explained the first course. Her reaction to Giovanni had been odd. Had she recognized the name? It seemed as if she had, but he could tell she didn't actually know the chef. She listened with interest as he explained their meal, and when he walked over to the curtained cart, where the food was served onto plates, her eyes once again found Reed's.

"This is the most amazing thing anyone had ever done for me," she said with certainty. "Thank you, Reed."

"You're welcome."

Giovanni brought them their soup, and Hope tasted it. She closed her eyes in delight and uttered a noise of pleasure that created the bulge in Reed's pants to harden uncomfortably. She was doing crazy things to his mind and his body, without even trying. And he could tell that she hadn't the first clue what a vixen she was.

He cleared his throat. "Tell me something."

"Anything," she said quickly. Then she recovered, and cut her eyes toward him across her bowl. "I mean, what do you want to know?"

"I want to know where you come from. Tell me about your family. You're different than any woman I've ever met, Hope, and I'm dying to know why."

She swallowed hard. He watched, fixated, as the delicate veins in her neck flexed with the movement. "What's so different about me?"

"I don't know, exactly. You're humble, for one thing. Girls as beautiful as you usually flaunt it, use it to get what they want."

She shook her head. "It's my exotic look. You country boys just aren't used to it, that's all. All this long, dark hair tends to drive you all a little crazy."

Her tone was teasing, and he grinned. "A lot of things about you drive me crazy. I can admit that. I'm hard as a rock under this table right now, and it's not because I'm not a master of self-control. It's you. It's everything about you."

He knew the rosy blush was coming, and smiled in response when it dawned like a brilliant sunrise on her face. "And that. You have a hard time reacting to it when I'm bold. Like you're not used to men showing you this kind of attention. And the way that you work with kids...and the way you are with Violet. You're almost like a mom to her. But you do have a mom, right?"

He was trying to slow down, trying not to bombard her with personal questions and his tumultuous emotions, but they were just rolling out of him like he couldn't control it. The desire to know everything about her was strong, pulling him like an ocean current. He couldn't help himself.

"I'm sorry," he said. "We're barely out of the first course, and I'm already getting personal. I'm used to just saying whatever the hell is on my mind. Just kick me if I'm too much."

Her foot nudged his calf under the table, and he chuckled. "Okay. Ask me something. Level the playing field."

Giovanni took away their empty soup bowls and placed salads in front of them. Hope nodded as she took a bite, chewing slowly.

He could watch her eat for hours. The way her jaw worked

each bite slowly and carefully through her mouth before she swallowed. Like she was savoring as much as she could for as long as she could. There was a crease in one of her cheeks that only showed when she smiled hugely, or when she chewed. Reed was mesmerized by it.

"I have a question," she said, breaking the spell that had him so frozen.

"Ask away."

"I know you play guitar and write music and sing, but what else do you do? Did you play sports in high school or college?"

He grinned. Hope was asking him questions about himself, and that made him very, very happy.

"Actually, yeah. I played tennis in high school, and I swam for my high school team and my college team."

She sat up straighter and her eyebrows rose. "You swim?" She glanced toward the ocean, and then back at him.

"I do. Why, do you?"

She nodded eagerly. "It's the only thing that helps all of the stress of the day just…fade away. I swim every single day. And I swam for my high school team, too, for a little while. Colleges were actually looking at me during my senior year, but I had to quit the team when we moved and I switched schools. Again."

Reed shook his head. "Wow, you must have been really good. What event did you do?"

"Two-hundred-meter butterfly and four-hundred-meter freestyle. I also anchored a couple of relays."

He tried not to look too impressed, but he was having an incredibly difficult time keeping his awe in check. "Why'd you have to move?"

She sighed. She stared thoughtfully into the distant sky, her brow furrowed slightly as she considered his question. Finally, she spoke. "My mom's pretty unstable. I mean, I think she has something consistent going now with my stepfather, Frank. But before that, she was all over the place. She's been married several times, and dated more men than I can count. I spent most of my childhood..."

Reed was leaning forward, and he frowned when she trailed off. "You spent most of your childhood what?"

She was staring down at her plate of food, but she was no longer taking small, sexy bites of salad. Just then, Giovanni appeared and asked if he could take their salad plates.

Reed nodded impatiently, waving the chef away. "Give us just a minute before you bring the main course, okay, Giovanni?"

The chef bowed and hustled their salad plates away to his cart.

Reed reached across the small sweetheart table and placed a finger under Hope's chin, raising it so that he could see her eyes. "What did you spend most of your childhood doing?"

She pulled back, and his hand fell away from her face. She shook her head, staring off into the distance once more, where stars were just beginning to dot the dark blue sky.

"I just don't want to ruin the beauty of this dinner by getting into my family problems," she finally said. "No offense, Reed, but you couldn't possibly understand my issues. Not coming from a family like yours."

Reed smiled wryly. "Oh, you think so?"

She shook her head, still not meeting his eyes.

"I'll agree to keeping the mood light, Hope. But don't mistake money for perfection where my family is concerned."

That earned him a startled glance, and he smiled sadly at her. "We're far from functional. Believe me."

He noted the doubt in her eyes. He gestured to the chef, who immediately appeared next to their table with plates of lobster.

"So," Reed mused around a bite of the deliciously tender shell-fish. "I swim every day, too. We're going to have to make plans to do a workout together sometime. Where do you swim?"

"In my stepfather's pool," she answered. She closed her eyes as she savored her meal, and he tensed. He had to physically keep himself glued to his seat. Hope sitting across from him with her eyes closed while her mouth worked to chew a bite of food just seemed like an invitation.

"I swim in the ocean," he remarked. "You ever try it?"

"I've splashed around in the ocean. But not for a workout."

"We'll have to change that."

After they finished their main course and shared a generous portion of chocolate cheesecake, dinner was over and they were both stuffed. Reed thanked Chef Giovanni and placed a hand on Hope's lower back as she also gave kudos to the chef. With an almost shy smile, she told him that it was the best meal she'd ever tasted. The sincerity in her voice warmed Reed from the inside out; he could pinpoint exactly where in his heart the heat began and identified each point of his body it spread to.

"Ready to go?" he asked her, leaning down to murmur in her ear. Her soft, sweet smell engulfed him.

"Where are we going?" she asked. She looked up to meet his gaze, and his nerves were immediately set aflame.

He turned her to face him but kept a tight grip around her waist. "You aren't ready to get rid of me yet?"

She slowly shook her head.

"Well, then," he drawled. "I guess I'm gonna take you to a little lookout spot I know."

She giggled. "Seriously?"

Hell yes. Seriously not wanting this date to end.

He guided her, minus the blindfold, back to the wooden bridge, where they rinsed off their feet at a spigot and replaced their shoes. It was fun to see her giggle as the water splashed between her toes. He made another mental note: Hope was very ticklish.

Thirteen

The morning following her date with Reed, Hope awoke on the surface of a pillowy white cloud. At least she felt like she did. She was still floating from the night before; her skin was aglow with the flush of happiness. As she sat up in bed and stared at herself in the mirror across from the bed, she couldn't remember the last time she looked as fresh and...hopeful. Like she was ready to take on the world in a bold, new way.

And it was all because of one date with a hot guy.

A guy who had treated her like a total goddess. His attentiveness was unreal—at least in Hope's mind it was. The way he looked at her, almost reverent, put her on a high no drug could ever compete with. She was literally giddy this morning, just thinking about him. And what was that feeling in her stomach? The jittery wings of butterflies? At just the thought of his name?

She looked down beside the bed, and her sky-high hopes plummeted when she saw Violet soundly sleeping, curled up into a ball, on the floor beside her.

She sighed. Violet stirred, and Hope nudged her gently with her foot.

"Again, Vi?"

With a groan, Violet rolled over on the white, fluffy rug and stared up at her sister. Her white-blond hair was barely mussed; its silky-smooth texture hardly allowed for a strand to be caught out of place.

"You know I can't do it, Hope," she said, her voice still groggy with sleep. "Sleep in that huge room by myself, propped up in that big-ass bed. It's like we're in that movie with all the alien wives. None of this shit is real. It will all disappear, and I'm not going to get used to sleeping in that kind of weird, parallel universe comfort. I'll take your floor over that bedroom any day."

Hope reached down to ruffle the younger girl's hair. It sliced right through her heart, hearing that Violet was unable to sleep in the comfortable bed sitting unused in the room Frank had had designated as hers when they moved into the mansion. She was right, of course. Wendy had never been in a relationship that lasted. And while Frank wasn't like the other stepfathers they'd had to endure—namely, he didn't put his hands on them, or drink too much, or snort cocaine on the coffee table—there was something about him that left Hope, and obviously Violet, deeply uncomfortable.

He seemed to say all the right things, and his business, for the most part, was on the legit side of the law. Although Hope knew that not all of the girls on the employee list for Silk were on the up-and-up, Frank's public rules were that it was simply a legitimate, upscale escort club, and that was it. What the girls did on their own time, Frank said, was up to them and had nothing to do with his company.

He treated their mother like a queen, and had never uttered an unkind word to Hope or Violet. But the girls had learned over the years exactly how to watch a man for signs of danger. And while Frank exhibited none of them, there was just something about his oily demeanor, about the way he hinted at the fact that he'd like Hope to be doing more for the business than she currently was, the fact that he speculated about how gorgeous Violet would be when she turned eighteen, the fact that rumors swirled around with the girls at Silk…he wasn't to be trusted. And he'd never once stopped Wendy from hurting Violet.

"Come on," Hope said, pulling her sister to her feet. "Time to get moving. Work for me and school for you."

Within forty-five minutes, Hope was dropping Violet off at school and heading to the Center for her long day of work.

At least it was work she considered rewarding.

She stepped out of her car, and a wolf whistle met her ears.

"Damn, girl," called Morrow as he strode toward her with two coffees in his hands. "From the looks of it, a date on Sunday night sure does agree with you on Monday morning."

And it was true that she'd taken a little more care with her appearance this morning than she normally did for a day at work. She worked with kids all day, so she was often known to rock jeans and her Chucks to work. But today she'd opted for red slacks, black ballet flats, and a sleeveless blouse that clung to her torso just the tiniest bit. Her hair was pulled back into a long, low ponytail and she wore a touch of bronzer and eye makeup.

"Thanks." She smiled. "Something made me want to dress up a little today."

Morrow rolled his eyes and grinned at her, showing off rows of shining white teeth. "Yeah? Could that something begin with an *R* and end with an *E-E-D*?"

She shrugged as she unlocked the door and they walked back to the office.

She settled in her desk chair and swiveled around until she faced Morrow, who was still leaning against the doorjamb with a knowing smirk sitting on his handsome face.

"Fine," she said, grinning. "It was amazing. Like, the most perfect date you could imagine, and then times that by twenty-five."

Morrow gave a low whistle. "So he pulled out all the stops?"

Hope nodded, a dreamy, faraway look in her hazel eyes.

"Good." Morrow nodded. "It's about time. And you deserve it."

"Yeah, maybe," answered Hope. "But, *God*, Morrow. Every time I think about it I feel like I might float away from the happiness and the hopefulness of it all, and then *bam!* I'm hit with the guilt. What I'm doing may be good for me, although it's not like I've ever seen a healthy relationship in my life and wouldn't even know where to start. But even if it is, it's not good for Violet. Reed is taking my focus off of putting away money for my sister and me. And the future I want to give her, that she deserves. And if Frank and Wendy found out about him…all hell would break loose."

Morrow nodded. "Yeah, it's a risk. But it's a risk you need to take, because it might be worth it. What if Reed is everything you ever wanted? What if he could even help you with the Violet situation?"

"What if he's the exact same man as every guy my mom ever dated or married?" Hope shot back.

"I think you'd already know if he was."

She sighed. "Time will tell."

She wasn't sure if Morrow was right. Reed was already seeming too good to be true. Didn't every man put his best foot forward in the beginning? She didn't know him well enough yet to know for sure whether he was truly as fantastic as he seemed to be.

She spent the rest of the morning working in her office, delegating different duties for Morrow to complete at a worktable in the corner, and the afternoon playing with and tutoring the kids who came to the Center for a full or half day in the summer months.

By four thirty, she was spent, and she was tired of checking her phone for a text or a missed call from Reed that never came.

Why hasn't he called today? Maybe he hadn't had a good time last night like she thought he had.

Is he wishing he'd never taken me out, or trying to avoid having to talk to me again?

Morrow was staying late to wait for a parent who'd neglected to pick up a child. He noticed how antsy she was acting, and practically ordered her to head home.

"A swim will clear that pretty head of yours," he insisted.

So she closed the door behind her and headed out into the parking lot in the muggy South Carolina evening.

She pulled her keys out of her purse as she walked, and a throat cleared just in front of her. She looked up, startled, and was instantly drowning in the sparkling blue abyss of Reed's eyes.

He leaned against her car with an easy, casual grace and looked good enough to taste in his slim brown pants, fitted button-down with the sleeves rolled up, and skinny tie. She noted the wide brown leather cuff present on his wrist, and smiled to herself. His father may have wanted him to present a certain look at the office, but he was always going to be Reed. She admired that about him.

She sighed with relief at the sight of him, and her face broke into a grin that nearly split her cheeks.

"Hey," she said as she pulled up short in front of him.

"Hey," he answered softly. His hands remained in his pockets, and she tried to hide a flash of disappointment that he wasn't pulling her into his arms.

He'd remained true to his word during the rest of their date and had kept his distance. He'd agreed not to make what they were doing completely physical, and he was taking it so seriously she was beginning to ache for the feel of his hands on her skin again, for the secure heaviness of his body pressed against hers.

"What are you doing here?" she asked a little breathlessly. Her wayward thoughts were causing her heart rate to accelerate in her chest.

He finally pushed off the car and stepped toward her. "I'm here because the Fourth of July is coming up this week. My parents throw a huge party every year. It's an all-day thing. During the daylight hours the people they know from the community and work come to network and discreetly get trashed while they talk business, and when the sun sets the younger crowd comes out to play."

"Oh," whispered Hope. Her breath was trapped in her lungs.

Reed watched her carefully. "Yeah. I had a good time with you last night, Hope. More than a good time, actually. And I wanted to know if you'd be my date for the party."

Hope studied him. "You could have called to ask me that, Reed."

He chuckled, and a lock of thick, dark hair fell against his forehead. She wanted to reach up and brush it away. His eyes were still staring so intently into hers she was having difficulty drawing a deep breath. "Yeah, I guess I could have. The truth?"

She nodded. Her heart was competing for a spot in the sprint medley at the Olympics, and her palms were growing damp with nervous sweat.

This is so absurd. Reed is a guy. I know guys like I know swimming. I need to calm the hell down.

Reed stepped closer and finally reached out to touch her. It was only one hand, but her eyelids fluttered as he grasped her chin firmly and stared down into her face. The strong, masculine grip sent her nerves into a frenzy and she clenched every muscle tightly to keep still.

"I missed you," he said, his voice low with sensuous heat. "I haven't stopped thinking about you since I dropped you off last night. I barely even touched you during that goddamn date and my fucking fingers are on fire with the memory of what it felt like to be wrapped around you. I needed to see you, so that I could stop feeling withdrawals from not being near you all day. I'm losing my ever-loving mind."

And with that, he stepped back, leaving a generous gap of distance between them that left her cold and hungry for his closeness again.

"So?" he said, his eyes flashing. "You wanna come?"

Finding her voice was difficult, but she managed it. "Yeah, Reed. I want to come to your family's party."

His face broke into a beautiful smile for the first time. "Is that all?"

"And..." she hedged. "I haven't stopped smiling since I left you and *Sharon* last night."

Now his rumbly laugh melted the doubt surrounding her heart, and she smiled at him in return.

"Who?" His blue eyes twinkled as he feigned innocence.

"Don't play that game with me," she said. "I *heard* you refer to her by name, remember?"

He shrugged. "I said I'd call her that until another woman entered my life who made me forget all about *Sharon*."

He bent and pressed a lingering kiss to her forehead. She sighed as his lips connected with her skin, and the chaste touch left a burning sensation when he pulled away.

"I'm glad to know you're as...affected...as I am," he said, his voice rough. "That's why I came here. I needed that."

"Glad to oblige." She breathed, struggling now in her effort to take in normal breaths through her lungs. Sharing air with Reed took away her ability to *be normal*. He affected her deep in her center, and she hated it and loved it at the same time. It was both exhilarating and terrifying.

He backed away, holding her gaze, and she was able to clutch her chest and take a breath. She noticed his truck parked on the other side of her car for the first time. As he rounded the corner of it, he winked at her and called over his shoulder as he turned.

"I'll call you later, gorgeous."

She nodded, and the truck roared to life. She stood there, staring, until he opened the passenger-side window, leaning over the center console to grin at her.

"Hope," he called, an eyebrow lifted.

"Yeah?"

"Get your sexy ass in your car. I was raised right. I'm not driving away until you do."

That broke her spell, and she nodded, a startled giggle breaking free. She got into her car and drove out of the lot, keeping Reed in her rearview mirror as she did so.

After one date with Hope, Reed knew he was standing in the deepest pile of shit possible.

He spent the entire next day thinking of nothing but the way her little red toenails curled into the sand, the way her petite, curvaceous body flowed like liquid in that long dress she wore, and how much he wished he had been able to feel that body pressed against him the way it had been in the past.

She was incredible in so many ways.

Reed felt as though he'd been an underweight boxer in a heavyweight fight, and he'd been knocked out with one perfectly complete punch.

And so the next day there was no way to stop himself from getting into his truck before the workday was even over, and driving over to see her. He'd never even been to the Center; he'd looked up the address online like a stalker and waited in the parking lot until she exited the building.

He felt like a crazy bastard. But after seeing her, he was a satisfied crazy bastard.

Take that back. He was far from satisfied, but seeing her, speaking to her, and knowing that she was in one piece alleviated some of the stress he was feeling at being so far away from her for the entire day.

He was losing his mind.

He loved it.

It scared the life out of him.

Fourteen

He'd never brought a date to the Fourth at the Hopewell ranch. He'd always been single, but he'd never ended up alone once the night was over. It was an occasion everyone in Nelson Island looked forward to every year, and each party went down in history as better than the one the year before.

He'd spent each day between their date and the party on the phone with Hope, or texting her. He couldn't stop. She was addictive. He'd even surprised her with lunch the day before at the Center, and she hadn't kicked him out the door.

The year Sam had arrived in town, Aston had fallen into the pool during the big event and ended up needing resuscitation. This year, Reed wouldn't be surprised if he were the one responsible for sending some poor asshole away in an ambulance. Hope would be in a bathing suit. And she didn't exactly belong to Reed, but he knew he'd be damned if any other dude there forgot she'd come with him.

When he arrived at her friend Morrow's to pick up Hope, he cursed under his breath. She and Morrow were sitting out on the front porch of his rental in the city, and she looked…she looked downright dangerous. More delectable than any woman had the right to look, especially when she was supposed to be someone's date and there would be other men present.

"Hope," he groaned as he jogged slowly up the porch steps. Both Hope and Morrow stood from their rocking chairs to greet him.

She looked self-consciously down at her outfit, and then back at him with a bewildered expression. "What? Is this not okay? Should I have dressed up more?"

He shook his head, disbelief filling his head. She really was clueless. Her white silky cover-up resembled a Grecian toga, only shorter. Her bronze skin glimmered in the sunlight and contrasted so starkly with the white of her little dress that Reed's breath caught in his lungs before he could exhale it. Her long hair, flowing gracefully from dark brown to light, hung free in deep waves that hit her hips in the back. A turquoise string snaked out of the top of the one-shouldered cover-up and wound around her neck. Reed's eyes lingered there as he imagined slowly untying the knot later with his teeth. She wore large brown earrings that jangled when her head turned and a brown cuff to match. He allowed his eyes to travel past the too-short hem of the dress down the smooth curves of her legs to where her brown sandals nervously tapped on the wood of the porch.

"Fuck *me*." He breathed.

Morrow laughed outright as he shot Hope an I-told-you-so glance. "She didn't believe me, man. Thanks for the, uh, blatant confirmation."

Hope glared at Morrow, and then aimed her steady gaze at Reed. "Is that supposed to be a compliment?"

Reed shook his head somewhat numbly to clear it, and then stepped up into Hope's personal space. He couldn't give two shits about the fact that her friend was standing right next to them—he needed to share air with her *now.*

"That's the best damn compliment I can come up with when I'm blindsided by that kind of view before I've even had my first drink of the day. *Damn*, girl. You just stole my breath from my lungs." He spoke closely enough to her ear that her shiver vibrated against his chest, and he was instantly hard in his swim trunks. Embarrassingly so. Only he didn't have the good sense to be the least bit ashamed.

She held her ground; she returned his stare, not backing away like he expected her to. She was reserved, but she wasn't afraid to go toe-to-toe with him. Turned on wasn't the right sentiment for how hot she was making him.

"Thanks," she whispered. "You haven't even seen me in my suit yet."

And there it was. The slight bit of rasp to her whisper and the blazing heat that flashed green in her eyes when she spoke those words was like a sledgehammer to the back of his knees, and he had trouble remaining upright. Luckily, Morrow slapped him on the shoulder, forcing him to stand up straighter.

"Morrow Mathis. Nice to meet you, bro."

Reed tore his eyes from Hope to meet Morrow's eyes. He held out his hand. "Reed Hopewell. It's nice to meet you, too."

Morrow cleared his throat and glanced quickly at Hope, then turned his gaze directly on Reed once more. "That night...the night you met her. In the alley? Thank you. For saving her. I would have murdered the dude if..." His voice trailed off and anger flashed in his eyes.

Reed nodded. He respected the man for caring about Hope enough to want to kick anyone's ass who hurt her. He understood the sentiment completely.

"I'd do it again," he answered honestly.

Morrow nodded solemnly, and a true sense of silent understanding passed between the two of them. Morrow was her friend, and Reed wanted to be so much more than that. But they both cared about Hope, so a bond was solidified.

"Have this girl here home at a decent hour," he said seriously. "She doesn't need the shit storm that comes with being late."

Mutual solidarity could only go so far. Hope's best friend was a virile, attractive, *straight* guy. Reed knew that they went way back and that their closeness was something he would have to get used to. But a tingle of irritation stuck him in the neck with Morrow's warning. Why was he picking her up here in the first place? She had a home. And why was he warning her about a curfew like she was sixteen instead of twenty-two?

"Got it," he answered. "Ready to go, Hope?"

Morrow chuckled and turned away.

She nodded to Morrow. "I'll be fine."

Reed stood at the bottom of the steps and held out his hand

to her as she descended. He put her in the truck and climbed behind the wheel.

"Question," he said as they began the drive toward the island.

"Yes?"

"Why Morrow's? What's the deal with me picking you up at home?"

She shrugged, looking uncomfortable. She didn't meet his eyes, which bothered him more than he wanted to admit.

"My parents are the last thing I want to subject you to," she finally answered.

"Why don't you just move out?"

She sighed. "I won't leave Violet."

He nodded, mulling it over. It seemed like an impossible situation. But he was sure that once they put their heads together about it, they could figure it out. If her parents bothered her that much, she shouldn't have to stay with them.

When he pulled onto Hopewell property and began the long drive up the paved path that led to the estate, Hope blew out a breath. Awe dawned across her face.

"What?" he said with a smirk, glancing at her. "Your stepdad's house is a mansion in its own right."

"I didn't grow up there," she said quietly. She gazed rapturously out the window as they continued. The property was lush; magnolia trees lined the driveway, and there was brightly colored greenery for acres beyond the driveway and the house. The stables and the horses weren't visible from here, but the estate was impressive enough without them.

"Where did you grow up?"

"In Charleston," she said vaguely.

He didn't want to push her, but he could hear that melancholy edge to her voice that appeared when she hinted about her past or the life she shared with her mother and her sister. It grated against his heart, and a coiled tightness pressed down hard on his chest when he glanced at the somber expression gracing her flawless face. Her profile nearly snapped his chest cavity in two open pieces, and then she turned quietly anguished eyes on him. His foot came down hard on the brake involuntarily, and he slammed the truck into park.

"Talk to me, Hope," he said, turning to face her. "I want to know."

"Want to know what?" she asked, her voice barely reaching his eardrums.

"What's making your face do that? I can't take it. You're too beautiful to be that sad."

"I'm not sad," she said bravely. "I swear I'm not. I just didn't grow up like you, that's all. You should feel lucky. Do you?"

He didn't miss the fact that she'd turned a question onto him, but he contemplated it anyway. He supposed he felt lucky for all the opportunities he'd been allowed because of his parents' prosperity. He knew he was lucky to have a sister who'd looked out for him and taken the brunt of the emotional baggage his parents' difficult marriage had inflicted on them both. But he didn't always feel lucky that his life's choices had never really been his own.

"Sure," he answered. "I feel lucky, most of the time, for what I've got. But that doesn't mean I can't empathize with someone who didn't have the same things."

"It's not just that I grew up poor, or that we didn't always know when our next meal was coming, or whether we'd make rent that month, or whatever. The poor part, I could handle. It was everything else my mother subjected me to, what she still subjects my sister to, that was the hard pill to swallow."

She gulped, as if she were still trying to swallow it, and then shot him another sad smile. "You know what? That's a story for another day. Today is a celebration, right? Independence and all that? Let's go."

He stared at her another minute before throwing the truck back into drive. He had a feeling, with her "independence" statement, that she wasn't feeling very free at all in her life. And he was going to find out why if it damn near killed him.

Because he could tell from the time he'd spent with her she was worth the work it would take to figure her out.

When they finally rounded the large house, walking hand in hand up the slate-stone walkway that led to the perfectly manicured backyard pool area, she gasped in surprise.

The place was decorated festively to the max. His mother surpassed herself every year, and the pool area was immaculate. There was smooth, gray stone surrounding the area beside the kidney-shaped pool, and a tent stood off to one side, sweeping white curtains held open with large red cloth fashioned into bows. A tiki bar had been set up inside, and guests were filing in and out of it with red and blue drinks in their hands. A row of loungers surrounded each side of the pool, and Reed pointed out Aston and Sam to his date.

"This is sick," she murmured. "I mean, in the best possible way."

"Yeah." He smiled. "It always is. Drink?"

She nodded, and he walked her over to the chair next to Aston. "A, you remember Hope. Hope, this is my sister, Aston. And her fiancé, Sam."

Hope smiled tentatively. "It's nice to see you again. We didn't really get to meet that night at the banquet."

"No, we didn't," said Aston, sticking out her hand. "I'm Reed's attack dog of an older sister. Nice to meet you."

"Easy, A," warned Reed.

"Oh, I'm just messing with her," said Aston, wafting one hand breezily in the air. "I'll be nice. Promise."

Reed looked unsure. Sam clasped Aston's hand in his and nodded to Reed. "Go get your girl a drink. I got this."

Reed was more comfortable with that. He trusted Sam implicitly, but Aston really was somewhat of a pit bull with other women. It could be that Reed usually only brought women he'd slept with on the first night, or was planning on sleeping with that night, around his sister while they were out at Sunny's.

But Hope was different, and Aston should already be able to see that.

He squeezed Hope's hand and leaned down to kiss her cheek. Her sweet scent practically begged him to stay. Swallowing, he went off in search of drinks in the tent. That was where, not surprisingly, he found the rest of his friends.

"Dammit, Reed," cursed Tate. "Why'd you make us get here so damn early this year? This shit is beyond boring until the sun goes down."

"Dude," Reed said with a laugh. "It's six o'clock. The sun will be down soon."

Tate grumbled, taking a swig of Corona. "Whatever. There's no women here yet."

Blaze's booming laugh filled the tent. "You need to get some glasses, Oliver. There're plenty of women. Just none that don't already know your game."

Tate looked extremely put out. Reed hadn't taken inventory of the female population of the party when he'd arrived like he normally would have. There was just no need to look at other women when Hope was around. It was an alien concept for him, but he wore it well.

"So, Reed," Tamara cut in, speaking for the first time.

Reed turned his attention on the redhead. She looked gorgeous, as usual. She was the girl next door with her coppery hair and light dusting of freckles, and her fair skin shone in the dim light of the tent. She was sipping a Corona just like her twin, and her lime-green bikini and matching sarong complemented her hair and skin perfectly.

"You brought Hope?"

He nodded, and Tate looked at him in surprise. He hadn't told Tate he was bringing her; he didn't want to deal with his shit about not bringing a date and all of that.

"You're fucking kidding me, right?" was Tate's flabbergasted response.

Reed held up a hand, and continued to look at Tamara. "Yeah. Getting her a drink. You okay?"

She nodded. Reed had a fleeting thought that he really needed to introduce her to some good guys. Then he realized that he didn't know any, other than the ones she already knew on the island.

Reed grabbed two rum and Cokes and turned to head out of the tent. "Y'all come on out here and hang out with us after you get a buzz going. Or before, in your case, Tate."

He headed back out of the tent, immediately searching for Hope's stunning form across the pool.

He found it all right, and she was staring up into the eyes of a guy he'd seen around the office but didn't know very well. Reed's eyes zeroed in on the man in question. He thought his name was Brent, maybe. He took in the hand that was resting lightly on Hope's knee from the lounge chair next to hers. Brent was leaning forward, and she was now looking down at his hand and frowning.

Reed's vision changed from perfectly clear and normal to a sharp, focused red, and the background noise of the party died down with the loud rush of blood pulsing in his ears.

His reaction was immediate, and primal. And definitely a little psychotic.

I'm gonna fuck Brent up.

Fifteen

Aston was actually being cordial. Hope had a completely different expectation of her than what she was getting. The girl could be the perfect definition of the phrase "Ice Queen." Her long, dark hair never had a strand out of place, and her tall, thin body was the same size and shape as a supermodel. Her skin was blemish free, and she rocked a tiny red bikini harder than anyone Hope had ever seen in her life. Her blue eyes were a shade darker than Reed's, and where his were warm and inviting with a hint of mischief, hers were icy and gave nothing away.

But Aston was being…nice. So Hope was happy that she could get along with a member of Reed's family. And Sam was just adorable. Like a big, hard teddy bear. A gorgeous one with a sexy tattoo across his stomach, but still a teddy bear all the same.

Suddenly, someone new popped into their little party. He swooped in, all white teeth and spiky blond hair and sly smile, and Hope looked to Aston with apprehension.

Aston rolled her eyes and shot Hope a what-are-ya-gonna-do look, and the guy introduced himself as working in the same office as Aston and Reed. His name was Brent, and he seemed harmless enough. Until his hand found itself resting on her knee.

The seemingly innocent touch jolted her upright, and she stared down at his hand in disbelief. In Silk, she was used to men taking liberties with her they normally wouldn't. Because they were paying for their time spent with her, and they expected to get their money's worth.

But here, in the free world where she had a choice, she never, ever let a man she didn't know touch her. And she was just opening her mouth to tell Brent as much, when suddenly Reed was beside her and in Brent's face.

"Hey. Did the lady ask you to touch her?"

Brent lips formed a seductive smile that he aimed at Hope. "Not yet. I was hoping that would come later. Why, Hopewell? You got first dibs?"

Reed's face darkened. "You're done here. Time to get out, Brent."

Brent shrugged, turning to face Hope. He rested a hand on her hip. "I'm gonna avoid the drama and get out of here. You want to come with—"

He was cut off as Reed's fist connected with his jaw. Brent's head snapped back at the impact, his hair falling forward over his forehead.

Small gasps and a couple of startled cries cut the air around them as Reed stood in front of Brent, who was now rubbing his jaw. He turned his head to the side and spit a mouthful of blood onto the gray, shiny stone at his side.

"What the hell, man?" he asked angrily. His voice was muffled due to the quick swelling of his jaw.

"If you touch her again I'll do more than just break your jaw. You hear me?"

Hope's mouth dropped. She stared at Reed, who was glaring ferociously at Brent, his chest heaving and his fists clenched by the sides of his black swim trunks. The tattoos winding their way up his arms flexed intimidatingly.

"I didn't know she was here with you!" protested Brent. He sounded angry but also a little scared. Reed clearly outranked him at work, and apparently hit harder than a freight train outside of the office.

Hope had seen enough. She stood, gulping a deep breath, and walked as calmly as she could manage to the tent where the drinks were being served. She dipped inside, letting out a gust of air in the much cooler darkness of the curtained space.

"Well, that was something," a soft drawl said next to where she stood leaning against the bar.

She turned to look, and a statuesque redhead stood nonchalantly next to her, a slim white cigarette hanging from her mouth.

"That'll kill you," said Hope automatically.

"Well, *something* will," said the redhead with a roll of her eyes. She took a long drag, and then put the cigarette out with a grind of her heel into the floor. "I'm Tamara. Longtime friend of Reed and Aston. My brother and Reed are roommates."

"Oh," said Hope, startled. She should have known. She'd only seen Tate that one time in the truck the night she met Reed, but he and Tamara looked so similar it was striking. "Are you twins?"

"You win a prize," said Tamara with a good-natured smile. Her sultry voice was making Hope's eyelids droop. The girl should really have a job as a nine-hundred-number operator.

"You saw what happened?" asked Hope with a sigh. "That was kind of embarrassing. And kind of..."

"Hot?" Tamara suggested. "Yeah. Reed in a nutshell. I've never seen him do that over a girl before though. So what'd you do to him?"

A smile tugged at the corner of Hope's lips, and she tried hard to mask it with a clearing of her throat. "What did I do to make him act like an insane person? Um, I don't know."

"That wasn't insane," scoffed Tamara with a wave of her beautifully manicured hand. "That was possessiveness. There's a difference. When you're dealing with a man like Reed, who knows exactly how to get what he wants and has no trouble exhibiting power except with maybe his father, that's the kind of pure, testosterone-driven reaction you're going to get if he thinks of you as his."

Does Reed think of me as his? Oh, God...

"Give us a second, Tam." Reed's voice shivered up Hope's spine as he appeared at her elbow.

Tamara nodded, and shot Hope a wink as she vacated the tent.

Reed leaned casually on the bar beside her, as if he hadn't just nearly broken a man's jaw for touching her. One half of her was horrified that a man could react like that in response to another male merely resting a hand against her skin. She'd never been the girl to have someone feel possessive over her. She'd never let any man get close enough to feel that way about her. How had Reed snuck in so close?

The other half of her still had tremors running along her skin due to the excitement and pure, nature-driven desire Reed had given her when he'd punched Brent. He'd hit him because he touched her.

Me.

She didn't know which of her two sides would win, but she could guess. Especially when Reed's liquid blue pools met hers.

"I should apologize," he said quietly. "For making a scene. For embarrassing you. I'm sorry."

She waited, tingling beginning to pulsate in her toes.

"But I'm not sorry I hit the pathetic bastard. I'd hit him again. Even if I hadn't brought you here, he had no right to touch you without your permission. And the fact that you're here with me means he doesn't get away with it. End of discussion."

"Oh, were we having a discussion? Because I thought you were just telling me how it was going to be."

He smirked at her. "Is there something you want to say?"

The tingling was now radiating through her legs, causing them to wobble slightly. Reed stared so intently into her eyes it was getting difficult to draw in the already stifling air around her. *Dammit! If those eyes weren't so piercing then maybe I could think straight.*

"I don't want a caveman in my life," she finally said. "I've met plenty of those. Actually lived with a few. It never works out well, in the end."

"I see," he murmured, entering her space. He twisted around so that he could place his hands on either side of her, bracing himself against the bar as he stared down. His dark eyebrows rose slightly, and one tendril of dark hair drifted down over his forehead. "And what part of their caveman behavior turned you off the most? Was it the fact that they'd do anything to protect you? Was it the fact that they'd beat anyone's ass who decided it was worth it to touch you? Was it that they put you and your safety first, above everything else?"

Now the air was entirely gone. His words had sucked the life out of the too-thin oxygen around her, and she was suffocating. Her feet were slipping on what felt like thin ice beneath her, and she was drowning in the blue depths of his gaze.

"No," she whispered.

"Hmm?" he asked, unblinking. "What was that?"

She closed her eyes, and the pressure of his finger on her chin forced her to open them again. To meet his stare head-on without relief. "I said *no*. None of that was what those men did for my mother...or me."

He continued to stare at her. "So, when you say caveman, you aren't referring to me. That was them. And this is *us*. Got it?"

She attempted to take a breath again, and failed. She just nodded.

Reed smiled, just a slight quirk of his full lips that had her nibbling on her lower one to keep from leaning forward. "Say you get it. So we won't have any misunderstandings about where I'm coming from."

Her knees knocked together. One of Reed's hands left the bar to wrap securely around her waist, effectively keeping her from collapsing into a puddle on the floor.

"I understand," she whispered, unable to look away.

She'd told him she wanted them to take away the physical portion of their…whatever this was. She badly wanted to retract that statement now. Because more than anything in the entire universe, more than water, more than food, more than *breath*, she needed him to kiss her.

He was reading every page of her need in her eyes; she could see his flashing a darker blue as he took it in. And the battle that went on in his expression as his innermost thoughts played out right in front of her. He sighed. And pushed back a step.

"Your drink is waiting at your seat, beautiful," he said with a slight bow. "And I took out the trash, so now you can sip it in peace."

With a *whoosh* all the air she'd been missing filled up her lungs. She released it slowly, counting to five internally.

"Thank you," she finally said. And she knew that *he* knew it wasn't just for the drink.

Sixteen

After the sun sank below the horizon, sending black shadows dancing across the glittering water of the pool, and crimson uplighting cast a hazy, red glow on everything, the atmosphere of the pool party really changed.

"We're off to bed, darlings," said Lillian Hopewell, hugging both Reed and Aston.

She turned to Hope, smiling warmly. "So nice to meet you, Hope. You've turned my little rebel upside down, I can see that. Keep up the good work!"

Hope smiled a genuine smile. It had been interesting meeting Reed's parents. They were the classic southern couple. Impeccable manners, sweet-natured personalities. They were clearly madly in love, but she'd had the impression from Reed that their relationship hadn't been the healthiest when he was younger. She wondered what that was all about, now that she had met them. The relationship between Reed and his father was definitely strained, but not alarmingly so.

Gregory bid them good night and followed his wife into their stunning home. As soon as the doors shut behind them, Tate let out a whoop.

"Let the real party begin!" he shouted.

Hope laughed with the rest of them.

Hope noticed as she looked around that everyone remaining at the party was probably under thirty. Some coworkers from Hopewell Enterprises (with Brent definitely missing), some of the friends that Aston and Reed grew up with, and some new friends they'd met along the way, all gathered to party out the rest of the patriotic holiday.

Tamara brought over a tray of shot glasses laden with golden liquid from the bar, and everyone in their small circle took one.

"Cheers to this being a life-changing summer for all of us?" suggested Tamara.

Everyone nodded and threw the shot back. Hope followed the burning liquid with a squirt of lime juice and a lick of salt from her wrist and sighed. She'd always had Morrow, but a group of friends to let loose with like this? Never. She suddenly wished she'd brought Morrow along with her. He would have really enjoyed the party and the people.

Next time.

"There's something I wanted to run by you," said Reed, tugging on her hand as he pulled her aside. The shot was beginning to unburden itself in her system, and she was feeling extra hot in the sultry night and the steamy heat that Reed seemed to give off whenever he was near her.

She looked up at him and cuddled in closer to where he stood. He smiled down at her.

"Shoot," she said.

"Next week, after the long weekend is over, I have to go out of town for a few days."

Well, that was a bummer. She hadn't been expecting that. She also didn't expect the deep wave of sadness that crashed over her when she realized she'd be far away from him for a length of time.

"Oh." She frowned. "Okay. For work?"

"Not exactly," he said, his eyes trained on her. "I've been invited to Atlanta by a producer. Someone who wants to cut a few songs with me, feel me out. He works with some pretty well-known labels."

Reed shrugged, cool on the surface, but she could tell from the tense set of his mouth that this meant something to him. Something big.

"That's amazing!" she said. "Oh, my God, Reed. You'll do great. I wish you all the luck in the world! Really."

He nodded, toying with her hands now in his lap. He'd towed her into one of the lounge chairs, and her legs were slung over the top of his long ones. "I want you to come with me."

Her breath caught in her throat, but she kept her tone measured and even as she answered, "You do?"

"Well, yeah. I kinda don't want to put a pause button on what we have going here. I like spending time with you. Do you have time you can take off of work?"

She did have time she could take off work. She never vacationed, and she knew that Morrow being there for the summer meant all her slack would be completely taken care of.

But what would she tell Wendy and Frank? And could she leave Violet for so long?

"I could," she said slowly, rolling her ankles absently as she thought about it. "I might just need to get some things situated with my family first. Could I let you know tomorrow?"

He nodded. "Sure."

She noted his frown but didn't ask why he wore it. *I'd rather not encourage the questions.*

Instead she stood up and untied the shoulder knot on her cover-up. "I think we're way past due for a swim, don't you? Remember all that talk about being able to beat me in the water?"

She let the white cloth drop to the chair behind her, and Reed's blue eyes grew wide.

The bathing suit she sported was of the tiny variety. A one-piece, with cutouts in very strategic places. She liked the way his pupils dilated when he let his eyes run the length of her body and back up again. She kicked off her sandals and stepped over to the edge of the pool, poised to dive into the water. Reaching up to tie her hair up in a messy knot, she narrowed her eyes at him.

"We doing this, Hopewell?" she asked, a playful lilt hanging on the edge of her voice.

Reed was sitting frozen in the lounge chair. As she stared at him, awaiting his competitive response, he tilted his head to the side. His mouth hung open slightly, and she wished she could bottle the moment up and save it. Or at least take a picture of

Reed's face the first time he saw her in a swimsuit. It belonged in a frame.

"You...have a tattoo?" he asked in a hoarse voice.

Her hand automatically rubbed at the spot on the back of her neck. Reed had only seen her with her hair down prior to this point. She turned around so that he could see the script.

THE CAGED BIRD SINGS

When she turned around again, Reed was silently appraising her with some kind of emotion in his eyes she couldn't read correctly if she tried. So she didn't. She inclined her head toward the pool instead.

He stood and ripped off his white tee. She swallowed hard at the sight of his sculpted chest and the rippling abdominals beneath it. His broad shoulders were even wider than she thought from beneath his shirts, and the sinewy muscles flexed fluidly as he stretched his arms over his head and walked over to join her poolside. His plain black trunks hung low on his slender waist, and the taut V of muscular perfection just above his hips suddenly caused her mouth to feel dry.

He met her eyes as he pulled up beside her, and she wet her lips. His eyes flashed dark blue.

"Oh, we're doing this." His voice was full of meaning she understood perfectly, and the frantic fluttering in her stomach intensified.

She dived in before they could establish a start for their race, and she heard his responding splash when she surfaced a second later.

They swam easily together, side by side, each keeping an eye on where in the water the other was. They ended up swimming an easy five laps, and emerged panting and laughing from the pool some minutes later.

"You're good," he said admiringly as he grabbed her hands to pull her easily out of the pool. "Really good."

"That's what happens when you practice every day," she said with a shrug.

He produced a white, fluffy towel from an adjacent lounge table and wrapped it around her, pulling her close. So close she could feel the heat from the night, or from Reed himself, growing between them.

"The more I get to know, the more I like," he said, his voice soft. It nearly blended into the croak of the bullfrogs in the shrubbery all around the yard, and she leaned in closer to hear him.

"Ditto," she answered. "Reed…I want to go to Atlanta with you. I'll try and find a way."

A grin spread lazily across his face. "All I had to do was swim against you? Hell, girl, we can swim together every day if it means I get what I want."

She smacked him on the chest, and the hardness of it resounded against her hand.

She stayed close to him for the rest of the party, so close that she'd committed the hard planes and lines of his torso to memory by the end of the night. Through the stunning display of fireworks closing out the evening, she stared up at the sky, appreciating the bright bursts of light and cannonlike thumps as Reed's hands trailed along her skin and sent repeated shivers of pleasure tingling along her shoulders.

Yeah, she was going to risk everything to make the trip with him next week. And he was making it so damn hard to feel guilty about it.

Something about Hope made Reed want to show up at all of her places on a daily basis, just to check on her. If he was being completely honest with himself, it would be more to mark his territory, to let all of the people she crossed paths with every day know that she was his.

Which was absurd, because she wasn't his. Not yet. And Reed knew enough to know that trying to make that happen would be like stamping the death certificate of whatever it was they shared. A commitment? That would ruin everything. She hadn't even given him a surefire signal that she was interested in a relationship. All he knew was that the more time he spent with her, the more unsteady his heart felt when he was away from her. She was beginning to affect his daily life, and he had no idea if that was a good thing or a terrible mistake.

"Come on, man," complained Tate. He groaned as he pushed the set of barbells toward the ceiling.

Reed stared down at his friend, his fingertips barely touching the ends of the weight Tate was currently pushing skyward. He knew this conversation was coming, and he didn't need Tate's permission to take the girl he couldn't get out of his mind on a trip. But he ran his plans by his friend anyway, against his better judgment.

"You're going to Atlanta, a way bigger city than this, and you're going to a fucking *music producer's* house to cut songs. You're gonna be in every man's paradise, and you're tying a weight around your ankle? What the fuck is wrong with your ass?"

Tate finished his tirade in a grunt of exhaustion as he let the weights drop to the floor beside the bench. They often caught a workout together in the gym at their condominium community, and today Reed had decided to mar their usually relaxed time together with the bomb about taking Hope to Atlanta with him.

"Look, man, I don't expect you to understand. But have you seen Hope? How the hell would I be able to screw around with other women when I have someone like her just waiting on me back here? Huh?" Reed ran his hands agitatedly through his hair, because he was fearful that Tate was right. Never in his life had he turned down an opportunity for an easy fuck and a good time. Never. But somewhere in the back of his mind he knew that even if he didn't bring Hope with him, he wouldn't be cruising downtown Atlanta on pussy patrol with the music execs.

Maybe a few months ago. But not now.

"God," said Tate, staring at him. "You've turned into a female, Reed. And I mean that in the worst possible way. You're going to turn down a chance at *groupie* pussy in order to come home to the *same old* piece of ass you banged the night before."

Reed busied himself with taking off his weight-lifting gloves and setting them carefully on the bench next to him, not meeting Tate's disbelieving gaze and not saying a word.

"Wait a goddamned minute," said Tate, his voice rising. When Reed still didn't look up, Tate let out a slew of curses.

"You tell me, right the fuck now, that you aren't bringing Hope with you to Atlanta on the off chance that she *might* fuck you, because you haven't actually nailed the chick to a bed yet. You tell me that *right now*."

Reed was silent, although his face was beginning to darken at the manner in which his friend was talking about Hope.

Tate raised his head to the ceiling and howled with laughter. "Now I know you've lost it. You've *lost it*, man. Your balls, my respect, all your damn marbles. What the fuck?"

"Shut the hell up," said Reed defensively. "You've seen her. She's the most gorgeous girl I've ever met. Of course sex was all that was on my mind when I first saw her. But then I walked in on that first situation I got her out of, and after that she was already different. It's not like I haven't been physical with her at all, but we mutually decided to lay off the sexual stuff. And now…fuck."

He let his head fall into his hands, his elbows resting on his knees. His fingers pulled at the strands of his hair with painful intensity as he ran over his relationship with Hope in his mind.

"Now I couldn't go anywhere if I tried. I take three cold showers a day, man, just because I remember what it's like to touch her bare skin and kiss those damn full lips. I'm turning into a fucking pussy, and I *like* it. I don't want anything else. Any*one* else."

Now Tate's expression was just comical. His mouth was hanging open in amazement, his wide green eyes staring intensely at Reed.

"Forget it, Tate," mumbled Reed. "I should be talking to Sam about this. Or Blaze."

Tate shook his head quickly. "Naw, man. I….I get it. I don't think I'll ever know what that feels like, but I get it. It's sad you haven't even bagged her yet to see if she's worth it, but *shit.* I never thought I'd see the motherfucking day."

Reed sighed. "Me, neither. And I swear to God, if you talk about her like that again, I'm going to smash one of these weights into your ugly face, roommates be damned."

Tate laughed. "My bad, man. Old habits."

Seventeen

It was an extreme stroke of luck. Wendy and Frank were going to Florida for a long weekend away, and their trip would overlap two of the days Hope would be gone. She spoke to the lead member of the housekeeping staff about Violet, ensuring that the woman would stay with Violet while Hope was gone.

"I'm going to be fine, you know," gasped Violet as she dragged Hope's huge rolling suitcase down the hardwood hallway toward the foyer.

"I know that," answered Hope, biting a strand of hair nervously. She swallowed down the guilt she'd been wrestling with over leaving Violet for a few days. "I had a long conversation with Maggie about it and she's on top of things. It's only going to be three days, sweetie. Just try and stay out of Wendy and Frank's way, and call or text me if you need anything."

"Yeah, yeah," scoffed Violet. "I can't believe you're doing this. It's so un–Hope-like."

Her devilish grin pulled a smile to Hope's lips. "'Un–Hope-like'? Well, maybe it's time for a little bit of that, don't you think?"

"Hells yes!" was Violet's resounding response.

Hope rolled her eyes. The roar of a V-8 engine outside drew her attention, and Violet laughed dryly. "There's your knight now."

Hope practically ran to the door, flinging it open to find a road-trip-ready, breath-stealing Reed jogging up the front steps.

"Hey," he said. He held open his arms, and she was drawn into them like a magnet.

"Hey," she said happily.

"Ready to go?"

She pulled back and gestured toward her stuff: her large suitcase and a smaller toiletry bag containing her bathroom supplies and makeup.

"That's it?"

She stared at her bag, and then back at Reed with disbelief in her eyes. "Isn't that enough?"

He nodded, laughing. "I lived with Aston for eighteen years. I tend to expect all women to be as high maintenance as she is. For a trip like this? She would have had three bags the size of your case and at least two for makeup."

Hope could only imagine what packing for a three-day trip would look like for Aston. She shuddered at the thought.

"What's up, Violet?" asked Reed. He walked over to the thirteen-year-old and held out his fist. She bumped it, and they made their fingers splay out in a faux explosion.

"Well, you probably are, judging from your reaction at the sight of my sister," answered Violet with casual grace.

"Vi!" exclaimed Hope. But Reed was doubled over in laughter. When he recovered, he shook his head at Violet.

"You're a dangerous one," he said with a wink. "You know way too much."

Violet sighed. "That's what they tell me. That's why they keep shoving my ass into these gifted classes at school. I keep telling them my gifts have nothing to do with academics, but they won't listen."

"Okay, Mouth," said Hope loudly. She stepped over to Violet and squeezed the girl to her in a big hug. "Love you. Paint me something pretty. Call me every three hours."

Violet rolled her eyes. "That's not happening, Hope."

"I know."

Hope climbed into the truck while Reed loaded her luggage under the cover in the back, and then they were on the road.

She glanced over at him as he drove. He was gripping the steering wheel with both hands, his eyes fixed firmly on the road ahead. Was he regretting his decision to bring her along? She'd never seen him so tense during any of their time together.

"Regrets?"

He glanced her way, jumping a little at the word. "What?"

"You're looking like you ate something that didn't agree with you. We're still in Charleston. We can turn back to my house if you want."

Now the wrinkles between his eyebrows creased together. "Why would I want that, Hope?"

She sighed. "Why wouldn't you? I'm not an idiot, Reed.

You're a musician, right? I know what musicians do on the road. And I'll definitely cramp your style. Plus, we haven't known each other but a couple of months. Too soon for a trip together, maybe? I totally get it."

She hadn't taken a breath during her spiel, so she sat back against the seat, trying to force the air to enter and exit her lungs properly. And trying to calm her pounding heart, which was threatening to shatter itself into pieces when he gratefully turned the truck around.

And the truck slowed, pulling over onto the shoulder and rolling to a stop. Hope closed her eyes.

"Look at me, Hope," Reed's voice ordered gently but firmly.

She opened her eyes and looked over at him. He was facing her completely and lifted the console between them to reach out and grasp both of her hands in one of his. A tremor reverberated through her mind and her chest as he squeezed them.

"Listen," he said, melting into her gaze. "I asked you to come with me because I couldn't imagine spending three days in a state different from the one you were in. That hasn't changed. I'm thanking my stars you agreed to come with me. I'm just sitting over here wondering why you did. We aren't... we're not... damn. I guess what I'm trying to say is that I want you with me. I'm just nervous as hell about fucking it up. I do that a lot, you know. Fuck things up. Just ask my dad."

She freed one of her hands to reach out to his face. He was warm, and his breathing was coming fast and heavy. His cheeks flushed as he looked at her, and she could see clearly that he was wide open to her, a state that he wasn't used to owning. And her heart slowed in her chest at the realization that he was just as scared about all of this as she was.

"I'm here because I want to be," she said. "And I didn't want to let you go without me. I would have missed you, Reed."

He leaned forward, so slowly she thought his muscles must have been aching with the effort, and she thought that he was finally going to kiss her again. She leaned forward slightly in anticipation, and her face grew warm at his nearness. He grazed his lips softly, painfully soft, against her chin and pulled back. It had only been a second, but she felt how warm and moist those lips were and she wasn't at all happy to see them withdraw back to their own space.

He started the truck and pulled back onto the road. This time, one hand was relaxed on the wheel and one was loosely gripping hers. His face was visibly more relaxed, but now she was the one on the edge of a cliff.

She'd slowed down their physical progression with just a few words, and he was taking it to heart. No matter what happened, Reed wasn't going to make a move until she told him to.

Shit. Damn morals are biting me in the ass.

They spent the drive together full of restless energy, talking about anything and everything. The four hours were filled with stories of Reed's childhood and how he and Aston were total opposites in almost every way except for how fiercely they loved each other. She told him about how she felt about Violet, and how she had tried her best to protect her from their mother's bad decisions over the years. She left out the parts where she would hustle the little girl to her room, passing men strung out from cocaine or heroin on their threadbare couch, and shielded her from many a beating given by a stepfather or angry, drunk boyfriend of Wendy's. She stepped in front of her sister more than once to field a blow to the face or body, and Wendy would scream at them to just get the hell out of the room.

It was glaringly different from the way Reed had obviously been raised, but when he grazed across the story of his parents' marriage, she could hear the edge of sadness in his voice. She didn't really understand what had happened, but it had hurt Reed. Maybe not physically, the way she had been hurt, but deeply inside of his heart and his soul. It had shaped him, had formed him into the man he was today and clearly affected the way he went about relationships, or didn't.

"So," she asked at one point. "When was your last serious relationship?"

He looked chagrined. "I've never had one."

She nodded thoughtfully, and he looked at her in surprise. "What, no shock? No grilling? Nothing?"

She shook her head, and he narrowed his eyes.

"Hope? When was your last serious relationship?"

She just stared at him, and he blew out a breath. "Whew. We're quite the fucked-up pair, aren't we?"

All she could do was nod.

When they arrived in Atlanta, Hope stared out her window in awe at the hugeness of the bustling city. Charleston was no small town, but it had nothing on the big-city vibe that downtown Atlanta offered. As they drove down Peachtree Street, tall buildings surrounded her; they passed large hotel chains and worldwide restaurant brands that she'd only seen on television. Reed caught her hungry intake of everything around her and squeezed her hand.

"You ever been here before?"

She shook her head. "Truth?"

He nodded solemnly. "Truth."

"I've never been out of Charleston. Well, except to go to Nelson Island with you."

He nodded casually, the tight way he held his jaw and the way he compulsively squeezed her hand in his letting her know he was floored by her revelation. "Glad your first time was with me."

She smiled. "Me, too."

He pulled into the garage at the Four Seasons, and the massive size of the glimmering, shining building intimidated her to no end. She held his hand as they walked into the glittering lobby and up to the check-in desk. He pulled out his credit card and addressed the attendant behind the counter.

"Reed Hopewell."

The young woman with elegant blond hair piled onto her head smiled brightly at Reed, ignoring Hope completely. "Of course, Mr. Hopewell. Mr. Castille has booked your suite and it's all ready for you. Shall I send someone to your car for the luggage?"

"Nah, I can bring it in," said Reed. He looked at Hope and raised a dark eyebrow. "Should I get you your own room?"

The woman behind the counter finally glanced at Hope, a hopeful lift in her expression.

Hope shook her head. "I think we can share, don't you?"

She hated the idea that he even needed to ask if she wanted a separate room. She wondered if the day would come where she and Reed would automatically know that they'd share the same hotel room. God, she hoped so.

Reed's gorgeous lips curved into a contented smile, and he nodded. He placed his credit card back in his wallet, and they received their room key cards from the disappointed employee.

When Reed used his key card to open the door to their suite on the thirtieth floor, Hope nearly lost her footing. It was the most beautiful block of space she'd ever entered, and she lived in Frank's mansion. The room was designed to be an urban getaway, and the clean, modern lines and stark color contrasts in the decor stood out as a bold reprieve from the traditional southern look she was used to back home.

"This is amazing," she said, spinning around in a slow circle so she could see everything. There was a spectacular king-size bed waiting in the center of the room, dressed in a thick, white comforter and sprinkled with red throw pillows. The white marble floors sparkled brightly against the gleam coming from the expanse of city lights pouring in through the wall of windows across the room. She turned a corner into the bathroom, and she knew she would lose herself in that luxurious space at some point during this trip. Especially the huge, claw-foot tub standing proudly in the center of the space.

Reed went to retrieve their luggage, and while he was gone she walked over to the windows and stared out at the busy city. Even after the sun went down, it seemed as though no one bothered to slow down or go indoors.

She loved it. It was new and exciting.

And it wasn't Charleston.

It wasn't where Wendy and Frank were bearing down on her to give more and more to the family business. More than she ever wanted to give.

Before she'd left, she had a conversation with Frank and Wendy about how she wouldn't be working the upcoming weekend.

"How do you plan to reimburse me for the money I'm going to lose by having my best girl not at work?" Frank had asked calmly.

"I don't know," said Hope angrily. "I can't work every freaking weekend, Frank. I need a break sometimes."

"Oh, do you?" asked Frank. "Well, if you're going to be taking breaks, I'm going to need you to step up what you are actually doing at work. Some of the clients have been offering monumental amounts of money for an entire date night package with you. I've been turning them down at your direction, but I think that needs to change. Especially if you want to keep your job and continue having weekends off time and time again."

"Time and time again?" asked Hope, disgusted. "This is the first weekend I'm asking. And I've told you a million times that I'm not a hooker. Ask another girl."

"Oh, I have asked other girls. They're actually thrilled about the shitloads of money the extra work brings in. You're the only one who acts like she's too good for the color green. Don't you love your sister enough to make your mother and me happy?"

Hope bristled at the mention of Violet. "Of course I love her. Why do you think I'm working so hard?"

"You're not working hard enough." His voice was final, as if he were stating a fact.

"What are you talking about?"

"I'm going to make this really simple for you, Hope. If you want to keep working for me, you need to keep my clients happy. Keeping my clients happy keeps me happy. And keeping me happy keeps your mother happy."

A deep feeling of foreboding enveloped her. She felt like she was being backed into a corner. How could she get Violet out of this house? If she went to the police, would they believe her over Frank? He'd use whatever connections he had to make sure that never happened, *dammit!*

Frank simply stared at her triumphantly. He knew he had her.

"I'll think about it," Hope finally said, the sour taste of defeat and shame threatening to bring her lunch back up from her stomach.

"You should," said Frank. "Not for too long, though. I think by your shift next weekend, you should be able to tell me something."

Hope had only nodded.

The dark memory subsided as Reed pushed through the hotel room door, pulling a cart with their luggage.

He unloaded it, placed the cart in the hallway, and then joined her at the window. He put his arms around her from behind, and she sank back into his firm chest gratefully.

"Hey," he said softly. He turned her around in his arms to face him. "You're trembling. What's wrong?"

She hadn't realized her thoughts had resulted in tremors, and she tried to take a deep breath to get a hold of herself. She shook her head and tried to smile up at him. "I'm fine."

It was a lie, and Reed knew it. "You're not. We don't have to share a room. We can go to dinner, and afterward I can grab another room for myself on this floor. There's no pressure here, Hope."

She took another deep breath to steel herself. It wasn't fair to Reed, she knew. But next week, there was a good chance she was going to have to sell her soul to the devil himself. And if that was going to happen, she was going to live as fully as she could until every last ounce of her old self was gone. Starting now. Tonight. With Reed.

"I don't want my own room, Reed. I'm glad I'm here with you. And I want you to know that what I said before, about us slowing things down, I'm done with it. I realize now that what we have isn't just physical, that I can talk with you and laugh with you and tell you…things. Tonight, all my cards are on the table. And we can order dinner in."

Eighteen

The muted, deeply buried sense of desperation in her voice was back. And if Reed were a better guy, he'd try harder to dig deeper, delve further beneath the surface to find out exactly what caused it and how they could overcome it together before he made any kind of move.

But I'm not a better guy. I'm just a guy.

And he had never wanted anything in his entire life like he wanted Hope at that moment.

The setting was perfect. The luxury hotel room was something out of a romance movie, and Hope couldn't have picked a better moment, a better place, to let her walls come crumbling down around them.

He'd watched those walls. He'd waited for them to fall. He'd removed one small brick at a time, one painstaking block of distrust and prejudgment after the other in order to get to this moment.

The moment when she said yes.

Yes to him, yes to them, yes to what they could be.

His eyes were glued to her face, watching for some sign that she wasn't really ready for this, that she was feeling pressure from him.

She stared right back, her steady, warm hazel eyes moist with promise and emotion.

"Are you—" Reed's voice was barely there, dry and scratchy, as though he'd just walked ten miles through the desert without a drop to drink. He cleared his throat, tried again. "Are you sure? Because Hope, you know I want to—"

She cut him off with an impatient shake of her head. And with that one movement, he was silent. Silent and diminished, small enough to fit into the palm of her hand. Or large enough to rain thunder upon the hotel with only his voice because of what Hope Dawson was currently doing to him.

She ripped her shirt over her head with a movement so swift, he hadn't even known it was coming. The beautiful piece of red fabric wrapping around her body beneath let Reed know that for Hope, this had always been a possibility. He'd come on this trip not even daring to dream she'd be ready for this kind of intimacy, but he'd been wrong.

Because now her hands were darting dangerously low, scraping against her flat, bronze belly, past the shining bar glittering softly at her navel and unbuttoning her jean shorts.

His eyes were riveted to her hands as they slowly slid down the zipper of the shorts and caught just a glimpse of the fire-colored panties beneath as she paused to kick off her Chucks. Which, he'd never told her, were the sexiest piece of footwear a woman like her could don in front of him.

When she had them off, her hands returned to her zipper, made quick work of it, and slipped steady fingers beneath the tops of the shorts to slip them down, down, down her curved hips and over her smooth thighs, and that was as far as Reed got before his mind snapped sharply into gear. He realized he'd been standing still the entire time she'd performed a not-so-subtle striptease in front of him, in his hotel room.

Their hotel room.

He moved, coming forward against her quickly enough to back her up, and he kept going until her skin was pressing against the cool glass of the window to the twinkling city beneath them. He was close enough to her that her breasts were pushing against his chest, her stomach flush against his midsection. Her eyes widened when he ground against her, letting her feel the erection that was struggling for freedom against his jeans.

"Hey, Hope?" he said, his voice low and dangerous now, where before it had been gentle and soft.

She looked up at him with big eyes, and he watched her tongue dance across her lips. He restrained himself from bending his head to capture that mouth, just for the time being.

"Yes?"

"I'm not the kind of man who lets a woman strip in front of him with no gratification of her own. You know that, right?"

She nodded quickly, and cleared her throat. "I just wanted to get the ball rolling."

A flash of heat engulfed him in a burning flame of desire, and he fought against it. This was Hope, and he had to control it. He had to take it slow, give her every form of pleasure in the process that he could muster. Because after tonight, he wasn't letting this woman go anywhere. Unless he was walking right beside her.

"It's rolling," he whispered beside her ear. He let his hands slip down her sides as he leaned closer and kissed the spot beneath her ear. She gasped, and a violent shiver rocked her body against the window. He smiled; usually sex was very...mechanical. He went in with the intention of getting the girl off and getting himself off and getting the hell out. Or getting her the hell out.

This was so totally different he almost needed a map to navigate the situation.

Almost.

Sliding farther down her body, he paused with his lips pressed against the swell of her breasts in order to enjoy the lushness of her sweet skin. He cupped their weight in his hands, and she arched her back, a moan escaping her parted lips. She tilted her head back against the window and closed her eyes.

"No," he ordered gently, placing a kiss on her jaw. "Eyes on me, baby. You're gonna wanna watch this."

She snapped her head back up, and he drank in the sight of her glazed eyes attempting to focus on him. He smirked at her and moved his hands down to squeeze her backside. It was round and smooth and perfect, just like the rest of her.

Her scent was nearly driving him to the point of no return, although he was keeping the insanity under lock and key as he allowed his lips and his tongue to travel south. He stopped again at her navel, darting his tongue out of his mouth to delve into the center; he tasted the cool metal of the body jewelry.

"This new?" he asked.

She shook her head. "Didn't know how you'd handle a piercing and my"—she moaned again as his tongue scraped against flesh—"tattoos."

Now he stopped altogether and pulled back. Disbelieving, he said, "I'm sorry. Did you say tattoos? Plural?"

She crushed her bottom lip between her teeth and nodded. The discomfort on her face was clear; she wanted him to continue his journey, but she didn't know how to request it.

So he smiled up at her and tugged the silver bar between his teeth and she jerked again with the pleasure of it. "Hope? Did you want me to stop here at this pretty piercing, or do you want me to go further?"

She mumbled something unclear, and he shook his head. "I couldn't hear that, beautiful."

"Keep going," she gasped.

Smiling, he moved his hands around her hips to grasp the crimson piece of fabric that was being used as a poor excuse for underwear and tugged downward.

Ah. There was surprise number two. A tiny drawing of a rising sun was inked on her supple skin just beneath her hip bone.

Reed swallowed. He was trying desperately to remain calm enough in this situation not to scare Hope off, but *damn*. And shit and fuck. Because that tiny tattoo tucked away in a place where only he could see it was causing his dick to throb harder inside his pants.

He kissed the ink, tracing it with his tongue, and Hope's tiny whimper drew his eyes up to her face once more. *Goddamn. Her skin is so damn sweet.* Her eyes were focused on him, but just barely. She tugged a handful of his hair in each hand, and he kept eye contact with her as he traced a line around the sun with his tongue once more. She shivered, and his fingers dug roughly into her skin as he quelled his own reaction to her undeniable pleasure.

"Reed," she rasped, her eyes silently begging.

"Yeah, baby," he responded. "I know what you want. I'm getting there."

She nodded and writhed her hips against his head, which nearly caused him to grab her in his arms and drag her onto the enormous bed, but he refrained. Because this time was about her.

Pulling the panties down and over her shapely legs, he allowed her to step out of them. He placed the material in his pocket.

"Hope," he said, glancing up at her again. She looked down at him.

"I want you naked. Unhook your bra and drop it on the floor for me."

She lazily reached up and did as she was told, and he watched intently as the gorgeous weight of her breasts popped free of their restraint. He swallowed thickly, wishing suddenly that he'd spent more time up there. But there was always later.

He used one hand to reach up and squeeze her right breast, rubbing a circle around her hardened nipple with his thumb. Then he used his other hand to trace a line from her tattoo to her dripping folds. His own personal playground.

"Oh, my *God,*" she cried as his fingers slid over her flesh. He released his own groan of need and want and *fuck,* pure, animalistic desire as her hips bucked against his face.

"Oh, so that's it," he said, his voice so strained it sounded foreign to even his own ears. "That's what you want?"

She looked directly into his eyes and tugged on his hair just hard enough to let him know she was serious. "You know what I want, Reed."

"Hell, yes, I do," he said, his own need evident in the deep husk of his voice. "Let me give it to you."

He pursed his lips and blew. His cool breath against her warm center wracked her body with delicious shivers and he held her tightly against him as he slowly dabbed her swollen clit with his tongue. She lost the use of her legs as her knees buckled beneath her, and his name was an almost incoherent whisper from her mouth.

He caught her by the waist, picked her up easily, and carried her to the bed. He saw her chest heave with a sigh of relief, but he chuckled and removed his T-shirt.

"No, baby," he said. "I'm not done with you yet."

The desire was crystal clear in her eyes as she watched him undress, sliding out of his shoes, jeans, and boxer-briefs easily before kneeling in front of the bed and pulling her by the thighs down to meet him.

"Lay back," he demanded. She did, resting on her elbows.

"Please, Reed," she whispered. Her breathing was ragged, and her hips kept twitching restlessly.

"You don't have to beg, baby," he answered. "You never have to beg."

And he plunged his tongue deep inside of her, opening her up and sweeping across her center with an aggression that sent her hips rocketing for the ceiling and her fingers clawing at the down comforter. He risked a glance at her face; her eyes were rolled back and his name was falling freely from her parted lips. His erection throbbed impatiently; if he hadn't been fully at attention before, he definitely was now.

"Reed, Reed, Reed," panted Hope. "God, *Reed*."

He wanted to drag her so close to the edge of reality that it would only take one thrust from him to send her reeling over the edge of it, and he could tell from her voice that's exactly where she was. Shit, he was damn near there himself. He rose from his knees and climbed on top of her; she opened her eyes and stared at him pleadingly.

"Hold on, gorgeous," he said, reaching for his jeans. "Let me get a condom."

She caught hold of his hand as he reached down.

"No," she said, shaking her head fervently. "I don't want it."

"Hope, we can't—" he began, caught off guard.

"We can," she cut him off. "I'm on the pill. We can."

Reed hesitated. He hadn't been with anyone since he met Hope, couldn't even if he had tried. And he made it a regular part of his health routine to get checked out. He could read it in her eyes how much she wanted this.

"Why, Hope?" he asked.

"I don't know when we'll get the chance again," she said softly, closing her eyes. "I want you. Just you."

How could he argue? How was he ever going to be able to argue with the beautiful creature lying bare beneath him, with all of her beauty, and sorrow, and perfection?

"Okay," he said, easing down on top of her. He wasn't prepared for how her slick softness would feel against his own throbbing erection, and his groan of blissful delight as he rubbed against her was mingled with her sharp cry. He knew how close he'd brought her to ecstasy, and now the frenzy took over. He wanted so badly to watch her face when she fell apart.

"You ready for this?" he asked. He just needed to hear it one more time; that she wanted him, that she was ready, that this was going to happen and she was fully on board with the game plan.

Just like earlier, she didn't answer with her voice, she answered with her actions.

She pushed her hips against Reed until just the tip of his erection was pressing into her entrance. His eyes drifted closed, and it was her turn to prompt him to keep them open. He did, focusing on her green-brown eyes and her cascades of dark hair splayed out against the pillow.

Angelic. That was the only word for how she looked at that moment. She needed him when he came into her life, needed him for her own survival at that moment. But somewhere along the way, the tables had turned, and now he needed her. Much more than she knew, he needed her. Maybe he'd saved her once, but she was saving him every day now, the closer they grew to becoming what he now knew they would one day be.

He was falling deeper into Hope, deeper than he'd ever been.

Now, at this precipice, he just needed to take the leap. Once he jumped, he would be hers. Whether they were ready for what was to come next or not, this one moment would change everything for them both. He knew it like he knew the color of the sky, or the letters in his name.

He jumped.

They shared a cry of joy, of the most painful pleasure either of them had ever endured as he filled her up completely with one measured stroke. He slid back out, and their matched exhalation mingled in the air around them. She was trembling. He was trembling, too, but he didn't break eye contact. He couldn't look away now even if he tried.

She clenched around him as he pushed back inside, deeper this time than the first time, and her voice escaped in a soft, pleading whimper. "Reed."

A thin sheen of sweat covered them both, and their hips joined up perfectly as their bodies found a matched rhythm. His chest ached at how softly and sweetly she gasped his name against his shoulder, her hips rising up to meet his. His arms held him hovering above her, but the muscles began to shake as her tremors vibrated beneath him.

Her eyes burned the brightest shade of green they'd ever been, hardly any brown at all, and she bit her lip to keep from screaming.

"Don't do that, Hope," he ordered. "If you want to scream my damn name loud enough for this entire Four Seasons Hotel to hear, then you damn well better do it. Because they all need to know that I'm here, and you're mine."

That was all it took to send her off spiraling toward the moon, and he watched her in wonder as she drifted back down to the earth from the heavens above, where he was starting to suspect she really belonged.

"Oh, fuck," she moaned.

That was all it took for Reed. Hope uttering the word *fuck* out of her perfect mouth somehow sent him roaring out of control. He pumped harder, faster into her, over and over again until his own release mingled with hers inside of her. Tremors rocked him as he lowered himself on top of her, her name just a breath off of his lips as he finished.

It took everything he had, every single bit of self-possession, not to utter the very scariest, most terrifying, three little words in the universe into her ear.

He felt it, but saying it would break everything. He knew that. So he kissed her neck, her shoulder, and then her soft, red, luscious lips.

But he said nothing.

Nineteen

He had called her *baby*. She let Reed call her baby, something she never wanted any man before him to do.

And she *liked* it.

She'd had sex before, with a boy she dated in high school. But she'd obviously never made love. Because, as she watched Reed doze peacefully beside her in their beautiful hotel room bed, she was sure there was no other explanation for what they'd just done.

Twice.

Never in her entire life had she been worshipped the way Reed had just worshipped her. Never had she been savored, tasted, *delivered* soundly into orgasmic oblivion the way Reed just did to her. Her body was humming in pure delight, aching in the loveliest way, singing in perfect attunement with the beautiful man lying next to her.

And now she regretted every single second of it.

Because now, she wanted it all. She wanted this man. She

wanted nights with him, she wanted days with him. She wanted vacations with him. She wanted to watch him sing at every single one of his shows.

And none of it would ever happen. She hadn't been honest with him. She gave herself to him, and she knew that he'd given himself totally to her. She suspected that wasn't easy for Reed. That maybe he'd never done it before.

But for some reason, he'd done it for her.

Why? Why me?

And even if he never found out on his own about Silk and what she did there, she could never go on like this with him without telling him the truth.

She rose from the bed quietly and grabbed a hotel robe from the closet. She wandered over to a chair in front of the picture window and sat, pulling her knees up and tucking her feet underneath her. She was elated, brilliantly happy for the very first time in her life. Then she thought of Violet, and she was dumped right back into misery.

She wasn't sure how long she stared out the window at the glittering lights of the city when warm, strong arms wrapped around her from behind.

"I fell asleep," he murmured into her ear. "Before I got to find your other tattoos."

Her face broke into a devilish smile. "I'll set up a scavenger hunt for you later. I do them for the kids all the time."

He leaned casually against the window in front of her. "Yeah? Hey, anybody else seen those tattoos?"

"Do you really want me to answer that question?"

His expression fell, and she smiled to herself. He was adorable when he was jealous. She'd seen jealous men before, more than once. But not one of them had ever made her feel like she was more important than the emotions jealousy stirred up inside them.

"No," he finally said. "Truth?"

"Yes. Truth."

"I want to make you forget anyone who ever saw those tattoos, except for me."

"You already have," she said honestly. "Since nobody has really mattered until you."

His expression softened to a level of sweetness that made her chest hurt. "Are we going to talk about where we are now?"

She knew he wasn't talking about their location, so she didn't bother being a smart-ass about it. Instead, she changed the subject.

"I'm hungry. Can we get a pizza?"

He studied her, holding her gaze long enough to let her know that *he knew* she was avoiding an important conversation. She wished she could just fall into his arms and tell him that she was his.

But she couldn't do that, not without being a liar.

"The universe has got to be shitting me. I've stumbled upon the only woman in a two-hundred-mile radius who gets hungry and asks for *pizza*?"

She giggled. Reed had officially turned her into a giggler. *God, what is happening to me?*

She had a fleeting, terrifying thought: she knew exactly what was happening to her. Oh, *no.* She'd never been the girl who dreamed about falling in love. She was the girl who dreamed about creating new, better circumstances for herself so that she could be free and independent. Stand on her own two feet.

Where the hell had Reed come from?

She pushed the three horrific little words out of her mind until she could pull them out later and really delve into what they might mean for her life. Or the sledgehammer they'd take to her plans.

They lay on the bed in their robes, eating pepperoni pizza and watching cable TV until the wee hours, and then they were an unconscious tangle of arms and legs in the center of the plush, king-size bed. Hope drifted off to sleep to the sound of Reed's steady heartbeat beneath her head, and the feel of his strong, secure arms surrounding her.

She awoke to the memories of the previous night burning through her veins, and instinctively reached out to pull Reed closer. Frank's voice and his ominous demand rang in her head, and she shivered. She wanted to feel Reed wrapped around her constantly until she had to finally set him free once and for all. But all she felt was cool sheets.

Without opening her eyes, she listened. A soft thrum of something beautiful drifted toward her ears, a melancholy melody pouring from a guitar nearby.

Reed was playing this morning, she immediately realized. She didn't want him to stop, so she kept her eyes closed and just enjoyed waking up to the sound of his tune. She could get used to this in the mornings. She wouldn't have to turn on a radio or a television. She'd barely need a cup of coffee if she could just wake up every day listening to Reed strumming away lovingly on his guitar.

And then his voice echoed around her, and her eyes flew open.

She hadn't heard him sing since that first night at the club in Charleston. She'd thought he was good then, and that was before she knew him. Now, with his sandpaper-and-silk voice served up to her on a platter of very physical and intimate memories, she was completely spellbound.

It was soft and hard simultaneously. He sang with a richness to his voice that suggested years of practiced tuning, yet there was a raw edge to it that told her he used his whole heart to pour out the meaning of the song.

She sat up in bed and searched for him. He was sitting by the window, and the sunlight created a bright sparkle to bounce off of the glass-walled buildings surrounding them. He wore nothing but a pair of black jeans, and his bare foot was propped up on the window ledge before him as he stared down at his instrument. His sleep-disheveled hair wasn't much of a departure from the messy look he usually sported, and his face was pensive, lips slightly pursed, eyelids heavy.

He was *beautiful.*

She swung her legs over the side of the bed and searched for her discarded robe. Putting it on, she padded over to the adjacent seat and perched on the edge of it. He looked up at her, his face breaking into a heart-shattering grin, and she gestured for him to keep playing. He did.

When the final strains of his song faded away into the morning, Hope brushed a piece of his hair from his face. He leaned into her touch.

"I missed you in bed right until I realized you were playing," she said.

His eyebrows lifted. "And then the missing me stopped?"

She turned her face to a mask of stone, nodding solemnly. "Yes. I can survive mornings without you in my bed, but I clearly cannot survive mornings without your guitar from this day forward."

His jaw dropped open, and she laughed. "Okay. Maybe next time you should sit *right next* to me so that I can reach out and touch you while you serenade me."

He contemplated this, and she wanted to kiss the wrinkly spot created in the center of his forehead by his meeting brows. "Do you plan on spending many more mornings in my company, Miss Dawson?"

She realized what she'd said then, and attempted to backpedal. "I mean…I don't know. Not if you don't want me to. We aren't exactly next-door neighbors, so…I just meant—"

His lips were suddenly on top of hers, shutting her up before she could continue her embarrassing stream of nonsense. All thoughts of the fact that she hadn't yet brushed her teeth this morning, of the fact that she hadn't even checked a mirror, about the fact that she should be a little self-conscious from all that they had done the night before, left her mind while his lips worked their magic on hers. He suggested, insisted really, that she open for his tongue, and she didn't need much convincing. He plunged inside, sweeping across her teeth and lips, and she couldn't stop the moan that cascaded out of her without much warning.

His answering grunt as he reached inside her robe and pulled her closer nearly set her on fire. She was immediately slick with need, made more so when both of his hands found their first destination. He squeezed her breasts hard enough to coax a gasp from her, and then his nose was brushing the skin of her chest as he took one already-firm nipple into his mouth and sucked.

"Oh, *Reed.*" Her voice was still raspy with sleep, and every muscle in her body tensed with desire for this man.

He responded by letting his teeth graze her sensitive skin, and she dropped her head back against her chair, spreading her legs open wide as she released a loud cry.

"Yes, baby," he said, his voice rough while his hands dropped to her thighs. "That's my girl."

His praise was strangely erotic; she wanted more and more of it. Tentatively, she scooted forward in the chair, perfectly aware that she was still wearing absolutely nothing beneath the plush white robe. She untied the belt and allowed the robe to fall open, exposing her body to him fully.

"Ah, hell." Reed licked his lips.

Her pulse leaped while her lips curved into an excited smile.

"Hope," he said, his voice strained and firm. "You're playing with fire this morning. Last night ruined me. You putting your body on display this morning is going to drive me insane. Are you saying you're ready for more?"

"Do I have to say it?" she said breathlessly, rubbing a hand up her bare stomach, past her little silver piercing, and up to cup her own breast.

His eyes zeroed in on her hand, and he shot to his feet. Before she knew what was happening, he'd thrust her out of her seat and turned her around. Bracing one hand on her stomach and one hand on the windowpane in front of them, he murmured into her ear. His voice gave her a delicious shiver, and she could feel him, hard as a rock, against her backside.

"You don't *have* to say it," he said. "But I want you to. I want you to say you want me to fuck you against this window, and then that's exactly what I'm going to do."

She didn't hesitate. "Fuck me against this window, Reed."

He plunged into her so hard she cried out, and the intense feeling of him filling her up so deeply, so completely, had her legs trembling within seconds.

Soft, gorgeous Reed sitting by the window strumming on his guitar had made her feel all warm and soft and cozy this morning when she awoke. But this Reed, this dark and slightly dangerous and *bossy* Reed made her want to do every dirty thing she'd ever thought about, slowly. To him, with him, for him.

Oh, God.

He eased out of her slowly, and then he pounded back inside, grabbing her hips and rocking them against his own with perfect precision.

"Baby, do you wanna come?" he asked fiercely.

"Oh, my God, yes!"

It was more than the truth. She really did want to come. Her insides were pulsing and clenching, and a deep ache had settled in her depths that nothing was going to be able to soothe but Reed. She rocked back against him and he practically roared with his own blunt desire.

He hissed through his teeth, and the sound sent a thrill of pleasure through her like she never thought she'd feel from hearing a man curse during sex. Everything about Reed and the way he made love to her was new, and scary, and invigorating. And damn sexy.

His hand slid down her damp body until it was resting on her pelvic bone, and his middle finger found her sensitive clit. He rubbed firm circles around her hot center while she writhed and pleaded softly for him to stop, or continue, or *something*. But he was relentless, punishing her from behind and loving her from the front, and she couldn't take it anymore. Her world fell, slid, crashed down around her and once again, their floor at the Four Seasons was introduced to Reed Hopewell in a big, loud way.

"I love that," he declared into her ear, softly now. He held her in place while she trembled all around him. "I fucking love it. My name falling from your mouth as you come is the best damn sound I've ever heard."

And then he crashed into her one last time, grunting with his own release and clinging to her with his strong arms circling her waist.

They slowly sank to the floor in front of her chair. A wayward thought occurred to her, but she was far too exhausted and satisfied to bring herself to care.

"I sure as hell hope those windows are tinted," she murmured, spent.

His chuckle tickled her ear. "I don't."

Reed wanted to stay in the damn hotel room all day. He wanted to order room service and just give it to Hope over and over again until they fell asleep, and then he wanted to start over when they woke up.

She was just that…addictive. He was crazily attracted to her before he'd actually had intercourse with her. He'd loved spending time in her presence, had damn near become a stalker just to be close to her and make sure she was okay.

But now…*now*? Now that he knew how she tasted and what her ass looked like while he plunged inside of her from behind? Now that he'd memorized every curve of her naked body and knew how her flawless face looked while she screamed his name?

Now he was gone. She could just go ahead and wrap him around her little finger, because he was completely hers. They had a little banter going, where one of them would say, "Truth?" and the other would respond in kind. And that was how he truly felt. He'd never been totally truthful with any female, especially not where feelings were concerned or about his family and his parents and the past.

That was going to change. Now. Today. He owed it to Hope to be truthful about the baggage that he carried and the fact that he was fucked-up due to his mother cheating on his father more than once during their marriage. He didn't know if he'd ever be able to trust a woman completely, even one as perfect for him as Hope was. She deserved to know that he was broken inside, unable to commit because he was *scared.* Scared of what would happen when he finally decided to jump over that ledge with a woman and be her one and only. And claim her as his.

Everything inside of him told him Hope was the one he could do it with, if there was one. He could share it with her, he could trust her. She wanted him, and only him. She wouldn't betray him, and she'd understand where he was coming from because her upbringing definitely wasn't all sunshine and roses.

So he'd tell her, and he'd let her save him. Because it was time.

He could see her from where he now stood in front of the microphone in the small, glass, soundproof booth. He wore large, black headphones and he sang with everything inside of him into the microphone as the producer outside the window gave him nods of encouragement and the occasional thumbs-up. He watched her while he sang, because he knew he'd never be singing to anyone but her ever again.

"That was incredible, Reed," said Phillip Castille as Reed took off the headphones and exited the sound booth. Phillip did something else with the board of switches and dials in front of him and nodded. "We got it, man. Three good cuts. You really wrote those yourself?"

Reed nodded. He still hadn't taken his eyes from the woman in the room, but he tore his gaze away and met Phillip's grinning one. "I did. I've had a lot of inspiration lately."

"I can see that," said Phillip with a knowing smile. "Keep her around, dude. You just killed it. There's no way a label won't want you."

Now Reed was incredulous. "Are you serious?"

"Absolutely," said Phillip. "I'm going to get these tracks packaged up and give 'em to the execs myself. They'll probably kiss me for finding you."

Hope stood, wrapping her arms around his waist and resting her head against his chest. "Congratulations, babe."

Babe. The first time she'd given him a term of endearment. Reed thought he could probably survive it if he jumped out the window right now. Surely he could fly if he tried.

"Thank you," he murmured, dropping a kiss on the top of her head. He turned to Phillip. "So that's it?"

"Yeah, man. I'm going to send a car to your hotel in a few hours so y'all can experience ATL in style. You good with that?"

Reed looked down at Hope, who nodded happily. "I think we're good with that."

Twenty

Hope stared down at herself, second-guessing letting Violet talk her into bringing the dress she now wore. She and Reed were going to go out in Atlanta tonight, and she just knew it was going to be all fancy clubs and velvet ropes. Violet had suggested she bring one of the dresses she normally saved for her weekend work for Silk. She agreed.

But now she wasn't so sure.

The dress was black, and short, and tight. Ruching stretched across her hips and thighs, calling attention to the curvy lines. The dress was cut high, just at her collarbone, and had long, tight, lace sleeves. The entire back was open, dropping to her tailbone, and at the top of her shoulder blades a strip of lace fabric linked the two sides together. She tugged at the bottom, trying to create length where there was none. It stopped midthigh.

"Thanks a lot, Violet," she said softly into the mirror. "Let's call attention to the fact that I'm practically a call girl."

She sighed. She hadn't brought anything else suitable to wear. She was going to have to step out of this bathroom, and Reed would finally see straight through to the center of what she really was. Cheap. Easy. Wasn't that how all men always saw her when she dressed this way?

She opened the bathroom door, ready to face the music. Reed was sitting in his favorite chair by the window, staring out at the city while he spoke softly to Aston on his cell phone.

"It was crazy, A," he was saying. "Someone seriously thinks I'm good. Like...they might want me. On a record label." He shook his head in disbelief.

Hope stood there awkwardly, wanting desperately to turn and flee back into the safety of the bathroom. Or better yet, all the way back to the safely of Charleston. Where everyone already knew what she was.

She cleared her throat involuntarily, and Reed turned his head.

He rose out of the chair to a standing position, and snapped into his phone, "I gotta go."

He slid the phone into his pocket and stalked forward.

"You can't wear that. No fucking way, Hope."

"You....you don't like it?"

Of course he didn't like it. He wouldn't want to be seen with a woman who dressed this way. Reed could have anybody he wanted. She should have...

"Really? You're asking me that? Baby, I love the damn thing. All that black, your hair is up and all elegant and shit. Fuck-me heels. You can't wear any of it outside of this room."

Anger immediately flared up inside of her. She hadn't wanted to wear the damn dress, either, but she sure as hell wasn't going to let him tell her she *couldn't*.

"So wait. Let me get this straight. You *do* like it, in fact the entire ensemble makes you think of the phrase 'fuck me,' yet you don't actually want me to wear it outside of this room?"

"Yes." Agitated, he scrubbed a hand across his jaw and stepped closer to her.

"So we're back to Caveman Reed?"

His eyes narrowed. "Didn't I already explain to you why that term didn't apply to me?"

"What are you trying to keep me safe from?"

"From all the stupid motherfuckers who are going to try to touch you while you're wearing that dress and those heels. I'm also trying to save myself. Because I really don't want to end up in jail tonight, Hope. Especially not when I'm on the brink of signing the deal of my life. Please don't make me get arrested. Please go and change your dress and shoes. *Please*."

Her lips twitched. Reed was really very adorable when he begged. Sadly, she wasn't going to be able to appease him, even though at this point she really wanted to.

"I can't change," she said, coming to him and wrapping her arms around his neck. "This is all I brought."

He groaned. "Oh, Jesus. You even smell like a slice of heaven right now. We gotta cancel the limo."

She smacked his chest. "We aren't canceling! I want to go out. Everything will be fine. I'll stick to you like glue, no one will dare touch me with you looking like an avenging angel."

She stepped back and appraised him. That was exactly what

he looked like when he wore all black. Right on down to the slim jeans tucked into loosely laced boots and an army-style blazer.

"Oh, man." He sighed. "You're really not going to change?"

She shook her head firmly, and her golden chandelier earrings jangled. "Nope."

He bent down and took a nip at her neck. "Fine. You really do look way too hot for your own good, you know."

Oh boy. If he was going to keep doing that, they weren't going to get out of the hotel after all. But he had given her the boost of confidence she needed. Now she'd almost forgotten why she was so squeamish about wearing the outfit in the first place.

But not quite.

The limo was waiting downstairs for them promptly at ten, and the front desk concierge who checked them in watched them with a forlorn expression as they exited the elevator and walked outside together, Reed holding the door open for Hope to exit first.

She kept her eyes on him once they were in the limo, a glass of champagne in their hand. Reed looked at his disgustedly.

"You don't like champagne?" she asked.

"I know since I have money, I'm supposed to," answered Reed. "But seriously, give me a longneck or a shot of Cuervo over the fancy shit every single time."

It was one of the things she loved about Reed. She knew he had money, probably a trust fund bigger than he could ever spend in one lifetime. He had nice stuff, and an amazing job, and everything seemed to come easily to him. But in spite of all of that, he was just a boy from South Carolina who wanted to drink beer in his favorite bar and drive a truck.

Unexpectedly sexy.

She looked around the limo thoughtfully, and then reached over Reed's legs to open a console embedded into the seat beside him. She pulled out two Coronas. She handed one to him, and then smirked at his beaming smile.

"Seems like Phillip figured that about you," she said with a shrug.

"Have I told you that you're pretty amazing?"

"Nope. But I kind of already knew it."

He pulled her close and they sipped Coronas as they rode, Hope staring out of the windows as the limo driver wound them through downtown Atlanta.

"Hey," said Reed suddenly.

Hope tilted her face up to look at him. He wore a serious look on his handsome, chiseled face, his blue eyes dark and brooding.

"I want to talk to you about something," he said softly. "Something I've never talked to anyone about before, except for Aston. After last night... this is different. I'm different with you. I want to talk to you about everything."

Her stomach tightened with something she didn't recognize. She should be happy that he wanted to open up to her. Maybe even share with her the real reason he had such a dark danger brewing behind his eyes, the real reason he was able to write songs with the truest sadness she'd ever heard.

But she wasn't sharing everything with him. *Is that fair?* She knew it wasn't. He was about to pour his heart out to her, and she hadn't decided to do the same for him.

Her stomach clenched even tighter, and she forced a smile onto her face.

"Let's not delve into unfamiliar waters any more than we already have, okay, Hopewell?" Her nervous laugh betrayed her true feelings of anxiety.

He sat back, a hurt look crossing his face before he was able to cover it with a frown.

"It's nothing bad, Hope. I just wanted to tell you about—"

She silenced him with a finger on his lips, and a shaky, light kiss to his lips. "Not tonight," she whispered. "Another time."

Stunned, he nodded. Then she watched a wall of insecurity build up, brick by brick, onto his face until all of his normal swagger was back in perfect position.

"Okay, Hope," he said with a shrug. "Whatever you want."

Sudden panic seized her as he turned to look out of the window. She knew deep down that she'd made some kind of grave mistake, but she was unable to see the silent distance she'd just created between them in a matter of seconds.

Twenty-One

The following day, after a long night of club hopping, VIP table with bottle service, velvet rope–lined clubbing with Hope, Reed was finally back home in Nelson Island. He had to wake up early for work the next day, but he needed a swim.

He needed to think.

The remainder of that night and the entire car ride home, she would barely let him talk. If he even attempted to take on a serious tone or change the direction of their light conversation, she practically threw on a pair of sneakers and sprinted in the opposite direction.

He didn't understand it, couldn't fathom what he'd done to cause that kind of reaction. That first night together and then the following morning was stellar, perfect, steal-your-breath fantastic, and he couldn't get her out of his mind. Her warm body lying next to his, sliding over his, melded against his...it was sheer, orgasmic perfection. And they'd never had a problem talking before, either.

But all of a sudden, she'd shut down. Put up some kind of cement wall that he couldn't even break through with a sledgehammer.

So he'd withdrawn, finally, and by the time he'd dropped her off at her house they were barely speaking.

He sprinted across the sand and dived into the ocean, pulling up to the frothy surface and cutting through the wall of water with his thick, strong arms. She'd rejected him, was what it came down to. He'd been ready to explain to her exactly why he was the way he was, and tell her that he was ready to just give everything to her, for the long haul, and she'd shut him down.

The shit hurt.

The shit killed.

So he swam. Until his body hurt just as badly as his heart did, and only then did he stop.

He dragged himself up the steps to the condo and into the shower. When he emerged twenty minutes later, the steam from the bathroom following him out into the hallway, Tate was sitting on the couch with a game controller in his hands, staring at the television with vengeance in his eyes.

"Die, fucker!" he screamed at the TV.

Reed rolled his eyes and dabbed at his face with the towel around his neck. Padding into the kitchen with bare feet, he grabbed a beer bottle from the fridge and sank onto the couch, staring blankly at the screen.

Tate glanced over at him. "What's up, man? Good trip?"

"It was and it wasn't."

When he didn't say any more, Tate glanced away from the

screen again and at Reed's face. He put down the controller. "Uh-oh. Trouble on the Island of Reed and Hope?"

"There might not even still be an island," snapped Reed.

"Naw, man," said Tate. "I've seen you with her. There will be an island. Maybe y'all just needed to come back to the mainland for a minute. But soon enough, you'll be in paradise again."

Reed stared at Tate, disbelief clouding his features. "Are you seriously talking to me like that?"

Tate mimed stamping his forehead. "Consider me whipped."

Reed smiled for the first time since he'd told Hope he wanted to talk to her in the limo. "I might have fucked it up."

Tate shook his head. "She's a chick. She'll want to talk it all over eventually, man. Just wait her out."

Reed nodded. "Okay. That's actually kind of good advice, Tate. You been watching that TV therapist?"

"Religiously. That's my shit."

"Uh-huh. You know, you could just go out and use your own advice on yourself. I've seen it now, man. It doesn't always have to be about how much pussy you can pull in a week. There's more out there."

Tate shook his head numbly. "Not for me."

Reed opened his mouth to speak, and then closed it again. He mulled it over in his mind, and then decided that it needed to be said. By someone. And it looked like he'd drawn the short straw.

"Look, man. It was high school. That was a long time ago. She's gone. Don't you think there might be another—"

Tate held up a hand to silence him. "I'm warning you, Reed. If you say her name I will come across this couch to punch you in your pretty fucking face. Don't say her name to me. And there won't be anyone else. Not for me."

Reed sighed. "Message received. Good night, man."

"Night."

Reed suffered through nearly three long, lonely weeks of no feedback from Hope. She barely responded to his texts and ignored his calls altogether. He was hurt, and tired, and had been through the wringer of emotions until he had finally settled on anger.

Red-hot, blood-burning anger.

He knew she'd felt the exact same thing he'd felt on their trip to Atlanta. And he'd spent over half a summer getting to know her and learning that he probably fucking loved her. There was no way in hell she didn't have those same feelings. He'd seen them in her eyes when she fell to pieces in his arms, by his hand. He'd *seen* it.

He'd been to her work, only to be intercepted by Morrow.

"Give her a little time, man," he'd said to Reed, placing a hand on his chest to bar him from entering the Center.

Reed sent him a look of pure anguish. "I have given her time, Morrow. I can't do this anymore. I just need her to say something. She just needs to let me know she doesn't want me to give up on her."

God, it had hurt him to utter those words. It sliced right through his gut like a newly sharpened blade. He didn't want to give up on her. Even as he said the words, he knew he probably couldn't. Before he'd met Hope, he'd been drifting. Wondering how he was going to make it another day dredging through the work at Hopewell Enterprises. Wondering how in the world he'd be seen for his music outside of South Carolina. Wondering how much longer he could trudge through life without someone to share it with. Meeting Hope, from that very first moment, had given him a new direction, an undeniable purpose.

He couldn't lose that now. When he'd barely begun to live it.

Morrow nodded; the sympathy was written all over his face. "Believe me, I know. She's stubborn. She had a plan and then you came along and smashed it to pieces. Just give her a minute to breathe. I swear to you, she's smarter than this. She'll come to you. Just wait."

Reed had heaved a painful sigh, climbed back into the Silverado, and driven back to N.I. alone.

Without his Hope.

"I can't do it," whispered Hope.

"You damn well better do it," said Frank calmly. "Or you'll be leaving my house."

"You can't do that!" Angry frustration nearly overtook her. Tears sprang to her eyes, and she brushed them away angrily and moved into Frank's space until she was inches from his broad chest. Wendy was out for the day, so she was having this battle with Frank and Frank alone.

"You are not taking my sister away from me! She is all that I have, and I'm the only safe place she's ever known! I *will not* sleep with Nathan from Silk. I'm better than that! I'm not a call girl!"

Frank laughed, rank spittle hitting her face. She wiped it away in disgust, turning her head.

"You're not a call girl? Really, Hope? What have I been training you to be for the last six months? You're a prude, so you had to work up to it. But eventually, all my girls sleep with the clients. That's just how this thing goes. You *will* give Nathan what he wants. You will. The end."

She stared at him, transfixed by the calm demeanor he maintained while he invoked horror in her very soul. He was a unique kind of monster, and her mother actually slept with him every night.

She nearly gagged.

"Okay, Frank," she said, because there was nothing else to say. She turned on her heel and left the room, shaking.

She walked slowly to the kitchen, where Violet was standing by the sink, tears streaming down her face. Hope only had to glance at her to realize she'd overheard her conversation with Frank. Violet turned watery, icy eyes on her sister.

"Oh, Vi," she said.

"You're not doing that," said Violet angrily. "You're not, Hope! I refuse to let you. You're no slut, you're my sister! I don't care what Frank says!"

"Vi—"

"No!" the younger girl screamed. "Just stop. I swear to God, if you think you're doing this, I will just get on a bus and run away by myself. Getting me away from them isn't worth this. I don't want you to...I can't let you lose yourself like that."

Hope stared at Violet. When had the girl grown up enough to know exactly what Hope would be losing if she sold her soul to Frank and his club for the money?

"I can't leave you," she whispered, torture scraping the edges of her voice.

Violet stepped forward and hugged her sister hard. "You won't. We can figure something else out. Okay? Just please tell me you won't listen to Frank."

Hope sucked in a shaky breath, and then nodded. "I won't listen to Frank."

She noticed a paper clutched in Violet's trembling hand, and gestured. "What's that?"

Violet looked down and her expression was startled. She'd clearly forgotten she'd been holding it.

"It's nothing," she mumbled.

She reached for it, plucking it from the girl's hands. "It's not nothing."

She scanned the paper quickly, and then frowned at Violet. "You have a school trip coming up? Why didn't you tell me?'

Violet swiped at the skin under her damp eyes. "I asked Mom, and she never signed the paperwork and sent in the form. I don't want to piss her off and ask her again. So I'm not going. I didn't want to bother you with it."

Hope stared at her incredulously. What did her sister think her purpose in life was? "Do you want to go, Vi?"

Violet shrugged. "I dunno. It's just some dumb museum."

Hope glanced at the paper once more. *Some museum my ass.* "It's the Art Museum, Vi. Of course you'll go."

She grabbed a pen from a drawer and signed her name on the paper. "I'll write you a check in the morning."

Violet nodded and disappeared upstairs to work on a project for school.

Hope leaned against the kitchen counter, a sigh escaping her. Violet was her first priority. Without Hope, Violet wouldn't get any of the things she wanted or needed. She wouldn't have anyone to go to when she was hurt, or when she needed help. She needed to keep her sister close at all costs.

And, with a sinking feeling, she realized the cost might be pretty damn high.

Miraculously, she was able to hold Frank off. It took every ounce of her energy to do her job at the Center, love the kids who so desperately needed someone to care about them, swim for the sake of her own sanity, make sure Violet had what she needed, keep Frank at bay, stay the hell off Wendy's radar, and then do it all over again the next day.

No time for Reed. No time to address the situation that loomed so large in the back of her mind that her head ached daily at the enormity of it. She had glimpsed heaven, even leaped high enough to grab a tiny piece of it. And then she just walked away.

I don't have time to deal with Reed.

At least that's what she told herself.

But a niggling feeling chewed away at her heart every day that went by and she ignored one of his calls, one of his texts. And after a month of that, a month of not seeing him at all since their trip to Atlanta where everything had changed, she knew she had to face it.

He called less. He barely texted. She knew she should let him go, just let him move on already like it seemed he was beginning to do. He had a future in music, a career on the stage that was going to be amazing. Without her. She was happy for him, proud of him for being strong enough to grab it.

She should leave it be.

But she just couldn't. Not after what they'd shared. So she grabbed Morrow, and decided to head to Nelson Island on a Friday night, when she knew Reed would be at Sunny's.

Twenty-Two

She was certain Frank was going to hit the roof when she told him she wasn't going to work that night. She knew there were girls who lived for the money these dates provided, and that she could be easily covered. But Frank loved to start in on her about how she was the favorite, about how every man in the club wanted a date with *her*.

But she held firm. The feeling that Frank was somehow sitting back, waiting for *something*, made her uneasy. It was like he knew something she didn't, that eventually there was no way she wouldn't do exactly what he wanted.

It scared her.

"I have to see him, Morrow," she said as she breathlessly climbed into the Tahoe.

"Good," he answered, grinning at her and patting her cheek like a grandmother. "I knew you'd figure that out eventually."

"Am I being an idiot?" she asked as they drove. She bit her lip tensely, worrying about what she was about to do.

Morrow kept his eyes on the approaching horizon as he crossed the bridge.

"Hope," he said over the rumble of the big vehicle's engine that reminded her so much of another big engine she knew and loved. "This is the first time in a month that you're *not* being an idiot."

She huffed.

He glanced over. "I mean that with all the love."

"Right."

They pulled up into Sunny's gravel parking lot, forced to park on the outskirts of the space due to a very large crowd. Judging from the look of the place, it most likely always drew a large crowd. Especially in August on a scenic tourist destination like Nelson Island.

"Oh, *hell*, no," said Morrow unexpectedly.

She looked at him, startled, and saw that his gaze was aimed at the rickety old building, which was leaning dangerously close to the edge of the pier on which it sat.

"Oh, come on, Morrow," said Hope impatiently. "We don't have time for you to suddenly be scared of falling into the ocean!"

Morrow raised a brow skyward. "Suddenly? I'm pretty sure that's always been a fear of mine. I'm not an Olympic-level swimmer."

"Then rest assured that I'll dive in to rescue you if we go down with the bar," she said wryly.

Then she wrung her hands as she stared up at the wooden door. "What if he doesn't want to see me, Row?"

"Impossible. He wants to see you, Hope."

But it wasn't impossible. She'd shut him out for a month. He very well may not want to see her. He could actually be in there with someone. He could have two beautiful, large-breasted girls in his lap as they spoke. Or maybe he was inside taking body shots off a blond as tall and leggy as Tamara or Aston.

Oh, God. I can't do this.

What had she been thinking? She had turned down Frank's demand more than once, but he would find a way for her to cave eventually. In the time Wendy had been married to Frank, Hope had never known him to fail at getting what he wanted.

And he wanted her to be the very face, and body, of his club.

Her phone chirped happily in her purse. She pulled it out and looked down at it, dazed by the darkness of her thoughts. Frank's name showed up in the soft blue glow of the screen.

She swallowed thickly, a slight taste of bile lingering in her mouth.

"I have to take this, Row. Go in and do intel for me?"

"Why do you have to take it?" he asked, suspicion alighting on all of his prominent facial features.

"Just give me a minute," she said, her eyes pleading with him not to argue.

He hesitated, just for a second, and then he nodded. As he bent down to kiss her cheek, he said, "You're damn strong, Hope. So *be* strong."

She nodded and watched as he disappeared into the bar. She stood in the yellow glow of the light above the door and answered her phone.

"Frank. I told you I wasn't working tonight."

"Yes," he said calmly. Judging from Frank's tone, he didn't have a care in the world. "That's why I'm calling. I'm concerned about you, Hope. I'm worried about the turn you seem to be taking. You're not taking work nearly as seriously as you used to."

She rolled her eyes. It was hilarious he thought she had ever taken work at Silk seriously. She only took Violet seriously.

"What do you want?" she asked.

"To set you straight," he said, his smooth, oily voice leaking out of the earpiece.

She sighed, exhausted with the bullshit. "About what, Frank?"

"About your job. About what's at stake. About what's in it for you. Listen carefully, Hope."

She remained silent, although her pulse was beginning to quicken.

He took her silence for confirmation that she was listening. "You will attend a charity event with our highest-paying client, Nathan White. Mr. White has requested you specifically for this event next week. You will attend."

Here it was. Here was where he'd threaten her relationship with Violet, or threaten Hope's place in his home, if she didn't cooperate.

"And you will give him the full, overnight package."

She waited, but Frank seemed to be done speaking.

"And if I don't?"

"Oh, there is no 'if you don't.' Because you will. *When* you do, I'll join ranks with you. I'll make sure your sister is no longer…burdened by your mother's temper."

Son of a bitch. Now Hope's heart was pounding like the hooves of twelve racing thoroughbreds. Frank had the power to end Violet's suffering all the time. Wendy would have listened to him a long time ago if he had insisted he wouldn't stand for the way she treated Violet. She would never want to risk losing Frank. All he would have had to do was speak up.

I guess he was just waiting for the right moment. Now he has me where he wants me.

With that thought, an idea began to unfurl in Hope's mind.

"Let me get this straight. I play nice with your Mr. White, spend the night with him"—she gulped at the thought—"and you will make sure Violet's no longer being hurt?"

"That's right."

She could hear the smile in his voice, and it made her want to hurl and shiver and throw something sharp at his smug face.

She was taking deep breaths now, too deep. So deep and in such rapid succession she was in danger of hyperventilating.

All she had ever wanted was for her sister to be safe. It made her sick to her stomach to think that doing exactly what Frank wanted was the only way she could make that happen.

Didn't Violet deserve the chance to finally be happy? And didn't her strong, smart, capable little sister deserve more than Frank's grimy guarantee that he would protect her?

"So, I will expect you to be ready when Nathan's car picks you up next Thursday night, yes?"

It wasn't really a question. Frank already knew he'd just laid a lifeline on her lap and driven away on the boat. It wasn't a matter of if she'd do it. It was only a matter of whether she'd do a good job.

She hung up the phone and felt her knees wobbling so violently they nearly knocked together. Her blood was making waves in her ears, and her equilibrium was suffering because of it. She was suddenly glad she'd worn flip-flops, because if she'd been wearing heels she would have already been eating gravel. Retreating until her back scraped the wood, she began to count. She counted silently, and when she reached sixty-five she was finally able to lean forward and grasp her bare knees without toppling over.

She breathed deeply once, twice, and regained her composure. Steeling herself for what came next.

The wooden door next to her opened, and Morrow stepped out.

"Row," she said, trying as hard as she could to keep her voice steady. Her relief at seeing Morrow was immense; it meant she could grab him and they could leave before she made the mistake of walking back into Reed's life only to run at a sprint right back out of it.

If Hope was going to follow through with her plan, she couldn't drag Reed into it. She could never be with a man like him. It wasn't in the stars for her.

"We have to—" she began.

She stopped talking when Reed exited the bar directly behind Morrow.

He hadn't seen Hope in close to a month, but the sight of her caused his body to shut down. He suddenly contracted a serious case of lockjaw, and the muscles in his legs clenched so violently he was in danger of pitching face-first into the sandy gravel.

But his brain, that wasn't frozen at all. It was operating on all cylinders, firing questions into his consciousness at five hundred miles an hour. And he knew that he must make his body work, because Hope was *here.*

"Baby." He breathed.

Shock permeated his core when she held up both hands in front of her body as if to ward him off. She stumbled backward two steps, and threw a panicked look at Morrow.

Who stepped up next to Reed and tugged at his arm.

Reed snatched his arm back from him and took a tentative step toward Hope.

"Hope, baby," he said carefully. "I'm so damn glad to see you."

She said nothing, just shook her head repeatedly and stood rooted to the spot. She seemed frozen, unable to speak or move, much like he'd been a few seconds previously.

"Look, man," started Morrow. "Let me—"

Reed crossed the gravel divide separating him and Hope and scooped her up over his shoulder, firefighter style.

"Reed!" she wailed from behind his back.

He stalked toward his truck, holding on to the back of her thighs more tightly than he'd ever held on to anything in his entire, privileged, fucked-up existence.

He wrenched open the truck's passenger door with one hand and tossed Hope onto the leather seat. Then he marched around to his side of the vehicle and climbed in, shutting and locking the doors behind him.

He looked back toward the bar's entrance, and located Morrow nodding his head and grinning like a fool. Then Morrow turned and disappeared back inside the bar.

Good.

Now he was truly alone with Hope, for the first time in weeks, and he was going to get some answers out of her if he had to keep her in his truck against her will for the entire night.

When he finally turned to look at her, his world flipped upside down once more. Her hazel eyes were wide, focused on him, and her chest was rising and falling deeply as she leaned back against her seat. She said nothing, only drank him in with those deep, soulful eyes.

"God, Hope," he choked out.

He opened his arms, and she launched herself across the bench seat, landing squarely in the hardened comfort of his chest.

He breathed again, really breathed, for the first time in a month.

She pressed her lips firmly upon his, and he finally crawled out of the deep, dark hole he had been clinging to since they'd arrived back home in Nelson Island from Atlanta. She was so warm, and soft, and curvaceous, and his fingers found their way under the hem of her shirt. Her responding sigh sent his mind into overdrive.

His arousal begged him to continue his exploration of her body, and he was so happy to oblige. He was hungry—no, ravenous—for her, and not just because he'd been deprived. It was because she had become more important to him than he'd had the courage to admit to himself.

His hand caressed the soft—so achingly soft—skin just above

the top of her black shorts, and her answering shiver was all he needed to function and survive. She snuggled closer, pressing her chest flush against his and squeezing her thighs against the rough fabric of his pants. She groaned at the friction that he knew was steadily building between those thighs, and he smiled against her lips, a genuine smile that lit up his entire face.

"I'm not letting you go," he whispered into the space under her long curtain of hair, which was giving them privacy.

She stiffened, her body freezing up so swiftly, he knew he'd said something seriously wrong.

She scuttled away from him, breathing heavily and leaning back against her seat once more. She squeezed her eyes shut, and he was certain his face was a mask of confusion.

"*What*, Hope?" he asked finally, after the silence was stretching on between them for what felt like years. "What the hell is going on with you?"

She didn't look at him when she responded. "You're going to have to let me go, Reed."

"Sure. As soon as you give me a valid reason that makes sense, I'll let you go. But I have no worries here, Hope, because I don't believe you can do that. I believe you're scared, and that's fine, because the thought of you and everything you represent to my life scares the shit out of me. So I *get* scared. I get being intimidated by something as big as what we're about to be. But what I don't get? Running. Shutting me out. I'm not gonna let you do that."

She opened her eyes, and turned to face him at last.

He was taken aback at how her face had changed in a matter of minutes. She was determined, clearly, and she was *angry*.

"I want you to let me go because this—us—isn't what I want. I mean, physically, you rock my world, Reed. I know you know that. Hell, I know I'm not the only woman who's told you that. But on an emotional level? You're not what I need. You're just not. I'm so sorry."

The words stunned him into silence. He studied her face, looking for the weakness. Looking for the tell. The chink in her armor that was going to tell him she was bullshitting him. But the chink didn't exist. She was calm, and she was serious. She meant what she said.

She may as well have stuck a straw into the center of his heart and siphoned out every emotion he had, because after those words he was dead. Completely dead inside.

"So, you're telling me good-bye right now? Is that what you're saying?" Reed used every ounce of strength he had to pull all of the emotion from his voice. She was dumping him before they had a chance to call themselves an item. But that's what they were; he knew that. They'd been on the brink, just about to jump, and then soar.

If he'd been looking at that moment, really looking, he would have seen that chink he'd been searching for moments before. Her head shook the slightest bit, and the corners of her mouth turned down as she struggled to contain her quivering lip. That full lip he'd sucked into his mouth on more than one occasion was her tell. And he missed it.

"Yes, Reed," she said, drawing her body up tight and keeping her voice steady. "That's what I'm telling you. Unlock the door, please."

He did as she said, and she climbed down out of the Silverado.

She pulled her phone out and her fingers began to fly over the keys as she walked across the parking lot to where Morrow's Tahoe sat on the outskirts of the gravel.

He wanted to scratch his eyes out, anything to stop himself from watching her walk away.

He hadn't tried everything. He hadn't told her he loved her. He hadn't explained how he came to be the man he was. He wanted to ask her to stay, because he knew his only chance at happiness was currently getting into another man's truck.

But he didn't do any of those things. Hope had made a decision. Hell, yes, it sucked. But it was hers to make. She wasn't the kind of woman he could force, and he wouldn't feel the way he did about her if she was.

He let her walk away.

Twenty-Three

Hope took huge breaths, attempting to fill her lungs with enough oxygen to keep her moving forward through this night that was created especially for her in the depths of Hell. It wasn't working. No amount of oxygen was going to get her through this.

She was gonna need some good ol' whiskey for that.

Normally, she never, under any circumstances, consumed more than one drink on a date for Silk. She knew what could happen to her if she lost herself, knew how quickly things could spiral out of control.

But tonight things were already as out of control as any situation could get. She kept telling herself that it was just one night, that she could do it easily and be done with Frank, Wendy, and Silk. She just had to execute her plan to fruition. Totally worth the sacrifice. It would just be her and Violet against the world, the way they both wanted it. She could do this.

But then she would see Reed's face in her mind's eye, and her resolve would shatter into a million tiny little pieces. She would feel his hands on her body, sink into the comfort of the warmth that was his body, and her fingers would itch to pull out her phone and just call him. Just tell him everything and allow him to take her away from it all. She knew he would have, if she'd been honest with him from the beginning.

He could have saved her.

And now, as she stared up into Nathan's baby-smooth face, she had a thought. Maybe if she'd sat down with Reed, like Morrow had suggested more than once, he could have figured out another way to help her save Violet from a lifetime of Wendy's destruction. He came from a powerful family, and he was so smart. Maybe he could have helped.

It was too late for that now.

"So," said Nathan. He was younger than she had expected, probably not older than thirty, and dressed to the nines. The gala in which he'd be introduced as the benefactor for the new wing in the children's hospital was being held at one of Charleston's oldest and most exclusive historic hotels. It was right in the heart of downtown. They'd even arrived at the event in a horse and carriage, one mode of transportation that still lived on in the coastal southern city.

"So," answered Hope, downing the remainder of her glass and licking the last drops of top-shelf whiskey from her lips. "It was actually kind of cool of you to do this for the hospital."

"Yeah," he said, smiling. "When you have the endless amount of money that I do, why not spend it in a way that gets people onto your side, you know?"

She nodded. Nathan didn't seem to care much about the children. He cared about promoting himself, fine-tuning his image in the public eye. For what, God only knew.

"Yeah, not to mention all the kids who are going to have care, now that they've expanded the cancer wing," she said dryly.

He shrugged. "That, too."

"Uh-huh."

She signaled for one of the men walking around in server uniforms to bring her another drink. She would never be able to get through the remainder of this benefit, much less an entire night, without it.

She was just beginning to experience the hazy edges of the liquor invading her world when Nathan leaned in close, too close, and whispered in her ear. Her stomach roiled at his proximity.

"You look absolutely stunning," he said.

She wore a red dress that hugged her curves before flowing out in billowing chiffon all the way to her feet, which were encased in Cinderella-esque bejeweled heels. Her hair was gathered into an elegant ponytail that hung all the way down her back, and her makeup was understated and glamorous.

She didn't feel gorgeous. She felt cheap. And later, she'd feel used. Too used to ever be worthy of any man's love again.

"Thanks," she replied, chugging her new glass of whiskey. Nathan watched her swallow it, nodding his head in approval.

She suddenly knew she would never be able to wait until she got upstairs. Leaning in close, she rose onto her tiptoes and whispered into his ear. "Tell me what you want me to do for you tonight. What'd Frank tell you the overnight package included?"

She listened carefully, nodding her head sporadically as he

whispered his dirty plans to her. When he was finished, she smiled.

"Thanks for sharing that with me, Nathan. I've got to, um, go get some air. See you in a minute."

Before waiting for his reply, she whirled and rushed for the exit. The ballroom was located on the eighth floor of the grand old hotel, and she rode the elevator to the lobby and rushed through the revolving door. She stood on the sidewalk, gulping hot, stifling air and thanking God she was no longer inside with Nathan.

For a while, she just watched people passing on the street. Women her age strolled by in groups of giggling friends, carefree. Couples sauntered by hand in hand, not conscious that the girl they were passing was about to make a choice that would change her life forever. She was utterly alone.

Except for Violet, who waited for her at home.

When Violet crossed her mind, she cringed at the memory of getting ready for the night.

"You promised," Violet said accusingly, her voice heavy with anguish. "You'll never be able to forgive yourself for this, Hope. Don't do it."

"Vi," Hope had answered, her tone even. "I'm just going to work for Silk, like any other night."

"I'm not an idiot, Hope! It's not any other night. I overheard Frank on the phone. Overnight package? You sold your soul so you could save me. I hate this!"

She grabbed Violet to her chest in a fierce hug. "I love you, Vi. I would do anything for you. And you're still so young. You don't know what staying with Frank and Wendy will do to you in the long run. Getting you out is my only priority. So I will do whatever it takes. And I could never regret that. You hear me?"

Violet remained still in her arms, and they hadn't spoken another word to each other before Hope left with Nathan.

She hoped that one day Violet would understand. Maybe next school year, when she could sleep in her own bed at night and bring friends home from school. Maybe when she didn't fear what state they'd find their mother in at any given time or what awful thing she'd say during one of her many insane rages, Violet would forgive her.

Reed pounded the tequila shot back, holding the liquid in his mouth for a moment to savor the smoothness of it, and then gulped it down his throat. He signaled Kelly, the regular bartender at Sunny's, that he was done.

"Aw, come on, man!" Tate stared at Reed. "One shot? After the shit week you've had, you only want one shot of Cuervo?"

Reed nodded. "After the shit week I've had, any more than one and I'll end up dead in a gutter somewhere, or locked up."

Aston narrowed her eyes. "Don't say shit like that, Reed. It's not funny."

"I wasn't making a joke."

Ashley, from her spot under Finn's arm, looked pensively at Reed. "She didn't even say why?"

"I don't want to talk about it anymore," Reed announced.

God, if they kept up the interrogation, he wouldn't be able to turn down another shot, and another, until he passed out right here on the wooden-planked floor of the bar. Or fell over the side and into the dark water outside of it. He didn't need to drown his sorrow in tequila, as much as he wanted to. He needed to drown it in lyrics to a song. But he'd been doing that steadily for the past four days, and Tate had finally dragged him out to hang with the crew for a night.

"It'll get your mind off of things," he'd said.

It was a big, fat lie, because all that the women in his life seemed to want to do was analyze Hope's behavior. He was over it. He couldn't wonder about it anymore. About her. It hurt like hell when her face blazed across his memory, and it nearly made him suicidal when he remembered what it felt like to touch her. To worship her body. To love her.

So he didn't. Instead, he wrote about it.

"So," asked Tamara casually, leaning forward to place her elbows on the table. She rested her chin on her delicate hands. "Hope's best friend? The Tomorrow guy?"

At that, Reed chuckled. "His name is Morrow."

"She didn't leave you so she could go and be with him, did she?" asked Tamara. The question raked thorns across Reed's ego.

"Hell, no." Reed's eyes flared at the thought.

Tamara nodded. "Just checking."

Aston grinned. "Why were you checking? You noticed he was hot?"

"Hey!" protested Sam from beside her. "Watch it, Princess. I'm right here."

"Yes, you are," she soothed, stroking his chin with a red-nailed finger. But she sent a wink to Tamara.

"Oh, there's definitely something about him," Ashley piped up. "Maybe it's that beautiful complexion, or that crazy-curly hair that hangs into his eyes. Or it could be all the rock-hard muscles that show through those button-up shirts he wears."

Tamara sighed. "I swear to God, I glimpsed a tattoo on his chest when one of his buttons popped open the other night."

Reed had had enough. Coming out tonight was a mistake, and he was just about to open his mouth to say so when his phone vibrated in his pocket.

He pulled it out and looked at the screen, frowning. He didn't recognize the number that scrolled across the face.

"Hello?"

"Reed?"

The sharp, frantic voice at the other end of the line was familiar, but he was unable to place exactly who it belonged to.

"Yeah?" he said into the phone.

"This is Violet. Hope's sister?"

Violet? What the hell is she doing calling me? Judging from the sound of her voice, she was worked up.

Hope.

Reed stood, plugging his other ear in order to reduce the background noise of the bar. "What's wrong, Violet?"

Even before she answered, his heart rate had kicked up to the point it usually only reached after he'd swum at least a mile.

She was choking back tears now; he could hear it through the phone. He was headed for the door of the bar before his movement registered with him, throwing a wave back toward his friends.

"Violet, it's okay, sweetheart. I need to know what's wrong, though, so I can help you. Okay? Please. Tell me what happened."

His calm request seemed to be what Violet needed to get herself together.

"It's Hope," she said as Reed climbed into the Silverado and cranked the engine. Violet's voice shook. "She's in trouble, Reed. I didn't know who else to call."

Every instinct in his body was screaming at him to get to her, to find out where she was so he could get there and save Hope from whatever trouble Violet might be referring to. But he had to calm down in order to get the information he needed.

"Okay, Vi, I hear you, sweetheart. Tell me where Hope is. I'm already on the way. I just need an address."

With a shaky voice, Violet recited the name of a hotel in downtown Charleston. Reed put her on hold while he plugged it into his GPS, and then raised the phone back to his ear.

"Violet? Are you okay? Do you need me to come and get you?"

She sniffled. "No, I'm fine. Just please help my sister before it's too late. Please."

Her voice had trailed off into a whisper he could barely hear, and his heart splintered at the idea that she was hurting this way, and that Hope being in trouble was what had caused it.

He assured Violet that he'd get there, and then hung up his phone. His foot pressed down hard on the gas pedal. He didn't think the Silverado had ever pushed a hundred miles an hour. He was about to test it out for the first time.

Twenty-Four

It didn't matter which air she took in, it was all stifling. Outside, inside, it all clogged her lungs rather than invigorated them. She turned to go back inside, and nearly ran smack into Nathan's chest.

He caught her, wrapping tuxedo-covered arms around her waist, and didn't let go. She resigned herself to stay in his embrace, as much as her body was screaming at her to jerk away.

"There you are." He stared down at her, his sandy brown hair slicked back from his face. "The benefit is almost over. Which means it's almost time for us to go upstairs."

She nodded dully.

"But first," he said as he turned their bodies to begin walking back into the lobby. "I need to have a quick word with your boss."

"What?" she asked, dazed. "Frank's here?"

Frank had been known to show up at Silk's clients' events, just to check up on his girls and make sure they were doing everything they could to keep the client happy. She should have known he'd make it a point to be here, at *this* date.

"He's right inside." Nathan's voice was as smooth as velvet.

They turned into the hallway that led toward the elevators, and his hands slid below her waist to cup her backside as he leaned in to whisper in her ear. Hope nearly went into convulsions, and she literally had to fight her muscles in order to keep her arms down by their side when all she really wanted to do was break her knuckles punching Nathan in the face.

"Get your *motherfucking* hands off of her."

Reed's voice came from behind them, back toward the mouth of the hallway entrance, and Hope whirled around to face him. A mixture of shock, relief, and dread showed on her body all at once. She sagged into the wall beside her.

"Reed?"

He strode forward, cradling her face in his hands. "Baby, what are you doing here? Are you all right? Did he hurt you?"

She glanced from Reed over to Nathan's outraged face. "Reed—"

The darkness in the dim hallway crept a little closer as Frank's huge form blocked out the light from the end. Hope jumped a little at his appearance and sucked in a breath at the sight of him. She closed her eyes, blocking out the impending scenario she had so often played out in her nightmares.

Reed cocked his head to the side, absorbing the change in her face and her demeanor. He turned to face Frank, instinctively holding his arm out in front of Hope in a protective gesture.

"Who the hell are you?" Frank boomed, his signature calm demeanor missing from his voice.

"I'm Reed Hopewell." Reed's voice was lethal. "Who are you?"

One corner of Frank's wide mouth tilted upward, and he flicked an imaginary speck of dust off of his tailored suit. "I'm her boss." He gestured mildly toward Hope, as if she were of no more consequence than a pesky fly.

"Her boss." Reed expelled the words from his mouth slowly. Then, clarity dawning on his face, he turned to Hope.

"This is your stepfather?"

"Oh, she didn't tell you, lover boy?" Frank tossed. "She works for me. For my escort service. She's one of my girls."

Reed clenched his jaw. "Hope?"

She looked distractedly between Frank and Reed, torn. With everything inside of her, she wanted to grab Reed, tow him outside to his truck, and ride away with him. She wanted to explain everything once they were far, far away from Frank and Nathan. She wanted to tell him how sorry she was that she hadn't told him sooner what her life was really like, and the reasons why she was employed in such a manner.

But there was a problem with actually going through with any of that. A beautiful, blond, precious problem. A living, breathing, loving issue that Hope would literally die to protect.

And her name was Violet.

She squared her shoulders and looked Reed straight in the eye. "He's telling you the truth, Reed. I'm out with Nathan tonight because it's my job. I get paid a lot of money to date rich men. It's a part of a club my stepfather, Frank, here"—she narrowed in on Frank's face with the most scathing expression she could muster—"set up a year ago called Silk. I cannot leave this date, and I'm not going anywhere with you."

Hope thought she'd memorized each and every precious expression that would ever cross Reed Hopewell's beautiful face.

She'd thought wrong.

The realization dawned on him with a sunrise of agony so fierce Hope expected to look down at his chest and see blood pooling in his shirt. But no bodily damage could have made his face look like that; and directly after the sunrise came the darkening. A storm of regret, rage, and—so much worse—disgust clouded his features.

"You're a *call girl*," he whispered. Nearly inaudible, his voice snaked up and around her already clenched heart and squeezed the absolute life out of it.

And then, she did grab his arm, pulling him down the hallway and past a very smug Frank. It was nearly automatic. She couldn't let Reed walk away like this. She owed him so much more than that.

I owe him everything.

"Where are you going?" Frank's cool demeanor was gone again. She didn't think she'd ever seen him depart from it so many times in one sitting. "You're on a date, Hope!"

"Nathan can wait!" She towed Reed toward a door at the back of the hallway, leading to an alleyway in the back. And then they were outside, in a place exactly like the one where they'd first met. They'd come full circle, and the nausea that rose in Hope's stomach at the thought of it nearly keeled her over onto her knees on the filthy concrete.

"Reed," she said urgently. "I am not a call girl. I swear to you, I don't sleep with any of them. No matter how much Frank and my mother want me to."

He stared at her. "You get paid? To date these men? And you've been doing it the whole time...oh my *God*, Hope!"

He ended his sentence with a choking sound, and then he rubbed his stomach like it hurt him. A sob ripped from her as she watched him, and she reached out to take his hand.

He stumbled away from her, shoving her hand to the side and backing up. He held his hands out in front of him, as if to ward her off from attempting to touch him again. He dug his cell phone out of his pocket and thrust it in Hope's direction.

"Do you see this, Hope?" he said. She was so confused by the strange, new tone in his voice that it took her a minute to realize he was holding out his phone.

"Yes, Reed," Hope said softly. "Why are you showing me your phone?"

"Because your sister called me tonight. Violet's the one that sent me here. She was completely torn up. And it's because of *you*. You're hurting her. So if you're not going to think about me right now, at least think about her."

He spat out the last words, and they hit Hope hard, like a sharp slap in the face.

Violet never trusted anyone. She only trusted Hope, as a rule. So the fact that she was worried enough about her big sister to call Reed, a man she only met a handful of times...it resonated with Hope. With the exception of herself, no one had ever been able to break down Violet's perfectly built walls of mistrust.

No one but Reed.

Her knees wobbled slightly, but to their credit, they continued to hold her up.

"Reed," she pleaded. "Reed, she...she shouldn't have done that. I'm fine."

He stared at a spot just over her head, and she longed for those intense eyes to land on her.

"Yeah," he said, a sarcastic bite in his words. "You seem fine. You're out with a guy who looks like he eats women like you for lunch. And this is a *hotel*. You aren't gonna sleep with him? Look me in the eye and tell me that again."

Instead of honoring his request, she closed her eyes.

"You should have known that I wouldn't be okay with this when I found out. And that I eventually would find out. And that you could have trusted me enough to tell me at the beginning, and then let me help you out of this shit."

And then his eyes did meet hers, and she regretted what she'd wished for. Because they were void of any kind of emotion. Reed had been brimming with what he was feeling. And now there was just...nothing.

Her heart was crushed to dust. Now she knew that even if she did get Violet away from her mother, her life would be nothing without Reed there to live it with her. How could she be everything to Violet when she was full of nothing on the inside? She impatiently brushed at the tears beginning to burn her eyes. Now wasn't the time to cry. It was the time to *fight*.

She opened her mouth to speak, but Reed held up a hand.

"I...yeah, I probably don't need to hear any more. And I probably don't need to see you again."

"Reed!" Her hands curled into fists, because he needed to know about Violet. He needed to know why she did any of this.

She could see that, although he had every right to be angry, he was so far off the mark about why she continued to work for Frank. He thought it was about the money. It wasn't.

"It's done. I can't...I'm done." He backed away a few more steps. His eyes locked on hers, and she sent every single form of voodoo psychic intuition from her heart that she could find and aimed it for him. It must not have worked, because he eventually turned and walked away from her.

Somehow, somewhere deep inside her, Hope knew it was the last time she'd see Reed again.

And she turned and retched right there in the alley where she'd met and lost the only man she'd ever be able to love.

"You need to eat something, man," Tate insisted.

His tone was slightly disgusted that Reed would allow himself to become so twisted up over a woman. They were normally brothers in arms. No attachments, no worries. Reed had gone and changed the game plan, and Tate didn't seem thrilled about the results.

The irony that Tate was insisting anything at ten o'clock in the morning wasn't lost on Reed. He was just too preoccupied to care much about it.

"Damn it to hell, Reed," Tate grumbled. "It's early in the goddamn morning. You will eat these damn-near-gourmet eggs I just cooked, or I will shove them down your pretty-boy throat."

Reed was unable to help his smirk at that, and he picked up his fork to shovel a bite of eggs into his mouth. They tasted like sand.

"There," he said, pushing back from the table. "Happy? I'm going for a swim."

A week had passed since he left Hope there in the alley in downtown Charleston. Seven long, unending days. He had no idea how he missed it. He was baffled by the fact that he'd nearly bared his soul and handed his heart over to a girl who wasn't merely cheating on him, she was getting paid for it.

It would be laughable if it didn't hurt so damn bad.

And yeah, it fucking hurt. Every part of his body hurt. Granted, he was probably setting Olympic records in freestyle swimming on a daily basis in order to cope, but his heart ached worse than his limbs. And it was such a brand-new feeling for him, he wished he could just rip the bloody thing out of his chest and burn it. Throw it into an incinerator.

Phillip Castille called and informed Reed that a record company based in Atlanta wanted to offer him a recording contract. Phillip wanted to get started on an album as soon as possible, and while Reed could work on a plan to go back and forth between Atlanta and South Carolina, it would really be more convenient if he just moved to Georgia.

He'd told no one. He hadn't signed the contract yet. He hadn't written a single line of music since he lost Hope, and he wasn't thinking that inspiration would be hitting him anytime soon. He went to work at Hopewell Enterprises, even dressing more tailored for the sake of his father. He threw himself into the work, closing a large takeover deal with a company in Japan just days after the incident in downtown Charleston.

His father was so proud.

And that irony wasn't lost on Reed, either, because as long as he was doing what Gregory Hopewell thought he should be doing, his father was happy. And Reed was miserable.

It was one of the nights when he was playing and replaying the same chords on his guitar, waiting for inspiration to strike him, that a soft knock sounded on the condo door. Tate was out, God knew where, and Reed wasn't expecting any visitors. He only wore a pair of gray sweatpants, and his hair was a mess of spikes all over his head. He hadn't showered, and dark circles were framing the underside of his eyes. He looked exactly the way he felt. Even his normally vibrant blue eyes had dulled, the life having left them when his Hope did.

"I'm coming!" he called to the insistent knocker.

When he opened the door to find his mother, Lillian, standing on the step outside, he was floored. He couldn't remember the last time she'd visited the condo.

"Mom?" he asked in confusion, scratching his bare chest. "What are you doing here?"

She frowned at him, taking in his appearance with a disapproving, motherly gaze. "I'm here to see my son. May I come in?"

He gestured past him into the condo, and she brushed by on her way in.

"Can I get you something to drink, Mom?" He hoped she said no; he didn't think there was anything but Coors, Corona, and water to choose from.

She shook her head, an impatient look on her face, and waved a hand in the air. "I'm fine, Reed. I'm really just here to talk to you a minute."

She took a seat on the couch, and he sat across the coffee table from her in an overstuffed chair. "To what do I owe the honor of this visit?"

She eyed him warily. "You look like hell, sweetheart."

His mother had always been incredibly loving and warm, if not a little flighty and shallow. But sometimes, especially when it came to her children, she saw things they tried to keep hidden deep down inside themselves. And she tried her damnedest to root it out and help them heal. Especially if it was a result of her own actions.

Lillian smoothed her sleek, dark hair, streaked with silver, behind her ears and crossed her ankles demurely. Reed rolled his eyes, because no matter what shit his mother was putting on the shelves, he wasn't buying. *Demure* was the last word anyone could use to describe the real Lillian.

"What's the matter, Reed?"

He settled back onto the chair, staring at a spot above her head. "I don't know what you're talking about."

"Really? Because at times, you're prettier than your sister. But right now you look a hot mess. And your father says you've been excelling at work. *Excelling*, Reed. At Hopewell Enterprises?" She shook her head knowingly. "Not my son. Not that you're not capable of it, but I know you. Your heart's not anywhere near that company. It's on a stage somewhere in a city with a hell of a lot more lights than Nelson Island, or even Charleston. Aston hinted at something going on with that girl we met on the Fourth...what was her name, Hope something?"

Without warning, hot moisture stung the backs of his eyes,

and he was unable to swallow past the lump that was forming in his throat. His mother, if nothing else, was attuned to him above anyone else, and she had hit the nail on the head. He couldn't stand to hear Hope's name from anyone's mouth, not even Lillian's.

"Talk to me, baby boy," she coaxed. "Your momma's here to listen. Not judge. That's your daddy's job."

He dropped his head into his hands and heaved a huge, shuddering sigh. She was right. If he didn't get this out, it was going to eat him alive. He wasn't going to survive it, maybe not even if he talked about it. The ragged hole that stood in the place where his heart used to be was killing him.

"Mom," he said, his voice cracking slightly. "God...I love her. I love her so damn much, and she broke me. I'm shattered because of this woman."

Lillian's face was something between heartbreak and determination. She clearly did not plan to fail her son tonight, no matter what happened.

"Tell me about it," she demanded gently.

The whole story came rushing out. He told his mother everything; about how he'd saved her from an assault when they met, about how he'd felt an immediate attraction to her, about how they'd been drawn into each other's arms that night at the banquet. He told her about how they'd decided to spend time getting to know each other, how he'd taken her on dates and set up a special dinner at the beach just for her. He explained how they ended up in Atlanta together and how he'd fallen in love with her, and then how Hope had pushed him away without an explanation.

When he finally got to the part where Violet called him with her panicked little voice, and what he'd found when he'd arrived at the hotel, moisture was clinging to his long, thick lashes, and his entire body was trembling.

"Oh, baby," said Lillian softly. Her hands were folded in her lap as she listened, and the occasional *tsk* or shake of her head was all the movement she made while her son poured out his heart. "I'm so, so sorry. Women can be complex individuals, sweetheart. I think there's far more going on with Hope than you can begin to imagine."

He shook his head. "I wanted to give her everything, Mom. Everything. And she betrayed me. She never told me what was going on. What's so complex about that?"

Lillian stared hard at Reed, the intensity of her gaze perfectly matching the heat with which her son usually pinned people down. "Reed, the entire time you were with Hope, did she strike you as a liar? Or a cheater?"

He contemplated, and then slowly shook his head. "No. At least I didn't think so. Guess I was wrong."

She shook her head, a sad expression entering her eyes. "This is my fault, Reed. Not yours."

He lifted his head to stare at her. "How can this be your fault?"

A tear of her own slid singularly down one of her perfectly made-up cheeks. "You have trust issues. It's why you've never had a serious girlfriend. And it's because of me. I know that."

He shook his head. Seeing his mother cry affected him in a way that nothing else in the world did. He just wanted to make her stop. "Mom, that's not true. You are an amazing mother."

She had been, in her own way. She was flighty, and a little thoughtless at times. Her affairs had definitely affected him, but he was younger than Aston when it happened and it had affected his sister even more deeply. She was his mother, the only one he'd ever get. And he loved her. He had forgiven her a long time ago.

She laughed ruefully. "Right. You mean, when I was home? And not doing God-knows-what with other men while your father worked his ass off to get the company off the ground?"

He'd never heard the truth actually fall from her lips. He knew she'd discussed it with Aston, and that she and his father had mended things long ago. But she'd never come right out and admitted her infidelity in front of her son.

It was a lot to take in, heavy and thick and…a relief. It was like taking a deep breath, hearing her admit the truth after all this time.

"You were young, but you knew what was going on," she said wisely. "And it hurt you. You've filed it away in your mind all these years, and you don't trust women farther than you can throw them."

He nodded. He couldn't deny the truth any more than she could deny the fact that she'd cheated on his father multiple times. The damage was done, and they all had issues to work through because of it. Lillian was nearly buried under a pile of guilt. Gregory always felt like he wasn't enough of a man, causing him to throw himself heart and soul into making the company bigger and better all the time. Reed didn't trust women, didn't give his heart away. And Aston still hadn't forgiven her mother for the hell she'd put their family through all those years ago.

"You're right," said Reed quietly. "All of that is probably true, Mom. So I have trust issues. But the point here is, I *did* trust Hope. Something inside of me recognized her as my other half, as the angel who was sent here just for me. But I was *wrong*. How am I supposed to come back from that kind of mistake?"

"What if you weren't wrong?" said Lillian. "I know you, Reed. I'm your momma. You're sensitive, you're guarded, and you see people in a way that's unlike anyone I've ever known. You've always chosen friends wisely, and I can't imagine that choosing the woman you want to spend the rest of your life with would be any different. Whatever you saw in Hope was there. You don't have the whole story, sure, but I know you didn't misjudge her. You need to find out what's going on with her. You need to go to her."

He stared at his mother in disbelief. "Why would I—"

"Oh, for God's sake, here's where the stubborn male part of you comes out to play. This isn't about your ego, baby boy, it's about finding happiness in a life that's usually too short to begin with. You said that girl's your other half? Then she's yours. And you need to go and get her."

Something inside Reed stirred. Some deep, ancient instinct told him that his mother was right, and no matter how bruised his heart and ego were, Hope still needed him. Maybe he *didn't* know the whole story.

Maybe she needed him now more than she did the very first time he'd met her. Maybe she needed him to save her all over again.

Standing, he kissed his mother on the cheek and ran—sprinted, really—for his truck. He didn't look back as Lillian shouted after him, her voice light with happiness and excitement.

"Stop at the ranch, honey! You know what to look for. Now's the time, baby boy!"

He nodded, more to himself than in response to her words, because at last he knew exactly what he was looking for.

He pulled out his phone the second he was moving, the sound of his big engine revving in the background as he made the call.

"Morrow," he snapped through gritted teeth when the other man answered. "Where is she?"

It didn't matter where she was, he was on his way to her. But first, he was going to stop at his parents' ranch and pick up his grandmother's antique engagement ring.

Twenty-Five

Hope sat in a rocking chair on Morrow's row-house porch, staring at the street beyond as a carriage pulled by two lazy horses clopped past on the old cobblestone. Her chin rested in one hand, an untouched glass of sweet tea on the table next to her, the ice in the glass melted long ago thanks to the heavy southern heat.

The screen door swung open adjacent to her, but she didn't move a muscle. She'd been sitting here for hours…no, maybe at this point it had been days.

She had an appointment with an attorney this afternoon. She was ready to fight for her sister, and she finally had the leverage she needed to do it. Only, in the meantime, Violet was still living with Frank and Wendy. They had taken away Violet's phone. Worry was ripping her insides apart.

After Reed left her in the alley, she couldn't bring herself to go back inside the hotel. She'd called Morrow to pick her up, and the entire story had poured out. Morrow had taken her home, where Wendy had thrown her stuff out in the driveway.

Without allowing her to stay and fight, Morrow had thrown her back in the car and taken her to his house.

She'd been unable to see her sister for seven days. She had no idea if Wendy was hurting her, but she could guess that Violet was suffering. And that alone could have killed her. But her heart was doubly broken, because she knew she'd never lay eyes on Reed again.

"Hey, girl," said Morrow, his voice not quite penetrating the malaise that hung over Hope over the last week. "I brought you something to eat."

His spirit remained strong and steady in spite of it all, and for that she was grateful. She counted on Morrow for so much more than he knew. And right now, she counted on him not to pity her, not to fall apart on her because she'd lost everything. She needed his strength above all else, and that was exactly what he'd been giving her.

"This too shall pass," he said. "At least that's what my grand-mamma told me whenever bad shit happened. And you know that for me, a lot of bad shit happened, Hope. She was always right. That meeting you have with the attorney, you're gonna get Violet back. It's only a matter of time."

She sighed. "I know. But I wish I could afford the best attorney out there. I know Frank will have the best backing him up, and with power on his side...it's still not a slam dunk."

The horse-drawn carriage, with its two blissful riders lounging back in the seat, taking in historic Charleston, ambled past and the street became quiet and empty. Hope thought it was fitting; the gaping cavity in her chest was exactly the same.

The plate of honey and biscuits Morrow had set next to her tea was fragrant, and she knew that the gnawing in her stomach was hunger; she also knew that once she filled it, the gnawing would only be replaced by nausea. She ignored the plate.

"Let's talk about Reed." Morrow crossed his arms over his chest.

Hope flinched. "I don't want to talk about him."

"I think you should. You need help with Frank, Hope. You can't do this on your own. Help is on the way. I want you to get ready."

"What do you mean, 'Help is on the way'?" she asked. "What kind of help?"

As she spoke, she was aware of a deep rumbling a few blocks away, one that she would never forget. One she thought she'd never hear again.

"Row?" she asked, aiming a heartbroken glance into his eyes. "What'd you do?"

He continued to hold her, but stared right back into her eyes as he spoke. "I know you well enough to know better, Hope. I did nothing, I swear. All I did was answer my phone."

She stood, raising a shaking hand to her eyes to shield the sunlight's glare as she searched and was rewarded with the only thing she'd wanted to see since the night in the alley last weekend. Reed's Silverado, skidding to a stop at the curb beyond Morrow's front walk.

"Reed." She breathed, one hand over her mouth and the other squeezing herself around the stomach.

The truck door slammed behind Reed's hurtling form and he

was on the walk, up the steps, and standing in front of Hope in two seconds flat.

Morrow kissed her cheek and nodded at Reed. Then he disappeared into the house.

"Baby," said Reed, his voice more full of anguish and misery than she'd ever heard it. More than she'd ever heard in anyone's. "I'm—"

She shook her head and took a step farther so that they were only inches apart. "Don't. Let me speak first, Reed. You deserve that much."

He nodded, his blue eyes soaking her up, hungrily absorbing her every feature, his ears taking in her every word.

"I didn't sleep with Nathan last weekend," she blurted out. It felt amazing to tell him that, because she knew he had spent the entire last week thinking otherwise. The words left her lips and she was lighter, freer, for having said them.

"That was the plan, that was the intention, but I would never have been able to go through with it, Reed. Even if you hadn't shown up that night. It's not who I am."

She sank down into her chair, and Reed pulled up the other rocker and scooted it over so that their knees were touching. He grabbed both of her hands in his, smoothing the skin on top with his thumbs. He just listened, which was more comforting than anything else he could have done at that moment.

"Me and Violet didn't have the best upbringing," she began. She explained to him about how Wendy had always struggled with stability and finding a man to fill the void in her life two daughters just couldn't fix. She told him how she brought home man after man, some who used, some who drank, and some who hit. She told Reed about what she'd seen in her living room at two in the morning on so many occasions, and about how she had to barricade her door at night merely to be left alone in her own bed.

Reed's sharp intakes of breath, muttered curses, and the pain in his eyes while he listened to her story nearly stopped her more than once, but she forged on because she needed to tell it, and he needed to know it.

"And then Violet came along, and I vowed that I'd never let my little sister see or experience half of the things that I had. So I tried to stand between her and everything, all the time. I took everything for her, from curses to sightings of strung-out users on our couch, to beatings from the men in our lives. I protected her from all of it as best I could. It's ingrained in me to protect her. If I hadn't, who else was going to do it? My mother?" She laughed bitterly. "And then, one day, I couldn't protect her anymore. Wendy got it into her head that everything wrong in her life was Violet's and my fault. I was big enough to fight back. Violet isn't."

At this point he left his rocking chair and his knees met the wood of the porch as he knelt at her feet. "I didn't know, baby. God, I wish you'd told me. I would have crushed Frank and Wendy with my bare hands."

"I know." She smiled sadly down at him. "I know you would have. I could feel something in you, Reed, from the first minute I met you. You were my hero that night, and I knew that was going to be who you were to me as often as I let you. I didn't want to drag you into my mess. I just didn't."

He pinned her down with a stare so full of emotion she was unable to look away. "I'm here now. And you're not going to be able to stop me from rolling around in your mess. I swear to God, I will help you through whatever situation you're in, and I will be the one pulling you through to the end of it. Because you deserve to be happy, Hope. More than anyone I've ever known. I'm going to make that happen, if it takes laying down my life to do it."

"It's not me that needs saving," she said urgently. "It's Violet. She's with Frank and Wendy, Reed. I've only been working for Frank because the money is good, and I've been putting it away so that I could start a life with Violet away from Frank and Wendy. I didn't have a plan for how to do it until the night he told me I'd have to start sleeping with clients. That night something clicked in my brain, and I knew how to get her out of there."

"How?"

She took a deep breath. "I...I recorded my date that night. At the hotel where you...saw me? His name was Nathan White. I recorded him telling me what he was going to do with me, and how it was all a part of the package that Frank presented him. I have a meeting with an attorney today and I'm going to hand over the recording. I can bring Frank down. We can tell them that Wendy's been abusing Violet. This can finally be over."

Reed wrapped his arms around her. "That's good, baby. That's really good."

She nodded. "I'm just worried it won't be enough. There are a lot of higher-ups on Frank's client list. None of them are going to want his business exposed."

Hot tears were streaming down her cheeks, and Reed wiped

them away with strong, sure thumbs. "Do you know what it means to be a Hopewell in this town? Do you? We'll use my family's team of lawyers. There's no way in hell we won't win a fight with Frank and Wendy. Especially with you knowing what you do about Wendy's issues, and Frank's business. Violet will be ours. I promise you that, baby. Do you trust me?"

She looked into his eyes. With everything she was and everything she had, she trusted Reed Hopewell.

"Yeah," she said, smiling for the first time in days. "I do."

The screen door banged against its frame as Morrow appeared on the porch, keys in hand. "I'm out of here, now that things are looking up. Y'all can have the house for a while."

He smirked at the two of them, and Reed shook his hand. "Thanks, man. For being on my side. For letting me know she was here."

Morrow nodded. "I'm always on *her* side, Reed. So you better be what's best for her."

It took longer than Hope wanted it to. But she would never forget the look on Frank's face when Reed's lawyers played the recording she'd acquired during the emergency custody hearing the following week. Violet waited in the hallway with Reed's mother, her arm in a sling, while Hope and Reed fought for her in the room beyond the big, wooden doors.

When they exited two hours later, it was with gigantic smiles on their faces.

Violet leaped up, an anxious question alight in her gray eyes.

Hope opened her arms. "It's me and you from here on out, Vi."

It felt like she was flying, making that declaration to her little sister. There would be a bigger trial later, because there were major charges pending against both Frank and Wendy for Violet's abuse and for the illegal business practices of Silk. There were more girls who would testify to the fact that it wasn't merely a dating service.

Reed wrapped his arms around both Hope and Violet. "If you two think you're leaving me out of this, you're crazy. It's the three of us from here on out. You good with that?"

Violet smiled, and Hope could see the effects that newfound freedom left on her sister's face. "I guess I can deal with that."

Hope looked up into Reed's grinning face, knowing that she owed so much to this man, for having faith in her even when she'd given him no reason to do so. "Thank you, Reed. For helping me save my sister."

He nuzzled her earlobe with his nose. "You're welcome. Anything for you. Tonight, we'll go back to the ranch so that Violet can spread out, okay? I have some things I want to talk to you about."

Hope looked up questioningly at him.

"I want to be totally honest with you," he said softly. "You don't know everything about my upbringing, just the way I didn't know everything about yours. It's not exactly the same kind of shit storm yours was, but it explains a lot about me and where I'm coming from. I want you to know it all, Hope."

"And that's why it's always been difficult for me to trust women," said Reed as he leaned back against the couch cushions in his bedroom at the ranch. "You're different, somehow. I knew it then and I know it now. After Atlanta, I wanted to bare my soul to you completely, but you started pulling away. I know now that was because you were scared of what we were becoming, and scared that you'd lose Violet because of it."

She nodded, reaching out to run the back of her hand over his cheek. "I was scared. I'm not anymore."

He nodded. Nerves fluttered in his stomach; he swallowed thickly in order to keep the bile down where it belonged. This was the only moment in his life that mattered, the only moment he'd looked at when a monumental change was about to take place. If she agreed, everything would change. If she didn't, everything was lost.

It's right, he thought. *It's always been so damn right with Hope.*

"Hope," he said, his voice strong despite the butterflies flapping their wings madly in his gut, "I love you. I love you so damn much it makes my bones ache, and nothing has ever hurt so good. I want you, now and forever, because without you none of the rest of this shit matters. You're it, Hope—you're my future. I want you to know that I would be saying this to you whether you'd told me everything you just shared or not. This isn't pity talking. It's love, and if you hadn't been so goddamned stubborn I would have told you how I felt a lot sooner."

Her beautiful face was slack, the shock registering in her eyes while he spoke, and her jaw hanging slightly open in the most adorable look of shock Reed had ever seen. *Wait till she hears what I'm gonna say next.*

He slid off the couch and onto his knees beside her for the

second time that day. If it was indicative of what was to come in their relationship, he knew he'd gladly stay on his knees for this woman for the rest of their lives.

He propped one foot out in front of him, his arm resting on his knee.

"Hope Dawson," he said, producing a tiny glittering ring from his pocket. She gasped, both hands flying to her mouth.

"I'd do anything for you. Anything. Will you do just one thing for me and make me the happiest man in the world? Marry me, baby."

A strange hiccupping sound was happening inside of her; she wiggled happily in her seat on the couch and then launched herself at him from where she sat.

"Oh my God," she gasped. "You seriously just proposed?"

He nodded, the picture of patience. "Yes. And you haven't answered me yet."

"*Yes!*" she squealed. "Yes, please, *God*, make me Hope Hopewell. Yes, Reed!"

He rose, laughing, and they tumbled onto the couch together in a fit of giggles, and he'd never been as happy in his life as he was at that moment.

When they paused, staring at each other, he held himself above her as she smiled up at him.

"Yes?" he asked, his voice full of awe.

She nodded, and finally his lips were touching hers. He hadn't kissed her in so long, and he missed the sweetness of her touch and her scent. Both enveloped him then as he sank deeper into her lips and her body, and an involuntary groan left him as his thickening erection told her how much he'd missed her. She moved her hips, pressing against him, and he silently begged her to stop. If she continued, he'd lose his shit before he got the chance to make their engagement official.

"That's my grandmother's ring I put on your finger," he whispered into her ear.

"It's gorgeous," she whispered back, allowing her lips to graze along his scruffy jaw. "Fits perfectly."

"You fit me perfectly," he said in a strained voice. "God, baby, I missed you. Don't ever take this away from me again."

She laughed. "I think by letting you put your ring on my finger I proved I won't."

He nodded, and smiled at her startled gasp when he yanked the tiny sundress she was wearing up to her hips. He stared down at the little purple panties she wore beneath and ran a finger from her pierced belly button down until his finger connected with damp heat. She shivered beneath him, and the intoxication that came with making her feel good overtook him.

"What did you miss?" he asked, snaking his finger under the panties and moving them to the side.

She hissed as he connected with her wetness, and he could barely hear her answer.

"I can't hear you, Hope," said Reed. "Tell your fiancé what you missed."

God. He had a fiancée. He was going to marry this girl. She'd said yes.

"Your—your tongue," she gasped. "I missed your tongue, Reed. And your fingers, and..."

"And?" he asked.

She stiffened beneath him as he took his finger away. He chuckled at her feisty glare. "Tell me."

She sat up on her elbows, and the fiery gaze she pinned him with made his dick twitch in his jeans. "I missed your cock, Reed. I missed it bad, and I want you to fix that right now."

"Oh, *fucking* hell," he groaned. He stood and stripped off everything as quickly as he'd ever done, never taking his eyes off of her as she pulled that sexy little dress off over her head.

"Now," she said again.

"What about my tongue?" he asked as he watched her sit up.

"Later," she breathed, pulling him down.

He sat, and she climbed on top of him, facing away.

"Baby," he groaned, leaning forward to swipe at the back of her neck with his tongue. "You're going to destroy me."

"This is your scavenger hunt," she told him, reaching up to pull her long locks aside. "Find your treasure, remember?"

He was so distracted by how beautiful she was from this angle, how amazingly wonderful she felt situated on top of him, that he forgot he was supposed to be finding another tattoo.

Leaning back, she captured his earlobe in between her teeth.

"Fuck," he groaned.

"Start hunting," she instructed. She positioned herself so that her entrance was hovering right over him. She moaned softly, and he closed his eyes.

"I can't concentrate," he hissed.

"Try. Hurry."

He opened his eyes and searched her smooth skin, running his hands along her back while his eyes roved every inch of her. He knew it wouldn't be somewhere he'd seen exposed, so he craned his neck around her petite shape until he found what he was looking for.

This one was tiny, an almost minuscule representation of a torch. He brushed it lightly with a finger. He couldn't believe he'd missed this one in Atlanta, but it was very small and nestled beneath her left breast at the top of her rib cage.

"What's this for?" he whispered, stroking it lovingly.

She turned in his lap to face him, looking deep into his eyes while she answered.

"It's for you," she said. His eyebrows lifted in surprise. "I got this for the man who dared to enter my life one day. I knew that with all the darkness I bring to the table, he'd need a light to see me." She shrugged. "You saw me, Reed."

She rose, then sank down onto him with such ferocity he cried out in unison with her, and wrapped his arms tightly around her waist as she began to ride him. He wasn't sure if he was holding on to her, or whether it was the other way around, but he couldn't unwrap himself from around her, even if he had wanted to.

She held his gaze, using her leg muscles to hold herself up, and then drop back down onto him at an increasingly rapid pace. He leaned forward to brush his lips against hers, and groaned as he felt her interior walls clench tightly around him.

Kissing her neck, he murmured, "That's it, baby, let go. I've got you. I'm always going to have you."

She continued to rise and fall on top of him in a pounding

rhythm. He helped her by hoisting her hips up and down right along with her, biting his lip with the pure ecstasy he felt.

With his name on her lips, she crashed into her orgasm with trembling limbs, and he allowed himself to release inside of her, washing away all of the pain and hurt and despair the last week of their lives had caused, leaving them both breathless and trembling, still holding on for dear life.

"I love you," he whispered, leaning his forehead against hers.

He marveled at the fact that he'd never said those words to a woman before her. Only her.

She stroked her hands through his hair. "Truth?"

One corner of his mouth turned up in a half-grin. "Always."

"I love you back."

Epilogue

I swear to God, if you two make out in front of me one more time I'm going to go drown myself in the damn ocean," warned Violet.

"Vi!" groaned Hope. "Language!"

Reed only laughed. "You mean the ocean you now love more than painting?"

Violet pointed a finger at him. "No, Hopewell. I love nothing more than painting."

She leaned back onto her beach towel, which was completely covered by the huge, hot pink umbrella staked into the sand behind her. Her head was brimmed by the largest beach hat money could buy. Violet wasn't taking any chances with the sun against her pale skin.

Hope, on the other hand, was slathered with sunscreen that made her skin gleam, and completely exposed in the glaring heat of the Labor Day southern sun. Her bikini was turquoise blue against her bronzed skin, and tiny.

"I'm so glad we came back here for the weekend," she said softly. "We have to come back a lot. I love this beach."

Reed leaned over to brush his lips against hers, eliciting a soft sigh from Hope and a gag from Violet. "We will come back as often as you want. Atlanta is only a four-hour drive away."

"You promise?"

"You doubt me?" he asked with mock hurt.

"Never."

"And next summer, if you want, we can get married on this beach."

"But Sam and Aston are getting married on this beach next summer."

"So?" One sexy eyebrow rose, and Hope wanted to kiss it. She restrained herself, for Violet's sake.

She leaned her head back and laughed into the bright summer sky. "Okay."

"Are you guys really going to stick me with Reed's parents tonight while you go have fun at a bar?"

"Violet!" admonished Hope.

"Yep," answered Reed simultaneously. "Hell, girl, I had to live with them for years. *Years*. You can endure one night with them."

Violet shrugged, but Hope saw the flash of happiness and appreciation in her eyes. Gregory and Lillian had taken an immediate liking to Violet, and over the past month, they had become the closest thing to grandparents she had ever known.

"Thank you," she said softly. "Both of you. For saving me."

They looked at each other, and then back at Violet.

"No problem," Reed said with a shrug. "It's kinda what we do."

"Row!" squealed Hope as she ran into her best friend's arms the second he walked into Sunny's.

Morrow glanced around him uncomfortably "Still hate this place. It leans too much."

Hope grinned. "Thanks for coming. You're going to be blown away by what Reed does."

"I better be," grumbled Morrow. "I need a shot. This place makes me nervous. And he *should* be good. He scored a record deal in ATL, didn't he? Took my best girl all the way to Georgia and shit."

Hope smiled at him. "He sure did. But I'm sure one of these days you're going to find a new best girl."

She led him to the table where the usual crowd sat, minus Reed, who was warming up with his guitar on the stage.

She introduced Morrow around the table, and everyone greeted him Nelson Island–style. A shot was passed to him almost immediately, and everyone raised their glasses in the air.

"To bright futures," Tamara said. "Reed and Hope's, Ash and Finn's little bundle of joy, and Sam and Aston."

She stopped, raising the glass to her lips. Hope leaned over and elbowed the redhead in her ribs.

"That's all?" she asked playfully

"Hell," Tamara answered with a roll of her eyes. "All that's left is Tate, Blaze, and I. I'm pretty sure that our futures are stuck in reverse. So yeah, that's it."

Aston shot Tamara a sidelong glance. "Tam. Lighten up, girl. Tonight is about celebrating."

"Yeah," Tamara answered, knocking back her shot and standing. "And I don't much feel like doing that tonight. Cheers, y'all."

Silence shrouded the table as Tamara walked out the door.

"Who was that?" asked Morrow, leaning into Hope's ear.

She shook her head, shushing him. "Someone should go after her."

Aston raised a brow. "We've all gone after her more than once when she's stormed out of this bar. And my brother's about to sing."

Hope sighed, pushing her chair back from the table. "Okay, then. Guess it's my turn."

Morrow stood up with her.

"Stay," she said. "I got her."

Morrow nodded, his eyes glued to the door where Tamara had just disappeared.

Hope found Tamara on the pier outside the bar. She sat down next to her, kicking off her sandals, and dangled her feet off the end of the pier.

"So, what's up?" she asked quietly.

Tamara shook her head, staring off into the blackness. "You seem really nice, Hope. Like… I totally see why Reed fell for you. But what's going on with me… it's not something you can just step in and fix. I'll be fine. I always am. Go on back inside and listen to your man sing."

Hope reached around the other girl, gently squeezing her to her side for a moment before she stood. She knew she wasn't going to be able to mend whatever ailed Tamara at the moment.

"Don't leave," she pleaded. "Take a break, and then come back in. Reed will hate having missed you when he comes offstage."

Tamara looked up at her with a small smile. "I'll see you in a bit."

When Hope returned to the bar, she shook her head at the group, and then focused on the stage, where Reed's first song was about to begin.

Halfway through his set, Tamara silently slid back into her seat at the table. Hope smiled at her.

"Thank you," she mouthed.

One side of Tamara's perfectly sculpted lips quirked upward, and she flipped her long, burnished hair over her shoulder.

Reed's voice carried them all to a different place in their minds, one where nothing bad happened to good people on a tiny little island in the South, and love never evaded those who deserved it.

Please turn the page for an excerpt from the first book in Diana Gardin's Nelson Island series,

Wanting Forever.

Available now!

One

Keep stacking those bales, son. When you're finished, we'll head back up to the main house and I'll let you go for the day." Leon, the ranch manager, scratched his forehead as he lifted his Stetson in the steamy, late afternoon heat.

"Yes, sir." Sam stood back from the hay bale and wiped the sweat dripping from his forehead. It was unusually hot for May. On a day like this, he'd guzzled two gallon-size jugs of water, and he'd need more by the time he was done. He'd lost his shirt hours ago, and the brazen heat sizzled into the now-golden skin of his chiseled torso.

When Sam finished spreading the hay through the pasture for the horses for the day, he met Leon in front of the stables.

"I want to run something by you, Leon. Do you mind?"

"Go ahead, son." Leon's expression teetered between tense and exhausted. He was down a few workers, which was why the ranch had hired Sam on as a temp without asking a whole lot of questions.

"How's the new scheduling procedure working out?"

"Savin' my ass. Your suggestion of having some of the trainers pitch in was a great way to get around the shortage of hands. You done a lot of this scheduling stuff before, kid?"

The corner of Sam's mouth tilted upward in a smile. He grabbed his shirt, lying atop the swinging barn door, and used it as a rag to wipe the sweat dripping from his chin. "A little bit. I helped the owner of the garage where I used to work with a lot of stuff like that. Ended up managing the place when I was eighteen."

They climbed into Leon's work truck and turned up the gravel path toward the main house.

"So, Sam," Leon began. He removed his well-worn Stetson and scratched his head. Replacing the hat, he glanced at Sam. "You plannin' on stayin' around just for the summer? Or you gonna be here in Nelson Island longer than that?"

"You know, sir, I really don't know yet. I'm just trying to figure things out. Taking it one day at a time."

Leon nodded. "I can understand that. You're young. What...twenty or so?"

"I was twenty-one last month."

"Twenty-one. You got a lot of road stretched out in front of you, Sam. Nelson Island is a great place to figure it all out."

"Thank you, sir. I can see that."

"And you moved from where?"

"North of here, sir."

Sam wasn't willing to go into details about exactly where he was from. Too much information may lead someone to draw conclusions about what he'd done back home, about why he was running.

Leon pulled the truck onto the circular driveway that curved into a horseshoe in front of the main house. He turned off the ignition and climbed out of the truck.

"Got any special plans this evening?" Leon asked.

"No," Sam answered, shaking his head. "I think I'll just go back to the tack house and crash for the night."

He nodded. "It's almost dinnertime, son. Shouldn't be skipping meals while you're doing all this hard work. Go on, then. I'll see you early tomorrow. Seven o'clock."

"I'll be there," answered Sam.

Leon headed up the steps leading to the front door.

Sam watched him go, thinking back to when he'd first met Leon on his way down from Virginia. He'd stopped at a gas station to fill up, and Leon had stopped him to ask about the Harley. They'd gotten to talking, or rather Leon talked and Sam listened. The ranch manager was looking for some workers. Sam ended up leaving the gas station and following behind Leon's truck while Leon led him straight over the bridge from Charleston, South Carolina, to Mr. Hopewell at his horse ranch in Nelson Island.

Sam shoved his hands in his pockets and walked around the driveway and down the stone-paved path through wooded land that led to the tack house.

Greenery surrounded the ranch, from old magnificent magnolia trees to palmettos flapping in the breeze. Lush, green pastures rose and fell gently with the rolling hills. The property was perfectly pristine due to Leon Jackson's running the place like a well-oiled machine. He was the man who made sure every job was handled, every animal was well looked after, and every building on the property was spic-and-span. Details and organization were law to Leon.

As he made his way through the trees, Sam had a flash of the night he'd left Duck Creek. He'd left Ever standing alone in woods so similar to these. The mountains of southwest Virginia accompanied him like a friend during his childhood, and the contrast he found on the coast of South Carolina was both comforting and disconcerting.

He couldn't wait to show Ever—just as soon as it was safe.

Walking into the tack house, Sam clicked the door closed behind him and stood just inside, surveying the living room.

Mr. Hopewell had fashioned several of the buildings on his property into guesthouses. He used the larger ones for actual guests and the couple of smaller ones as houses for the hired help who needed to stay on the property. Sam qualified, as he had no other place to live on the island. Most of the staff drove to work. Leon lived in quite a nice house only a couple of miles away, with his wife.

Leaning against the door, he pulled the well-worn sheet of stationery out of his back jeans pocket. He pulled it out and began to read.

Sam,

If you only knew how it felt being in Duck Creek without you, you'd come running back to me. I know you don't want to do

that. But I really am miserable here without you. The only silver lining about you being gone is that my dad is gone too. He can't hurt me anymore, thanks to you. And Hunter.

I've known you my whole life, Sam, and I've known I loved you for the same amount of time. We've never been so far apart. How are you? I know you can't e-mail without access to a computer. I was so excited to get a letter from you. Letters are more romantic than e-mail anyway. So I've written you this one. Maybe it will make you a little less lonely if you read it at night before bed.

Thank you for asking Hunter to take care of me while you're gone. He's been doing just that. Hovering a little, but I appreciate the help he's given me. I was able to use the insurance money from Daddy to pay off the house and car. Now I only have to worry about the monthly bills, and my job at the bakery is doing a pretty good job of covering that.

Without you, Sam, none of this would be possible. I'd still be terrified to sleep in my own bed every night. I'll be forever grateful.

I want this to be over soon, so we can be together again.

Love you forever, and

Ever

His daily readings gave Sam the strength he needed to stay away from her. Until the whole thing with her father's death blew over, they had to stay apart.

He carefully folded the letter on its worn creases and placed it back into his pocket. Then he wandered over to the desk in the corner and waited.

The phone on the desk jangled a few minutes later. He picked up the cordless handset.

"Hello?"

"It's me." Hunter's gravelly voice.

"I know."

"How are you, man?" Worry laced the edges of Hunter's tone. He'd always taken care of Sam. He took the big brother role way too seriously, if you asked Sam. They were only eighteen months apart.

"Couldn't be better, considering. The Hopewells have been real nice so far. Can't do much better than that. There's been a lot of fixing fences, cleaning out barns, and lifting heavy-ass feed bags, but the money's good. It's not like I haven't done hard work before. So I'm gonna be okay here, Hunter."

"Glad to hear it."

"How is she, Hunter?"

He couldn't wait any longer to hear about Ever.

"She's missing the shit out of you, Sam. Like you'd expect. I try to drive over most nights after work to check on her. But sometimes I leave the site too late. On those days I call to see if she needs anything."

"Good. Keep doing that, Hunter. You keep taking care of her, since I can't right now."

"Sam...look. You could come home if we'd just—"

"We've been through this. It's not going to happen. This is the best way for everyone."

"How's it the best way for you, Sam? You're on the run. I never thought you'd—"

"Just stop. We don't need to rehash this over the phone. What's done is done. No one will understand the truth except the three of us. Now, do your damn job and take care of Ever."

"Done, man." Hunter sighed.

A rhythmic knock sounded on the heavy wooden door of the tack house. Sam glanced at it quickly.

"I gotta go, Hunt. Stick to the plan. Love you, bro."

He hung up the phone and strode to the door.

When he opened it, the slick grin of Reed Hopewell shone up at him from the stoop. Reed leaned against the doorjamb, looking casual in a pale blue T-shirt and jeans.

"What's up, man?" he drawled. "Dad sent me down here to ask you to come on up to the main house for dinner tonight."

Sam stepped back so Reed could come inside. He closed the door behind him.

"Yeah, okay. It's always nice enjoying a meal up there."

The too-familiar panic began to set in deep in Sam's bones.

"That's what Dad does. He treats all the help like family." He smiled playfully and slapped Sam on the back.

Sam chuckled, not quite relieved. He'd been invited to the main house a couple of times for dinner since he'd been working at the ranch. Each time his heart ended up in his throat, anxiously waiting to hear that his short-term employment was terminated. Or worse...that the sheriff would be there waiting to haul him back to Duck Creek.

Mr. and Mrs. Hopewell didn't seem to suspect a thing. They

were gracious employers and seemed to want to include Sam for purely innocent reasons. They claimed they didn't like thinking of him always alone, fending for himself.

"All right, man. Let me change and I'll be right out."

Reed sank onto the soft plaid couch, propping his scuffed boots up on the coffee table. Then he straightened, staring at the couch cushions with eyes full of doubt.

"You haven't been..." He glanced pointedly at Sam, and then back at the couch.

Sam caught his gist, and cleared his throat. "Uh, no. Definitely not."

"Cool. Just had to ask. So my sister's in town for the summer. Mom and Dad have asked the kitchen staff to do it up right. It's gonna be bangin'."

"Oh yeah?" Sam called as he walked to the bedroom, stripping off his work clothes as he entered the attached bath.

He showered quickly and changed into a fresh pair of jeans and the nicest shirt he owned, a striped button-down. He preferred T-shirts to shirts with collars. But if he was having dinner with the Hopewells, he'd play the part as best he could.

"My sister stays gone most of the year. So when she's home for the summer, they really go all out."

Sam nodded. He was aware of the Hopewells' other child, a girl who attended college in Louisiana. She hadn't been home during his time in Nelson Island, so he'd never met her.

"I'm ready," he told Reed.

"All right, dude. Let's head on up."

Their easy conversation as they walked up the path brought

Hunter back to the forefront of Sam's mind. Reed, although younger than he and Hunter were, was friendly and good-natured, with a wild streak and a wicked sense of humor. He'd just completed his senior year of high school, so the summer stretching ahead of him was the last he'd spend as a carefree teenager.

When they arrived at the main house, all of the windows were alight. The front doors swung open, and Mrs. Hopewell stood at the top step, waiting for them.

"Sam." She greeted him with a sweet smile. "I'm glad you could join us. We know you must get lonely down there all by yourself. What were you going to eat for dinner if Reed hadn't come to drag you on up here?"

His answering smile was impossible to prevent. "Peanut butter on crackers."

She frowned. "See? Fate intervened at just the right time."

"I guess so, ma'am."

"Well, come on, boys. Appetizers are being served as we speak."

She took off down the hall. Sam marveled at the sheer size of the home's interior. His entire trailer back in Duck Creek would have fit in the foyer.

He and Reed followed Mrs. Hopewell down the hall. The ivory-paneled walls flashed by Sam as he went. His eyes traveled up to the high ceiling, where a large crystal chandelier hung over an ornate fountain in the center of the entry. He was used to seeing family photos covering the walls of houses he'd entered, but not here. Expensive-looking tapestries and paintings adorned the paneled walls.

At the end of the entry hall, they turned right and entered the massive dining room. A huge rectangular glass-top table was laden with china. The middle of the glossy surface was completely occupied by a centerpiece dripping with flowers and fruit. The flickering of candles set the entire room aglow.

"Wow," Sam murmured under his breath.

"I know." Reed nudged him hard in the ribs with an elbow. "You'll get used to how the other half lives, my friend." His voice was barely loud enough for Sam to hear. "Like fucking gluttons."

A laugh rumbled up from Sam's chest, but he smothered it just before it could escape.

Gregory Hopewell sat at the far end of the table, and he stood as they entered.

"Sam, my boy! Good to see you!"

His hearty voice filled the dining room. Sam had never once heard Mr. Hopewell's voice do anything other than boom. Mrs. Hopewell smiled at them from the other end of the gargantuan table.

"Come sit, boys. We're waiting on Aston, of course, but try some of the miniature crab cakes."

Sam was still trying to figure out why they were waiting for a car when Reed's sister swept into the room.

"Ah! There you are, sis. Sam Waters, meet Aston Hopewell. The one and only."

Reed smirked at Sam, as if he were expecting a certain reaction from him.

Sam held out his hand. "Nice to meet you, Aston."

The girl who took his hand shook out a long tumble of dark hair, pulled off to the side to hang over one shoulder and pinned in place with a glimmering clip. Her crazy high heels and short white sundress showed off her tanned legs to perfection. Her face was exotically beautiful, her bright blue eyes a stark contrast to her raven-colored hair. The clear gloss on her lips made her mouth look deliciously kissable. For the briefest moment, Sam wondered what she'd taste like.

"Hello." Her voice was strong and clear. She rolled her eyes at her brother. "They bringing in strays again?"

"Always," Reed answered solemnly.

Sam quickly brought himself to reality...and Ever. Aston was the opposite of the girl-next-door type, completely unlike anyone Sam had ever met back in Duck Creek.

As Sam pulled out Aston's chair for her, he caught her mouthing, "Is he for real?" toward her brother.

Reed merely smirked, then motioned at a chair for Sam next to his seat.

"Now that Her Highness has arrived, can we eat?" Reed grumbled.

"Don't tease your sister," Mrs. Hopewell admonished. "Louise?"

A tiny woman carrying a tray of dishes bustled into the room.

Sam gazed around the table as he ate, trying to take mental notes so that he would be able to describe it all perfectly to Ever in his next letter.

"So, Sam," Mrs. Hopewell began. "Greg has told me how lucky Leon feels to have stumbled upon you earlier this spring. We're glad you're with us. How long do you plan on staying in Nelson Island? Do we get to keep you past August?"

Sam took a bite of a crab cake, chewing slowly to savor the delicious flavor. He thought of the best way to answer her question so as to discourage any further wonderings.

"I'm not sure, ma'am. I'd like to stay on at least until the end of summer. My plans depend on, uh, a friend back home and a special situation. So after summer ends I'll have to play things by ear. I'm grateful to y'all for having me, though. I really needed the work."

"Dude, you've gotta drop the 'ma'am' thing. I can't take it much longer." Reed leaned forward, lacing his fingers together above his plate.

Sam shook his head. "Can't help it, man. It's called manners. You ever try them?"

"Oh, low blow, Sam! Low blow. You don't need to impress them, dude. They clearly already love you."

Mr. Hopewell cleared his throat. "Stop it, Reed. Sam, don't listen to him. We really do appreciate your hard work. We want you to know that you can think of yourself as part of the family while you're here."

"Yeah, right, Daddy." Aston rolled her eyes skyward again. "One of the family who works in the fields, right?"

"Actually," Mr. Hopewell began, "Leon has seen some management potential in Sam. He told me about the improvements you've made to the efficiency of the ranch. But you realize raising horses is only one arm of Hopewell Enterprises. Most of the capital comes from our energy division. And finding efficiencies is our biggest goal there. Leon mentioned that you were employed in automotive repair previously?"

Sam nodded. "I worked on a lot of cars at the garage back home. None ran on alternative fuels, but I know something about it. I rebuilt the engine on my Harley myself."

"Well, if you're interested, I thought you might help out my assistant. She's got her hands full with a brand-new baby at home, and Leon found a few more people to do day-to-day labor at the ranch. I thought this could give you the opportunity to learn more of the business end of things. You remind me of a young me. I didn't grow up with the kind of advantages my children"—he shot pointed glances at Aston and Reed—"enjoy. I had to work my way through college, and I started Hopewell Enterprises from the ground up. You're a hard worker and I think all you need is a break and the right hand guiding you."

"I don't know what to say, sir—"

"Of course, I'll increase your hourly wage as befits the new position," Mr. Hopewell added.

"Mr. Hopewell, that's beyond generous. I don't even know what to say."

Sam had been so busy worrying about how he could help Ever for as long as he could remember, that he'd never thought much about what came next for him. His 3.5 GPA in high school had gone untapped because, even though he was scouted by some D III schools for football, he hadn't ever been able to think about leaving her and going to college. Her father would have never let her go.

"Just think about what you want for your future, son. That's all I'm asking. And I can help put you on the path to get there."

Sam nodded slowly. "Thank you, sir. I will."

Louise brought out the main course, Cornish hens laden with dried fruit and tiny pearl onions and potatoes. Sam inhaled every bite, dimly aware of Aston's crystal blue eyes burning into him from across the table.

About the Author

Diana Gardin is a wife of one and a mom of two. After that, writing is her second full-time job, and she loves it! Diana writes contemporary romance in the Young Adult and New Adult categories. She's also a former elementary school teacher. She loves steak, sugar cookies, and Coke and hates working out.

Learn more at:

DianaGardin.com

Twitter: @ DianaLynnGardin

Facebook.com/AuthorDianaGardin

www.ingramcontent.com/pod-product-compliance
Ingram Content Group UK Ltd.
Pitfield, Milton Keynes, MK11 3LW, UK
UKHW022258280225
455674UK00001B/85

9 781455 560486